PRICE OF LIFE

Also by Danielle Singleton:

Safe & Sound
Do No Harm (Joseph #1)
The Enemy Within (Joseph #2)
The Containment Zone

Connect with the author online:

www.daniellesingleton.com
@auntdanwrites
www.facebook.com/singletondanielle
www.daniellesingleton.wordpress.com

Price of Life

Danielle Singleton

ISBN: 0692446389

*****

To Joshie:
For The Future

"Children are the living messages we send to a future we will not see."
~Neil Postman

AUTHOR'S NOTE

The story you are about to read is fiction, but the world in which the story takes place is all too real. The facts and figures quoted in the book regarding human trafficking are true, pulled from the latest governmental and international reports.

Slavery did not end in 1865, as many Americans believe. It continues to this day and exists in nearly every city in every country in the world. Every day, tens of millions of people work for a life that is not their own. A majority of those people are women and young girls who were forced into prostitution. The average life expectancy for these sex slaves is six years. Drugs, violence, and disease show no mercy.

I wrote this book in part to help raise awareness of this global tragedy. To that end, I will donate 10% of all book sale proceeds to organizations that either provide support to trafficking victims or work to eradicate slavery once and for all.

If you would like to learn more about the fight for freedom, you can visit www.enditmovement.com. You can also join my #endit team at https://secure.enditmovement.com/team/DanielleSingleton.

Thank you for your support in this most important cause.

God Bless,

Danielle

ACKNOWLEDGMENTS

Thank you to the One who makes all things possible. Ad maiorem Dei gloriam.

Thank you to my Reading Committee for your continued assistance and support. I rely on y'all more than you'll ever know! A special thanks to you, Madre, for once again being my sounding board. I'm sorry to ruin the surprises for you!

Thank you also to Mel Meyer and the Out of Darkness organization. You provided invaluable insight and knowledge and I am sincerely grateful! I hope the contributions to Out of Darkness from these book sales will help in your continued good works.

I'd also like to make special mention of another author, Patty Kelly, whose groundbreaking study of Mexico's modern brothels (*Lydia's Open Door*) served as a launching point for much of my own research. The same appreciation goes to Benjamin Nolot and Exodus Cry for your amazing, heart-wrenching documentary (*Nefarious: Merchant of Souls*). An absolute masterpiece.

To Hope Combest, Danielle Hargrove, Page Barron, and Maureen Stewart for your name suggestions – thank you!

Of course, thank you to my readers for continuing to support my writing career and ask me when my next book will be published. Your enthusiasm motivates me to deliver stories worthy of your readership!

And, as always, thank you to my big baby, Gus. Even though you stole (and ate!) a few pages of this draft, you're still the best assistant any author could ask for.

I hope y'all enjoy the story!

Y un mensaje especial a las víctimas de la trata de personas en América Latina – aunque no soy una víctima de este crímen horrible, aunque no he vivido el infierno como Uds. han hecho, espero que este libro se abre a los ojos del resto del mundo y ayuda a poner fin a la esclavitud que persigue a la humanidad. Mis oraciones y mis pensamientos están con Uds.

Price of Life

*****

"If slavery is not wrong, nothing is wrong."

Abraham Lincoln

ONE

Cries of pain rang out through a tiny village home and Aurelia Dominguez's grandmother wiped a wet towel across the teenager's forehead.

"Respira," the older woman said, continuing to soothe the granddaughter she had raised from birth. "Breathe. The baby is coming."

"I know it's coming!" Aurelia screamed in response. "Get it out! Get it out now!"

The abuela sighed and did her best to not use this opportunity to lecture the soon-to-be mother. She had told the girl time and time again to stay away from the city – to stay away from guys who only wanted one thing from her. But Aurelia loved the attention, loved the men, and they loved her.

And see where all of that loving has gotten us, Abuela thought. *Sixteen, unmarried, alone, and with a baby.*

Abuela dipped the towel back into the bucket of water and squeezed it over Aurelia's head. Late July in the tropical nation of Honduras was always sweltering. Highs in the 90s, lows in the mid-70s, with a humidity so stifling that outside felt less like a town and more like a sauna. As if a steam pipe followed people everywhere they went, spraying misery with every step.

Air conditioning was unheard of in the villages dotting the dense jungles of the Central American country, fans required electricity that also wasn't present, and the best many could hope for was a moment's rest on a cool dirt or concrete floor.

It was on such a floor that Aurelia Dominguez found herself one hot, sticky day in 1997. The sixteen year old was in labor, giving birth to her first child in the middle of a two-room hut.

Of Mayan and Chorotegan descent, both tribes native to Honduras, Aurelia's own mother gave birth to her at age fifteen and promptly abandoned her on the doorstep of her grandparents. Aurelia's father, she had been told, was a security guard from the capital city of Tegucigalpa whose only lasting contribution to the girl's life was her bright green eyes.

1

Six hours and a thousand screams later, the latest in a long line of Dominguez women was born. Her mother named her Luisa, and was happy to see that the little girl inherited her father's fair complexion. *That will help her in life*, she thought, wanting young Luisa to be able to avoid the discrimination she often faced because of her darker, indigenous skin color.

"You and me, mijita," the teenager cooed. "We're going to conquer the world together. Just you wait and see."

****

Even though she started out with the best of intentions and had the undying support of her grandparents, Aurelia's world conquest took a back seat to other types of conquests in other back seats. A short fourteen months later, baby Luisa had a little sister. The birth of Josefina was complicated, though, and Aurelia almost bled to death before she made it to the hospital in the city of San Pedro Sula. After that, there would be no more siblings for Luisa. In a twist of fate, the near-death experience was one of the best things that ever happened to Aurelia – saving her from many more mouths she couldn't afford to feed.

Luisa, the oldest, didn't know about her mother's medical struggles. A bright, inquisitive child with straight black hair and matching black eyes, Luisa gravitated toward the calming presence of her great-grandmother. The older woman was a year shy of fifty when her first great-grandchild was born, and the staunchly Catholic woman embraced the two young girls as her chance to get their family back on the right track. Aurelia soon left the village to find work (and male attention) in the city. After her husband died when Luisa was two, Rosaria Dominguez clung even tighter to the things she loved the most: her God and her great-granddaughters.

Life was hard, with Rosaria, Luisa, and Josefina having to scrape together an existence based on charity from the Church and what little food they could grow in the small garden by their house. Luisa and her sister felt loved and supported, though, and their lack of material possessions created no sense of longing. They couldn't miss what they'd never had. In a country where two-thirds of the

2

population lived in abject poverty, poor was the norm for the girls. Life was hard, but they were happy.

All of that happiness ended when Luisa was twelve.

TWO

On a cool February night, when Luisa was twelve and Josefina was eleven, their great-grandmother died in her sleep. Tests would have revealed that the sixty-one year old had congestive heart failure, but all the girls knew was that Abuela went to bed one night and didn't wake up the next morning.

"She's in a better place now," the local priest, Father Daniel, told them after they laid their great-grandmother to rest in a grave behind her house. "She's gone to live with Jesus."

Tears streamed down Luisa's cheeks and she hugged her sister so tight that the younger girl winced in pain. "Why did she leave us?" Luisa asked Father Daniel.

"She didn't choose to leave you, honey. I know it's hard, and I know you're sad. It's okay to be sad. But your great-grandmother lived a good life, and God decided that it was time for her to go back to Heaven."

Josefina pulled away from her sister's hug. She had black wavy hair like her mother, and her apple green eyes were blazing at the religious man sitting next to her at the house's only table.

"I'm not sad," Josefina declared, and Luisa could see in her face that her sister was telling the truth. "I'm mad. How come Abuela gets to live with Jesus and we have to go live with *her*?"

The little girl's head jerked in the direction of their mother, Aurelia, who was standing on the front porch. Luisa followed her gaze to see her mom reclined against the open doorway. *Flirting with a guy, as usual*, she thought.

A surprised Father Daniel paused for a moment, then sighed and shook his head. "I don't know, honey. There are some questions we have to wait to find out the answers to."

The miniature green-eyed dragon continued to spit fire in the direction of the full-sized version of herself. Although the girls' great-grandmother had been careful to not speak ill of their mother, Luisa and Josefina weren't blind. They saw when Aurelia showed up drunk or high, and they knew that the only time she visited them at all was after yet another boyfriend kicked her out and she needed a place to sleep. But now, as the only living relative of the two children, Aurelia would be forced to take custody of them.

Sensing an end to her carefree, drug- and sex-addled life, Aurelia was squeezing out every last minute of freedom that she could on the steps of her grandparents' home.

Inside, tears continued to stream down Luisa's cheeks. When Abuela died, Luisa's happiness died with her.

And now we have to move to San Pedro Sula, the twelve year old thought. *To an apartment in a neighborhood that even Father Daniel said is too dangerous for him to want to visit.* Luisa sighed. *Josefina is right. Abuela is so lucky. She gets to live with Jesus – we have to live with our mother.*

****

Father Daniel used the van that belonged to the parish to help transport Luisa and her sister to their new home with their mother in San Pedro Sula. The two pre-teens didn't have many possessions to move, but he felt it was the least he could do. Señora Dominguez had been so kind to him during his time in their village, and she loved her great-granddaughters with all of her heart.

The priest didn't know what Aurelia Dominguez did for a living, and if he was honest with himself he didn't want to know. Steady, honest work had never been the twenty-eight year old's style. Father Daniel had his suspicions, and most of them involved drugs and prostitution. He hated sending the two young girls to live with her, but there was nowhere else for them to go. Years of violence in Honduras had created more orphans than there were orphanages to house them, and people in his parish village were barely surviving on their own – none of them could afford having two extra mouths to feed.

Driving through the city, with a hungover Aurelia in the passenger seat beside him and the two little girls in the back, Father Daniel surveyed his surroundings. Wide colonial streets with open-air markets, small shops, and independent hotels dotted the landscape of San Pedro Sula, along with far too many funeral homes. Everywhere – on walls and windows and the sides of buses – were murals and posters proclaiming the love of Jesus. *If only people would follow his example*, the priest thought with a sigh.

After several minutes, the church van turned onto Calle Principal in the Rancho Coco neighborhood of the city. Located in the northwest corner of San Pedro Sula, Rancho Coco was a less than desirable part of town. An area where gangs often dumped the bodies of people murdered elsewhere.

Father Daniel pulled the van to a stop in front of a run-down apartment complex.

"This is it?" he asked, looking at the building that appeared to be falling in on itself. Decades-old concrete, iron railings and outdoor walkways, barred windows, and uneven doors revealing shoddy workmanship. Tiny black specks dotted the buildings' walls and were, upon closer examination, bullet holes.

"This is it," Aurelia answered, nodding her head. "Let's go girls. Say goodbye to the father and get out of the van."

Josefina, with her wavy black hair, bright green eyes, and emerging curves that would soon make men go wild, hopped out of the van and joined her mother on the sidewalk. The rail-thin Luisa, all arms and legs and long, straight black hair, lingered in the vehicle.

"Thanks for the ride, Father Daniel," she said in a voice barely above a whisper.

"You're welcome, Luisa," he responded with a smile. Daniel liked Luisa. Smart, sweet, and inquisitive, she was also a regular attendee at mass with her abuela.

"Luisa – let's go!" Aurelia barked from outside the van.

"Bye," the little girl added before climbing out into the oppressive afternoon heat.

"Bye," Father Daniel repeated, but by that point Aurelia had ushered her daughters inside the apartment building. The priest crossed himself and said a prayer for Luisa and Josefina. *God help these girls. No one else in their life will.*

THREE

In the beginning, Luisa was surprised by how well her mom pulled herself together. She picked up various temporary jobs answering phones, washing dishes, and working in a clothing factory. Luisa and Josefina weren't in school – after a boy in their building got shot walking to class, their mom said they didn't need an education. She would bring home books for them to read, though, and the girls didn't mind that they only left the one-room apartment a couple times a week. They had a decent amount of food to eat, their mom was sober, and they had each other.

It could be worse, Luisa often thought.

Threadbare carpet covered the floor of the apartment, and the girls went diving in dumpsters around the building to find old blankets to use as makeshift cots. A small mattress in the corner served as their mom's bed, while a large cardboard box was repurposed into a table. The apartment's lone decoration was a cross . . . two small pieces of wood that Luisa found, nailed together, and hung on the mold-stained wall next to her cot.

They had six good months together, Luisa, her sister, and their mother, but then it was back to how things were before. The girls' mom, Aurelia, had managed to pull herself together for a while, but then she went back to the drugs and the drink and the men with so many tattoos that they almost changed races from mestizo to black.

Aurelia never brought her boyfriends back to their rundown apartment, though. Not because she was concerned for the girls' welfare, but rather because Aurelia Dominguez knew that, at twenty-eight and with years of prostitution behind her, she would be far less desirable to the men than her two young, pure daughters. Aurelia didn't want to share the attention, so she kept them hidden away out of sight. One of those many, many men might have been Luisa's father . . . the little girl didn't know. *Probably not*, she thought.

Another six months into her stay in San Pedro Sula, one year after her great-grandmother died, Luisa awoke one morning to the sound of keys jangling and scraping against the lock on the outside of their apartment. It was a common sound and happened whenever her mother was too drunk or drugged to figure out how to unlock the door. Luisa climbed up off her pallet on the floor and shuffled over to the window, still half-asleep. After checking to make sure that it was indeed Aurelia making all of that racket, Luisa flipped open the locks and let her mom inside.

The tall, curvy woman who looked like the life-sized version of Josefina stumbled into the apartment. After several steps, she stopped and stood up straight. Glazed eyes surveyed the room before coming to rest on her younger daughter, still asleep on the floor.

"Ugh," Aurelia growled. "I forgot about you." Turning her head to the side, she saw Luisa standing by the door. "You too. Ugh. Why are you still here?" she slurred, her eyes struggling to stay open and her body swaying under the influence of last night's adventure.

"You two ruin everything," Aurelia added, swinging her arm to motion to her two daughters and causing herself to fall to the floor in the process. Luisa rushed over to help her mom, only to be met with a sharp slap across her cheek.

"Get away from me. You ruin everything," her mother repeated, curling up into a ball on the floor. Years of drugs and alcohol had made Aurelia look older and uglier than she truly was, which was bad for business. Particularly when they discovered she had kids. The night before, the man she had been sleeping with for three weeks found out that she had two young daughters at home. When Aurelia declined his offer to 'share some fun' with all three Dominguez women, he kicked her out.

"I'm tired of you two brats stealing all of my money and ruining all of my fun," the drunk woman growled. Somehow making it back onto her feet, she walked over to the corner of the room and ripped a piece of cardboard off a box that had contained books during earlier, happier times. Aurelia found a pen on the floor and scribbled a message on the cardboard, then staggered over to the apartment's one window and placed the sign there.

After her mother crawled into a fetal position and fell asleep, Luisa opened the door and stepped out onto the landing to read what her mother had written. There, in scribbled handwriting, was the sign that changed the young teenager's life.

Se vende: 2 niñas.

For sale: 2 girls.

It only took a couple of hours before men and women alike started knocking on the door, each wanting to see the two niñas and asking how much they cost. For the first time in six months, Luisa saw her mother smile.

She and Josefina were the property of a lowlife named Manuel by the end of the afternoon. They were twelve and thirteen years old.

FOUR

The girls' new owner, Manuel, let Luisa and Josefina stay with their mother one last evening, mainly because he didn't have anywhere to keep them overnight. Manuel was a trafficker, a drug and human runner called a coyote, and he wasn't equipped for storage of merchandise.

That last night in San Pedro Sula was one of the best they ever had, with Aurelia staying sober and happy given her new influx of cash. Luisa and her sister both fetched $50 US, which combined was more money than their mother might earn in six months of odd jobs and prostitution. For the first time in her life, Aurelia wished she had more children. More daughters. *Easiest money I ever made*, she thought.

Aurelia made sure to give her daughters advice on how to keep their new owner happy and how to survive in the world they were entering. It wasn't because she cared what happened to the two young girls. Rather, she didn't want the man who bought them to come back to her with buyer's remorse. There was no telling what he might do to Aurelia to get his money's worth.

"The only value a woman has is what she can give to a man," the girls' mom said that afternoon after their buyer left the apartment. "Remember that, Josefina. Your body and what it can get for you – that's what you're worth."

While Aurelia Dominguez left her younger daughter with those words of 'advice', the woman knew that her older daughter was different. That her grandmother, the girls' beloved great-grandmother, had taught Luisa about hopes, dreams, education, and living a life to be proud of. So after telling her second-born that she could never amount to more than a whore, Aurelia turned to face Luisa. Her apple green eyes stared straight into her daughter's, and Luisa noticed how the leather wrinkles on her mom's face betrayed how many lifetimes she'd lived in her twenty-nine years.

"No seas estúpida," she hissed. "Don't be stupid. Do what they tell you to, and don't cause trouble. This is the best your life will ever be. Dreaming otherwise will get you killed."

****

Early the next morning, a bright February day full of warmth and sunshine, Manuel returned to claim his property. It was the dry season, which most people preferred for the cooler temperatures and prettier weather. Luisa liked the wet season, though. The second half of the year, June through December, brought more humidity and higher temperatures, but it also brought rain. Cool, refreshing rain that washed the streets clean. In the wet season, the gutters ran clear with water and the air smelled of grass and flowers and life. In the dry season, the gutters ran red with blood and the world smelled of death.

A different kind of death filled the air around Luisa that morning. The man who bought her and her sister looked only slightly older than their mother and was a short, pudgy, smarmy looking character with a patchy beard and even patchier teeth. Before leaving the apartment, Luisa saw her mother sign several different pieces of paper that Manuel then placed in a folder, rolled up, and shoved in his back pocket.

"Let's go," he barked, grabbing each girl by the arm and marching them toward the door. "We have a lot to do today."

****

Manuel, the gruff man who communicated in grunts, head jerks, and waves of his handgun, first took the girls to a small internet café where he made copies of everything their mom had signed. The next stop was a liquor store. "I don't usually come here," Manuel said, "but it's going to be a long fucking day and you two brats are already on my nerves."

A six-pack of Salva Vida, Honduras' most popular beer, rode shotgun next to Manuel while Luisa and Josefina sat huddled in the backseat of the vehicle. The girls' captor called it a car, but it wasn't much more than a heap of metal on top of four wheels. As the group of three ventured north on CA-13, farther and farther away from San Pedro Sula into the dense, mountainous jungle, Luisa prayed that the car would break down so she and her sister could escape.

Please God. Please make the car break down. Please.

11

Sixty minutes farther into the journey, when they reached the Caribbean coastal city of Puerto Cortes, Luisa stopped praying for the car to die. Empty beer bottles now rolled in the passenger floorboard, and as the road veered south along the coastline and back into the jungle, Luisa prayed that they would crash. *Six beers in an hour and a half had to make the driver drunk, right? If we crash, Josefina and I can escape.* Luisa made sure that both backseat passengers had their seatbelts on in case of a wreck. *Please God*, she thought, *make the car crash. Please.*

Without realizing it, Luisa's prayers changed from silent meditations to whispered pleas.

"What was that?" Manuel yelled, whipping around in his seat to look at her – all the while still driving at breakneck speed through an area near Honduras' Cusuco National Park.

"N-n-nothing," she stammered.

"I heard you," the man growled, then pulled a pistol off of the dashboard and pointed it backward at Luisa.

"Quit praying," he commanded. "God isn't answering prayers today."

FIVE

Three hours after leaving the apartment in San Pedro Sula, Luisa, her sister, and their new owner arrived in the border city of Corinto. It was much busier than Luisa expected, although she didn't have many expectations and didn't even know where they were until she saw a sign demarcating the Honduras-Guatemala border.

Manuel parked his dump of a car in a large, almost full lot and stepped out into the midday sun. He opened the passenger door and leaned his head down into the backseat.

"I'm your good family friend Manuel. Your mom asked me to take you up to Guatemala to visit relatives there. Speak only if spoken to. If you mention a sale, or my gun, I will kill you both and then go back to San Pedro Sula and kill your mother too. Do you understand me?"

The girls' eyes grew as wide as saucers and their heads bobbled up and down in agreement.

"Good. Now get out."

Manuel escorted Luisa and her sister through two massive sandstone buildings, Customs and Immigration, and each time the story was the same. He was a family friend, the girls had relatives in Guatemala City, and their mother asked him to take them there.

Luisa could see that the people working behind the counters knew Manuel was lying. Their eyes darted back and forth between him and the girls, with a look on their faces that was a cross between pity and disgust. But with all of the paperwork in order – his passport and driver's license, the girls' birth certificates, a notarized letter of permission from their mother, vehicle title and registration, and a temporary car import permit from Guatemala – there was nothing that the immigration officials could do. He was a coyote on his way north, one of thousands that they saw pass through the checkpoint with children in tow. They assumed his destination was the United States, but not all made it that far. At best, this Manuel Cardona character had been hired by the young ladies' family to transport them out of Honduras and to the United States. At worst, he was trafficking them as part of the international sex trade. The

Customs and Immigration officials didn't know which, and they had no means of finding out.

The paperwork was all in order, so they were stamped 'approved' and sent on their way. After a similar stop at a much less elaborate building on the other side of the border, Luisa found herself back in Manuel's dusty old car and headed inland.

"Another eight hours," Manuel said, his words still slurring from the beer, "and we'll be in Quetzaltenango. Then I can sell you whores and go back home."

****

Three hours after crossing the border, Josefina leaned over to her sister.

"I've gotta go," she whispered.

"Go where?"

"No," Josefina said, glancing down at her lap. "I've gotta *go*."

Luisa sighed and her body tensed with nerves. The last time she spoke to Manuel, an hour earlier when she was thirsty, he had pulled the car over to the side of the road, climbed in the backseat, and punched her in the stomach with the back end of his gun. "Next time you talk," he growled, "I'll hit you in the fucking face. I don't care what it will do to your sale price."

Part of Luisa, a large part, wanted to tell her sister to ask Manuel herself about going to the bathroom. *She's the one who needs to go, not me*, Luisa thought. A second later, the young teenager shook her head. *No, she's my little sister. I'm older . . . I should ask.*

"Umm, excuse me, sir?" Luisa said, her voice not much above a whisper.

"I thought I told you not to talk!"

"But, sir –"

"What?!" Manuel said, again turning around to look at the girls without stopping the car or slowing down.

I really wish he'd quit doing that, Luisa thought. *No, wait, I don't. Maybe one time when he does it we'll crash.*

"What could possibly be so important, huh?"

"Josefina needs to go to the bathroom," Luisa replied.

"Who the hell is Josefina?"

14

"I am," the little girl said, raising her hand as if she were in a classroom.

"Damn women," Manuel said, jerking the car over to the shoulder of the road and slamming on the brakes. "Why can't you piss out the window like a man would?"

Josefina opened her mouth to respond but Luisa squeezed her arm to keep her quiet. Some questions weren't meant to be answered.

Climbing out of the car, Manuel flung open the rear passenger door and pointed to the roadside grass with his gun. "Go on then. We don't have all day. It'll be dark soon and I have to meet my buyer before ten o'clock."

Josefina crawled over her sister and out of the car. Standing next to her captor, the pre-teen barely came up to his chest. "Can you . . . can you turn around?"

"What for?"

"So you don't watch me? I can't go if people are watching me."

"Tough shit. Go pee and whatever else. Now."

Josefina's hands trembled as she undid the button on her denim shorts and slid them and her underwear down her legs. She then squatted down low to the ground and, after several seconds, started to relieve herself.

Manuel's laughter filled the late afternoon air. "Look at that – squatting down like the little bitch that you are. Get used to that position, puta. It's gonna happen a lot."

Luisa's sister finished going to the bathroom, stood up, and pulled her clothes back into their proper position.

"Alright. Let's go. We have another five hours until we get to Quetzaltenango."

SIX

Manuel's buyer, a slimy, pale-skinned man named Rogelio, was waiting for them when they arrived in Guatemala's fourth largest city. In a back room of a rundown hotel on the outskirts of Quetzaltenango, the Guatemalan in his early sixties made Luisa and her sister strip out of their clothes and walk back and forth in front of him so he could 'examine the merchandise'.

Smiling and nodding, Rogelio liked what he saw. "Well done, my boy," he said to Manuel. "Well done. I can tell from their ages and the way they're trembling in fear that they're untouched. These two will fetch a high price at the market."

Luisa saw the older man give the coyote 150 US dollars, and Manuel handed him a large brown folder in return.

The young Honduran smiled. "Fifty percent return on investment for one day's work. I don't know why anybody still transports drugs anymore. People are way more profitable."

Rogelio nodded his head in agreement. "Money is good. The money is definitely good. Now take yours and get the hell out of here."

Luisa's first owner did as he was told, leaving her and Josefina alone in the hotel room with this new, second one – tired, hungry, naked, and terrified.

****

The next morning, Day Three in Luisa's life as a slave, she was loaded into the back of yet another car headed to yet another destination.

And another owner? Luisa couldn't help but wonder. Seventy-two hours earlier, when her mother told her she was going to be sold to "whoever is dumb enough to want to buy you," Luisa hadn't known what to expect. *Working in a factory somewhere, perhaps? Maybe picking corn or other crops on a large farm? Living in a –* Luisa shuddered – *a brothel? Whatever I expected, it wasn't this. Why do they keep selling us? And where are we going?*

16

One of the teenager's questions was answered when, three hours later, their car arrived in the small Guatemalan border town of La Mesilla. Large green signs hung over the road with words printed in Spanish and what Luisa thought might be English.

Mexico, she read on one of the billboards. *He's taking us to Mexico.*

In a moment of déjà vu, Rogelio turned around in his seat and faced the two girls sitting behind him.

"I'm your Uncle Rogelio. Your mom asked me to take you to Mexico to visit relatives there. If they ask, we're going to Tuxtla Gutiérrez. Don't speak unless spoken to. If you say a single word about anything that has happened on this trip, about being sold or the fact that I have a gun in the console, I will shoot you both square between the eyes and then feed you to my dogs. Do you understand?"

Again, Luisa and Josefina's eyes grew wide and they nodded their heads up and down.

"Do you understand?"

"Sí Señor. Yes sir."

The man nodded. "Good."

As the car inched closer to the border, Luisa looked out the window and saw dozens of people walking around. Some appeared to be waiting on something, while others looked like they were doing business of some sort.

"Jungle runners," her owner said, in a rare moment of explanation. "Coyotillos. Poor suckers pay the runners to take them across the border at night, through the jungles and past the immigration checkpoints. Terrible business, but as you can see people do it all the time." He shook his head. "If the Federales don't snatch you up, the jaguars in the jungle will. They love to feast on little girls," he added with a crooked smile.

When Josefina gasped in fear, Rogelio laughed. "See how lucky you are to be with me? I don't even have to bribe the immigration officials. Not with these letters signed by your whore of a mother. We're crossing legally, chiquitas. See how lucky you are to be with me?"

Rogelio continued smiling all the way through the checkpoint, playing the part of the happy uncle taking his nieces to visit their family members in the southern Mexican city of Tuxtla Gutiérrez.

17

Part of it's true. We are going to Tuxtla, he thought, still grinning and chatting with the immigration officials. *That's where the girls get sold and I get paid.*

****

Rogelio de la Varga was a veteran of the trans-American black market trade routes. For decades, the Guatemalan had traversed Central America and Mexico with illegal merchandise. Drugs, guns, and women. Mostly women lately, ever since the government crackdowns on drug-running made those items too risky for his taste. Women, though, were very profitable and surprisingly easy to transport. *Besides*, he thought as he drove north through the state of Chiapas, *if I'm pulled over in a car with a pound of cocaine, I'll get arrested and sent to jail. If I'm in a car with these two girls who don't say anything, I'll be let go. Yep*, Rogelio nodded, *humans is the business to be in right now.*

Another three hours in the car, including one stop in Comitán for gas, brought Rogelio and his two pieces of merchandise to Tuxtla Gutiérrez. He used to take his drugs, guns, or girls straight to the cargo trains in the city of Arriaga, but that route was too dangerous now. *Way too many police and military milling around and sticking their noses where they don't belong*, Rogelio thought.

As the capital city of the state of Chiapas, Tuxtla's 500,000 residents provided the perfect amount of cover for criminals like Rogelio. And at only eighty miles away from Arriaga, Tuxtla was the next best thing.

Unlike the girls' two prior owners, Rogelio did not have a buyer lined up when they arrived. After driving around the city for a couple hours, meeting the right people and asking the right questions, he found what he was looking for: the market. The slave market in Tuxtla was never in the same place twice for fear of being caught by the federal police. Local cops sometimes knew where the market was; often they didn't, but it didn't matter. As long as the Federales were kept in the dark, the slave traders felt safe.

That day's sales were happening in the gymnasium of an abandoned school. *Fitting*, Rogelio thought with a grin, *since most of them are kids.* "Alright, chiquitas," he said, standing in the middle of the Dominguez sisters and wrapping his arms around their shoulders, "let's go make Uncle Rogelio some money."

SEVEN

Unlike their previous, one-on-one sale transactions, the Dominguez sisters' experience in Tuxtla was a free-for-all of frightened teenage girls with men (and women) buying and selling them like cattle. Walking into the abandoned school, Luisa saw that it must have been empty for several years. Dirt and dust covered every square inch, spider webs booby-trapped the halls, and overturned chairs and scattered desks revealed that academics was the last thing on the minds of the community's children.

The auction took place in a gymnasium, the cavernous remains of an ambitious attempt at establishing an American-style, school-based sports team. Hardwood floors that once shined bright were now beginning to rot, bleachers remained closed and locked up against graffiti-covered walls, and the basketball goals sat untouched and without nets.

Administrators at Municipal High had dreamt of being the first in a new wave of *fútbol* and basketball dominance, with students becoming local stars and crowds paying money to fill the gym and chant their names. In some respects, the vision had come true. The room was once again full of teenagers, the girls were the stars of the show, and adults came from far and wide to watch the spectacle unfolding before them. Each person in the audience paid a cover of $20 to enter and sit in one of hundreds of folding chairs spaced out around the room.

But this was a different kind of show, and the stars' names weren't being chanted as much as they were demanded.

Luisa and Josefina were herded to the center of the room where they joined scores of other young women like them.

"Take off your clothes," a bearded man barked. Looking around, Luisa saw that the rest of the girls were either naked or in the process of undressing. She looked at her sister and nodded once, and both stripped out of the dirty, sweaty shorts and tank-tops that they had been wearing since they left Honduras. It actually felt good, in a way, to rid her body of the filthy garments. That is, of course, until Luisa saw the even filthier stares coming from the men surrounding the merchandise for sale.

20

The auction organizer, the one with the beard, pushed, shoved, and grunted the girls into position at the steps of an elevated wooden catwalk. One by one, the naked young women in the line in front of Luisa took their turn walking up and down the runway. After what seemed like forever, it was her turn.

Luisa closed her eyes and took a deep breath, then climbed the stairs in front of her. One. Two. Three. Standing at the top of the catwalk, her eyes scanned the gym and saw hundreds staring back at her. Eyes that roamed up, down, left, and right as the men tried to determine if Luisa was worthy of their money. She saw many men nod their heads and smile. Luisa's combination of youth, beauty, and fair skin made her one of the highest-rated items up for bid. She shuddered, and for a second Luisa thought she might vomit right then and there in the center of the stage. *It was one thing with one guy in the hotel room, but this?* Luisa closed her eyes again and her heart pounded so fast that she thought it might beat right out of her pre-pubescent chest. *I can't handle this.*

The young woman had never been a showboat like her mom – much preferring the quiet life exemplified by her beloved great-grandmother. Whereas Aurelia and Josefina could always be counted on to entertain guests with stories, songs, and dances, Luisa was usually found in a corner by herself reading her abuela's Bible or in a neighbor's barn petting their horses.

This kind of attention, nearly five hundred people staring at her naked body as she paraded up and down a stage, was too much for Luisa to handle. After she made it back to the end of the catwalk and climbed down the stairs, Luisa collapsed on the rotting wooden floor in a heap of nerves and tears.

Luckily for both Dominguez sisters, unlike many auctions in Europe and the Middle East, the Tuxtla sale did not allow 'product sampling' before purchases were made.

"Female up for sale. Item Number 417," the announcer said over a crackling microphone. "This one's a steal, gentlemen. Coming to us all the way from Honduras."

A few buyers in the crowd grumbled when they heard that Luisa was a foreigner.

"What's that?" the announcer said, turning his head to speak to his assistant. "Oh, excellent. Ok everybody . . . even better: two Hondureñas for your purchasing pleasure. Items 417 and 418. Get them together and the seller will cut the price. Starting at $150 total. Do I hear $150?"

"Yeah, I got $150," said a man near the stage.

"That's $150. Do I hear $175?"

"$175."

"$180," countered the first bidder.

"$190," called out a voice from the back of the room.

"$195," argued the second bidder.

"$200."

"Alright," said the announcer with a smile. "We've got ourselves a determined buyer in the rear of the gym. "Anybody want to top that? We're at two girls for a total of $200."

Silence filled the auditorium, accented only by squeaky chairs and smokers' coughs. Luisa and her sister were good merchandise and the crowd knew it, but they didn't have the money on hand to go any higher. Girls of slightly lower quality could be had for much better prices.

". . . going once? Going twice? Sold to the man in the back." The auctioneer banged a hammer against the podium – the closest thing he could find to a gavel. "Go on over to the side table and make your payment. Next is Item 419: a pretty little thing from up the road in Oaxaca . . ."

Luisa stopped listening to the auction and focused instead on the person coming forward to claim her and her sister. *Thank you, God, for keeping us together. Thank you thank you thank you.*

The man who bought Luisa and Josefina was dressed in baggy jeans, a dirt-stained white t-shirt, and sneakers that looked from a distance like they had holes in the toes and soles. He also appeared to be only a few years older than they were – less of a man and more of a boy still. He handed the auction treasurer $200 cash – $100 for each of them – and Luisa noticed that the money was once again US dollars. Nobody wanted to be paid in local currency.

Marching his property out of the gymnasium, the new owner, Antonio, told the girls in no uncertain terms that he wouldn't hesitate to shoot them both if they misbehaved. Except this time, unlike the men before him, Antonio didn't promise a quick death with a shot between the eyes. "I'll shoot you in the arm, and the leg, and the stomach . . . then I'll let you lie on the side of the road and bleed to death. It can take hours sometimes. Maybe days. Don't make me do that to your pretty little bodies."

If the seventeen year old slave trader was talking extra tough, it was because he felt he had to. The two girls he bought in Tuxtla – one tall and lanky, the other short and curvy – were his first venture into human trafficking. He'd only dealt with willing travelers before, and they didn't fight back. Wouldn't try to escape their guide. *I can't let that happen with these putas*, he thought.

It took the group of three almost a day and a half to travel from Tuxtla to Arriaga . . . Days Four and Five of Luisa and Josefina's enslavement. They walked some, hitched rides in the back of passing trucks, and spent the night in a lodging house along the road. Antonio paid $11.50 each for the privilege of sleeping in a room with fifteen other immigrants.

Later in his career in human trafficking, Antonio would figure out that any money spent hiring a car to drive from Tuxtla Gutiérrez to the trains in Arriaga would be more than made up by the time he saved. Even further down the road in what would become a very profitable business venture, Antonio would purchase his own car and forgo traveling on the trains altogether. But, at that moment, Antonio hadn't figured it out and barely had two pennies to rub together, so he hitched. And he hiked. And he hoped to God that the two little girls hiking with him would be worth the hassle of moving them up to Oaxaca.

****

The area surrounding the train depot in the otherwise sleepy city of Arriaga was bustling with activity. Migrants from South and Central America joined Mexicans in waiting for the cargo trains known as La Bestia – The Beast. When the trains rolled through town, hundreds of immigrants at a time would climb aboard the roof and sides of La Bestia and ride that way for hours or even days. Despite the many dangers associated with 'The Train of Death' and a recent government crackdown on the illegal travelers, it was still the cheapest, fastest, most reliable way north through the thick, green jungles of southern Mexico.

23

Only thirteen hours on La Bestia, Antonio thought, *and we'll be in Oaxaca. Where I can get rid of these two pests.*

At that moment, the 'pests' were sitting on the ground, drawing flowers and other images into the dirt while waiting on the train. Their new owner-escort watched them from a few feet away. Antonio was only seventeen himself, a wiry, gangly heap of arms and legs who grew six inches the previous year but hadn't filled in the extra space yet. *And I won't for a while*, he often thought, *at least not until I can afford more food.* He had tangled black hair, honey brown eyes, and deep brown skin that looked a shade or two darker than it really was because he never took the time to take a good, proper shower. Without parents to look after him and working a job that saw him only interact with slaves or other smugglers, the teenage orphan saw no need to scrub behind his ears. Antonio didn't remember his parents . . . they either died or abandoned him when he was a toddler, and the people at the Catholic Church-run orphanage where he grew up didn't know which. When he was eight, the boy of mysterious origins was adopted by a local businessman who was more interested in what he could get from Toño than what he could give him. Children made great vehicles for transporting drugs or escorting immigrants past government checkpoints, and Antonio's adoptive 'father' had an agreement with the local priest: financial sponsorship of the orphanage in exchange for a steady supply of pint-sized pack mules.

Before his growth spurt, Antonio had worked as a coyotillo – guiding undocumented migrants across the Guatemalan-Mexican border and through the jungles of southern Mexico to Arriaga, where La Bestia awaited. But now, at six feet two inches tall, Antonio had the stature to be taken more seriously. And, after nine years as a coyotillo, he had the experience to not only escape the grasp of his guardian but also to graduate on to more difficult parts of the human trafficking trade. Legitimate jobs in the legitimate economy were beyond the scope of the teenage career criminal. The black market was the only world he knew, and the two malnourished girls currently under his care were his first big scores. *All I have to do is get them to Oaxaca alive*, thought Antonio, *and I get paid.*

While the Dominguez sisters earned their mother $50 each in Honduras, Antonio would make $400 per girl when he sold them in Oaxaca. *$450 net profit, including expenses. For three days work.*

He shook his head and smiled. *I'd have to work almost six months at minimum wage to make that much money.*

The closer the girls got to the red light districts of Mexico City, Monterrey, and Tijuana – or even the big payday of the United States – the more they were worth. Antonio knew that whoever bought Luisa and her sister from him in Oaxaca would turn around and double profit again in a northern city, but he didn't have the connections, the experience, or the cojones to enter that world. Not yet.

Looking over at the girls again, Antonio saw that the older one had her arms wrapped around the younger one and was rocking her back and forth how a mother would rock a baby. His thoughts flashed back to his first journey north. With his parents either long dead or long gone, young Toño had been 'rescued' from an orphanage by a local drug smuggler in order to run backpacks full of marijuana from the border to various towns farther north. He was eight, and terrified.

But now . . . the young man sighed. *I know that route like the back of my hand.* A year of running drugs and eight years of running people made Antonio one of the best – and most sought after – coyotillos in the region. *It's this route that I need to master now.*

The faraway whistle of a train caught the young man's attention.

"Get ready," he called out. "La Bestia is coming."

EIGHT

Just as passengers on a regular, non-cargo train had to buy tickets, Antonio, Luisa, and Josefina did as well. Gangs patrolled the boxcars of La Bestia, charging anywhere from fifty to one hundred dollars per person to ride atop the speeding cargo train from its origin in Arriaga to all points north. Because of the unconventional manner in which immigrants got on the train – running, jumping, and climbing, hoping not to fall – tickets were bought once everyone was already on board.

After Antonio paid their fee and the tattooed gang member moved on to the next person, Luisa leaned over to her captor.

"What happens if you don't pay?" she asked. Despite the young man's threat of a slow, painful death, Luisa wasn't as afraid of him as she had been her two previous owners.

"They throw you off," Antonio replied.

"Like, at the next stop?"

He shook his head. "Like, right away. They stand you up, grab you by the shoulders, and throw you off the train."

Luisa and Josefina gasped in unison and the coyote rolled his eyes. "Stop looking so damn surprised all the time. Shit ain't even started to get real for you two. Ain't even started."

****

A few hours into their journey, halfway between Arriaga and the first stopping point of Ixtepec, Luisa and her fellow train passengers began to get restless. Riding a train in a passenger seat for that long would be bad enough, but spending the time on the hard, metal roof of a boxcar was miserable. At one point, when Josefina tried to stand up to stretch, Antonio grabbed her arm and yanked her back down.

"Are you insane?" he yelled, his voice carrying over the screeching sound of La Bestia on the tracks. "You don't stand up on a moving train unless you have to. Shit," he added, shaking his head. "If you fall off this train and get yourself killed I swear I'll find your body and fucking kill you all over again myself."

26

When their owner laid back down on the roof, Josefina glanced over at her sister. A look that Luisa couldn't quite recognize filled the younger girl's eyes. "Did you hear that?" Josefina asked. "He cares about us," she added in a whisper, and Luisa realized that the look was one of contentment and appreciation.

The older sister shook her head. "No he doesn't. Not like that. He only cares about keeping us alive so he can sell us when we get wherever we're going. He doesn't care about you. Not like I do. Not like Abuela did."

Josefina's eyes hardened and she stuck out her chin. "Abuela is dead, Luisa. She's not coming back. Get over it."

Right then the two girls heard a man yell, then several more people joined the chorus and a woman started to wail and cry.

"¡Gonzalo!" the woman screamed, and two passengers grabbed her arms to keep her from jumping off the top of the train. "¡Gonzaaaaaaalooooooooooo! Nooooooooooooo!"

Everyone within hearing distance turned to watch the spectacle unfolding on the boxcar behind Luisa's.

"What happened?" she asked of no one in particular.

A man sitting a few feet away turned his head but kept his eyes facing backward toward the screaming woman. "Somebody fell off the train," he explained. "Her husband, or son maybe."

Another passenger nodded his head. "I saw it happen. He stood up and walked closer to the edge. Looked like maybe he was gonna take a leak. Lost his balance and he was gone."

Luisa gasped and covered her hand with her mouth.

"You mean . . . he's dead?" asked Josefina.

"No way he survived that fall," the first passenger replied. "Not on this part of the tracks. Not moving at this speed," he added, motioning down toward the spinning wheels of the cargo train as it rumbled through dense green forest.

"See what I'm saying?" Antonio interrupted, glaring at the Dominguez sisters. "That's what happens when you stand up. You fall off the train, break your neck, and then have the jaguars and monkeys and wild pigs battling over the remains of your dead, rotting corpse," he said, with the fury, drama, and fascination that only a seventeen year old boy could give the topic.

"Ewwwww," both girls replied in unison.

27

"Eww is right. So unless you want to be like him, don't stand up."

"But . . ." Josefina said.

"But what?"

"But what if I have to go to the bathroom?"

"Hold it. We'll be in Ixtepec soon enough. Or piss your pants. I don't care. Just don't stand up."

A nearby passenger, the one who explained what happened to the man who fell, leaned over toward Luisa and Josefina. Yellow, crooked teeth smiled at the girls. "It's okay," he said. "Everybody who rides these trains has had to pee their pants at least once. Happened to me last time I rode. No shame in it at all."

"You . . . you've been on here before?" Luisa asked.

Their new friend nodded his head. "Second time for me. Had to start riding the train after they built up the road checkpoints so much. We used to bribe the guards, you know? Give them a little money and they let you pass. Now?" He shook his head. "The price has gone way up. Some of them won't even take money. It's the damn United States' fault too. They keep giving all kinds of money to Mexico to stop immigrants from coming up from Central America. Don't they know that people only come to Mexico in the first place to get to the US? They're the reason we want to go, and they're also the reason why we can't make it there. Fucking gringo bastards."

Another man sitting nearby nodded his head in agreement. "This is my fourth time making the trip north. I got all the way to the US border once, but then I was caught and sent back."

"Why do you keep trying?" Josefina ventured to ask. Luisa admired her little sister for that. Even though she was younger, Josefina was a lot braver than Luisa.

The man shrugged his shoulders. "It's better than the alternative. Staying in my hometown and getting charged extortion fees I can't afford from the paycheck I don't get from the job I don't have . . . all to the gangs so they have mercy and don't kill me. Knowing the whole time that they might still kill me anyway." He shook his head. "Making it to the United States is my only chance at success in life. I mean, I have a cousin in Tegucigalpa who is doing it 'the right way'," he continued, making air quotes with his fingers. "Eleven years and thousands of dollars paid to a lawyer, but he's still in Honduras. Waiting. No," he said. "I don't have that much time or that much money. So I ride the train." The man paused and looked over at Josefina. "What about you, chiquita? Why do you keep riding La Bestia?"

"This . . . this is my f-first ride."

"They're with me," Antonio interrupted, wrapping his arms around Luisa and Josefina's shoulders.

"You their brother?"

"No."

The truth dawned on the older man's face and he cut his eyes back and forth between the girls and their captor. Antonio lifted his arm off of Josefina and used that hand to pull up the hem of his t-shirt.

Rays of sun glinted off the metal of the pistol shoved in his waistband.

"Oh," their new travel-mate said. "Well, okay then."

Turning his back away from the group, the man shot one last glance at the two girls. Luisa would've sworn she saw pity in his eyes. Something that said 'I wish I could help you, but I can't'.

NINE

All of the train's illegal passengers jumped off before they reached the city of Ixtepec. There would be a cargo inspection at the train depot, and immigration officials were there waiting to arrest anyone without proper identification. While Luisa and Josefina had forged their way through checkpoints in Honduras and Guatemala, there would be no more false documents or lies. Only good old-fashioned smuggling from that point forward.

The sisters managed to jump off the moving train without too much trouble. Walking through the outskirts of Ixtepec was the more dangerous activity, since they had to be on the lookout for anyone who might try to arrest them. Antonio and his property made that part of the journey on foot, and finally reached the point where they would reboard La Bestia once it passed cargo inspection. After a dinner of a bag of chips and a can of Coke – the most they had eaten in days – Luisa and Josefina curled up beside each other in a patch of grass and fell asleep.

Luisa woke up the next morning to the sounds of people yelling and footsteps running over dirt, grass, twigs, and the rock gravel that lined the train tracks.

"Wake up, wake up! Now!" a male voice yelled. "The train is early! Wake up!"

Luisa's eyes flew open and she saw her sister and Antonio standing over her. Josefina tugged at her sister's shirt. "Come on! We'll miss it if we're not ready!"

If Luisa had the time, she would've reflected on how much she and her sister had changed over the course of the past six days. They were now hardened, seasoned travelers – sleeping outside on the ground, watching as people were robbed and beaten on the journey, and knowing how fast to run to be able to leap onto the moving train. If she had time, Luisa would've thought that thirteen and twelve were no longer appropriate ages to convey all that the girls had experienced in those few short days. But she didn't have time. There was a train to catch.

The young teenager stood up and brushed dirt and leaves off of her tank top and shorts.

"Come on, c'mon!" Josefina said again.

The sisters held hands and climbed up to the edge of the woods, careful to not get too close to the railroad tracks. They were on the northern edge of the city, having slept there to avoid the cargo inspection in town that morning. The trick now, the girls knew, was to wait until the engine passed so the conductor wouldn't see them. Then they had to run as fast as they could to keep up with the train and time their jump to leap onto one of the platforms, open boxcars, or ladders. Anything, really . . . whatever they could hold onto.

Luisa, Josefina, and Antonio saw the conductor roll past, waited a boxcar or two, and started running. The train wasn't moving too quickly yet since it left the station minutes earlier. Their escort had told the sisters that some train conductors intentionally went slower for longer in order to give migrants a better chance of jumping on. Others sped up as quickly as they could to prevent the hitchhikers. This train, Luisa was relieved to discover, seemed to be closer to the former than the latter.

Picking up their own groundspeed, Antonio and Josefina jumped onto a passing platform, landing with a thud next to large, industrial-grade tractors. Once she saw that her little sister was safely aboard, Luisa jumped on too.

"Good work, chiquitas," the coyote said with a huff while he tried to catch his breath. "Settle in . . . you know the drill. We'll have one more stop later today where we have to jump off and get back on, but after that the next time we get off we'll be in Oaxaca. Where I get paid and get rid of you brats."

TEN

The Train of Death, as it was also known, stopped again a short distance down the tracks in Tehuantepec, a bustling city of around 60,000 people that was one of the largest in the region. Known as a center of indigenous Zapotec culture, Tehuantepec was more than double the size of Ixtepec and required La Bestia riders to jump off before reaching the train station where Mexican immigration officials would be waiting.

To Antonio's relief, the Dominguez sisters navigated the jump with ease. They were old enough to be able to climb down without much assistance, but still young enough to not fully realize the danger in what they were doing.

Unlike Ixtepec, which had an entire miniature economy set up to cater to the travelers, the area around Tehuantepec's train station was barren. No vendors selling food and clothing; no relief shelters run by the Catholic Church offering refuge to the tired and weary. Just several hundred people leaning against concrete walls and scribbling in the dirt with sticks, waiting for the next train to come by so they could continue north.

"Not all of the trains stop here," explained Luisa's new friend, the middle-aged man making his fourth attempt at reaching the United States. He took a liking to her and her sister and had been talking to the girls throughout the day. "That's why there's not more set up. All of the trains stop in Ixtepec, but not here. Besides, they know that we all got food and clothes and whatever else a few hours ago, so it doesn't make sense to try to have a business here."

Luisa nodded her head in acknowledgement and gave the man a small smile. He had a kind heart, she could tell, and she was happy to have found a friend along the way. Six days into her new, uncertain life, Luisa clung to anyone and anything that didn't seem like a threat. *Survival is what matters now*, she kept telling herself.

When the train whistle blew and the next round of cargo steamed closer, Luisa and the rest of the travelers gathered whatever belongings they had with them and walked up to the tracks. Josefina was standing beside her on the right, with Antonio on the other side of the young girl. To Luisa's left was the man who was quickly becoming her immigration mentor, José Luis. Luisa smiled when remembering how they had exchanged names while sharing a candy bar that he bought in Ixtepec. *Josefina and I are so lucky to have met him*, Luisa thought while watching the train's engine come into view. She knew that they would be separated soon, with the girls getting off La Bestia in Oaxaca while José Luis continued north. But Luisa was grateful for the encounter anyway. A few kind words and a shared Snickers had done wonders to restore the teenager's shattered faith in humanity.

The train continued to steam toward the station, this time appearing to slow down the bare minimum while rolling through town.

"Shit," Antonio said. "This one isn't stopping here. Come on, you two. We've gotta catch it anyway. The next one won't come through until tomorrow," he added, starting to run beside the tracks. "Let's go! Come on!"

Luisa and Josefina did as they were told, not yet having the worldliness or self-awareness to realize that if they let Antonio get on the train and then didn't follow him, they would be free. Such a maneuver was beyond the thoughts or skills of the girls, though, so they too chased after the speeding train.

"Come on come on come on!" Antonio yelled, running while holding onto a platform ladder with one hand. "Let's go!"

After the coyote jumped aboard the train, he reached down and pulled Josefina aboard. Luisa was next, running as fast as she could and jumping as high as her short legs would allow, grateful for Antonio's assistance.

Luisa turned around, looking for José Luis.

Older and out of shape, he was struggling to catch up to the train.

"Run José Luis!" she yelled. "You can do it! Run!"

Battered sneakers pounded the dirt and gravel as the veteran traveler willed his body to go faster. The man's chest heaved up and down from exhaustion, and just when Luisa was about to give up on him making it on board, José Luis grabbed the platform ladder like Antonio did a minute earlier.

Luisa breathed a sigh of relief.

Looking up to where he would jump, José Luis didn't see the large chunk of gravel lying in his path. His foot tripped, his ankle rolled, and that brief pause was enough to tear the man's hand away from the ladder and suck him down beneath the train.

The first thing Luisa heard was a thud, following by a deep snapping, crunching sound as José Luis' legs were caught on the railroad tracks. Train wheel after train wheel rolled over the man's body, with steel sparking, blood spraying, and screams filling the air so terrifying that they made Luisa nauseous and she felt like she was being crushed to death too.

"Noooo!" Luisa yelled. She dropped down to her knees on the boxcar platform and looked back to where her friend lay. The train rolled on and José Luis settled farther and farther into the distance, but Luisa's hysterics remained. Tears streamed down her cheeks and she sobbed inconsolably, with Josefina doing her best to comfort her older sister.

Antonio, to his credit, didn't force Luisa to stop crying. While Josefina was lucky enough to have been looking the other direction, Antonio wasn't and joined Luisa in watching the other man get sucked under the train. He had seen a lot in his nine years in the trafficking trade, but nothing near as gruesome as that. Antonio shook his head. *Dios mio. What a shitty thing to happen.*

Long after José Luis' body disappeared into the distance, Luisa could still see him. Still hear him. Every bump in the tracks made her jump, thinking that they hit someone else. Every scream from another passenger – happy, sad, or otherwise – made Luisa's nausea return. And jumping off the train when they arrived on the outskirts of Oaxaca was the single most terrifying experience of the young girl's life.

ELEVEN

As Luisa sat on a sidewalk in an abandoned shopping center near Oaxaca, the teenager tried to take stock of what had happened to her. A mere eight days earlier, she had been living with her mother and sister in a one-room apartment in the Honduran city of San Pedro Sula. Now, a week later, she was in a strange country with a strange man who appeared set to do what each of her other 'owners' had done before him: buy her, move her somewhere else, and sell her for a higher price. The rapid set of sales was unusual but not unheard of. Each successive owner was only interested in the Dominguez sisters for how much money they could make him, and, without the infrastructure necessary to keep any of the girls for themselves, Luisa and Josefina were passed along the line – climbing the food chain of black market human sales.

First there was Manuel, who took Luisa and her sister from Honduras to Guatemala. Then came Rogelio, who brought the sisters into Mexico. Their third owner was Antonio, yet another trafficker who braved La Bestia to sell the girls at market in Oaxaca. And on this day, the seventh day, Luisa and Josefina met Orlando. Owner number four.

The girls didn't know it at the time, but Orlando was less an owner than he was an independent contractor. The chain-smoking, black-haired, black-eyed man worked for a notorious Mexican slave trader named El Agente, which loosely translated to The Broker. Similar to buyers for major clothing department stores, Orlando's job was to go to slave trading sites in Oaxaca, Tijuana, Cancún, and other cities and locate prime 'merchandise' for The Broker. While he was free to contract with other top-flight sellers, Orlando made more than enough money and stayed plenty busy as a buyer for El Agente.

On that day in Oaxaca, Orlando purchased eight girls for his boss. All were young, ages twelve through sixteen, and all fit the general profile that brothel customers wanted: beautiful, relatively inexperienced, and with a light-skinned, 'European' appearance. To have all four of those qualities, like Luisa and Josefina both did, was a rare and valuable combination. The Dominguez sisters each commanded the highest price of the day: $600.

Loading all eight girls in the back of a large delivery truck, Orlando chained the doors shut and climbed in the driver's seat.

"Next stop," he said, "Mexico City."

****

The drive from Oaxaca to Mexico City took a little over six hours, with Orlando's truck rattling up Routes 135D and 150D past a series of towns with indigenous names like Asunción Nochixtlán and Tehuacán. They also passed through Puebla, a vibrant city in its own right that Orlando often visited when on the hunt for new merchandise.

In the back of the truck, Luisa and Josefina sat huddled next to each other in a corner. A few of the other girls tried to make conversation, but the Dominguez sisters were too exhausted to be interested in talking. Seven days of travel, little sleep, and even littler food had drained the young Hondureñas of every last ounce of energy that they possessed.

Luisa's eyelids grew heavy, and her head bobbed up and down a few times before coming to rest on her chin. A happy dream soon filled her mind – one of love, safety, and home.

In the fuzzy camera lens of her sleep state, Luisa saw the village where she grew up. It was small, with only a couple dozen families living in the vicinity, and was a solid half day's journey from the metropolis of San Pedro Sula. The Dominguez family home was small and rudimentary, with only three rooms – kitchen, living room, and bedroom – and an outdoor toilet one hundred yards away from the house. The walls were sunbaked clay mixed with concrete cinderblocks, and Luisa was never quite sure where the blocks had come from. The roof of the home was patched and thatched and worked remarkably well, even during the rainy season. The home had a wood burning stove where Abuela cooked, the mattress that Luisa and Josefina shared was stuffed with straw, and the living room doubled as a second bedroom at night.

It was perfect, Luisa remembered, and she smiled despite being asleep. Village life wasn't easy, to be sure, but it was good. Her abuela loved her and wasn't shy about showing it. They were happy and blessed to have each other – something Abuela thanked God for every day during her prayers.

The truck screeched to a halt and Luisa awoke with a start, having slid across the floor during the abrupt stop. She would have slammed into the front wall if not for several other girls in her path.

"We must be close," one of them said with a nonchalant air that made her seem much more confident than she was. "Traffic gets worse in the city."

"Close to where?" Luisa ventured to ask.

The other girl shrugged her shoulders. "Beats me. Mexico City, maybe? Guadalajara? Monterrey? Who knows. Who cares. They're all the same."

Luisa wondered what had made the other passenger so jaded, but she didn't dare ask. Truth be told, she didn't want to know. Because, truth be told, Luisa knew she would find out for herself soon enough.

As the truck wove its way through the never-ending traffic, Luisa held her sister's hand and reflected once more on how far the two girls had come in one short week. *Mami always said she wanted to visit the big cities in Mexico*, Luisa thought. *She said people in the United States were snobs, but that she wouldn't mind living in Mexico. Maybe even its capital, Mexico City. And now we're here and she's not.* Luisa sighed. *I wonder if she would've ended up here too if she sold herself instead of us?*

TWELVE

On a quiet residential street in the upscale Polanco suburbs of Mexico City, at the end of a row of elegant homes, sat the house of Señor Enrique Lopez-Garcia. Of average height with a slowly-expanding waistline, the forty-seven year old Lopez-Garcia was an art collector and dealer, and his life reflected his profession. His clothes blended the latest fashions with a traditional classic look, and his house could have been profiled in any decorating magazine. The gardens were immaculate, the grass and trees freshly trimmed . . . even the stucco security wall surrounding the property was decorated with a beautiful landscape mural. He had twenty-four hour, round-the-clock security guards, but that was the norm rather than the exception in his posh neighborhood. Señor Lopez-Garcia was a nice man and a good neighbor, known in the area for carrying candy in his pockets for the local kids and giving excellent 'friend discounts' on the paintings he sold from his gallery.

Those kind gestures and Enrique's sunny disposition helped make him one of the best-liked neighbors on the street – so much so that the other residents didn't complain about the extra traffic created by clients visiting his home gallery or delivery trucks dropping off new merchandise. It also helped that Lopez-Garcia's house was the last one on the street and had a separate driveway around the side where the trucks could go to unload. Indeed, the business operation ran so smoothly that many of the neighbors forgot about it most of the time.

On that particular Thursday night, well after dark, a large white delivery truck rolled down the street and pulled to a stop in front of the Lopez-Garcia side entrance. The hiss-pop from the brakes spread into the damp air, but the truck's driver made no other movements. No horns were honked; no intercom buzzers were pressed. Orlando sat in the truck. And waited.

After a few minutes, the ten-foot gates in front of him swung open and Orlando drove through them into a large concrete courtyard. He smiled as he put the truck into park. *Pay day*, he thought.

****

Luisa and her fellow passengers huddled as far away from the exit as they could. Some knew what they were in for at El Agente's house, having been to similar locations before. Others, like Luisa, were less sure what was going on. But the girls all had one thing in common: none of them wanted to be there.

Metal chains clanged against the truck seconds before the back doors swung open and Orlando stood in front of them, smoking a cigarette while accompanied by two large, imposing looking creatures. All three men held guns in their hands.

"¡Muévanse!" the man in the middle commanded. When no one moved, he pointed his gun into the cargo hold. "I said move!"

Screams of fear escaped the girls' mouths and they scrambled forward to exit the truck. It was so tall that Luisa had to first sit on the floor and then jump down to reach the ground.

It was dark outside, but the night air had a thickness to it that she couldn't quite figure out and didn't quite like.

"Move!" Orlando barked again, and Luisa was herded forward through an open doorway into a large, dimly-lit room.

When all of the girls from the truck were inside, another person – a woman this time – swung the double doors shut behind them. Luisa heard what sounded like a large chain and lock being snapped into place, and lights turned on to illuminate what the Hondureña could now see was some kind of warehouse. The floor and walls were concrete, and the ceiling looked like it was metal. Large, wooden crates and empty painting easels lined one wall while a row of cots covered the opposite side. Close to a dozen girls sat in the makeshift beds and stared at the new arrivals. There was also a smaller room in one corner, and the lack of a door allowed Luisa to see a sink attached to the wall. *Must be the bathroom.*

"Where are we?" Josefina asked, whispering in hopes that the scary woman guarding them wouldn't hear her.

"I don't know. It doesn't look like somewhere we would live."

"This is the sale warehouse," another girl said, inching her way over to the sisters. "They make us take off our clothes, a doctor checks you for diseases, and then they give you a grade. After that,

39

the chulos come in and pick which girls they want. Then they take you to wherever you'll be working."

"Hey!" the female guard yelled. "No talking!"

Luisa and Josefina both ducked their heads in embarrassment, but the other girl, the one who knew so much, smiled at the guard and blew her a kiss.

"Oh my God – are you crazy?" Luisa hissed.

Her new friend shrugged, with long black hair falling over her shoulders. "She won't do anything to us. If we're bruised and beaten up then we'll have a lower sale price, which means she gets a lower commission. Relax," she said, wrapping her arm around Luisa's waist. "Enjoy these next few days. We get food, showers, a real doctor's visit, and don't have to work any. This is my second time for sale here with El Agente. It's like a vacation."

A vacation? Luisa thought. *She thinks this is a vacation?*

Luisa's face mirrored her thoughts and the other girl laughed. "Stick with me, niña. I'll take care of you."

"T-thanks," Luisa managed to reply.

"I'm Bianca, by the way," she said, stepping back and extending her hand in greeting.

"Luisa. And this is my sister, Josefina."

"Sister, huh? Well, don't count on getting bought by the same pimp. You can stand next to each other and maybe you'll get lucky, but it probably won't happen. And if you get different grades from the judge?" Bianca shook her head. "Then you can definitely forget about it."

Bianca turned and looked at the younger Dominguez sister. "Josefina, right? How old are you anyway?"

"Twelve."

"Dios mio. They keep buying younger and younger girls. And you?" she asked, looking back over at Luisa.

"Thirteen."

Bianca nodded her head. "That's how old I was the first time I came through. But I was one of the youngest. I'm fifteen now. Twelve?" She sighed. "Mierda."

THIRTEEN

Several yards away from the warehouse in the main residence, Enrique Lopez-Garcia stood in front of a mirror examining his appearance. Even though he was only going to inspect the arrival of a new shipment of female merchandise, Enrique wanted to look perfect. Hair combed, teeth cleaned, clothes pressed and fashionable. Nothing but the best for The Broker.

A native of Mexico City, Lopez-Garcia grew up in a less desirable part of town and from a young age was determined to be successful. And rich. After studying art history at the Universidad Nacional Autónoma de México, Enrique landed a job as an assistant at an art gallery. It was grunt work and he made little money, but the bright, polished young man soon gained a reputation in the art world for his keen eye. Within three years of graduation, he opened his own gallery.

One evening, during an exhibit, a customer commented on a pretty waitress and said that she would "fetch quite a price" on the market. Intrigued, Enrique asked the man what he meant.

That was the night that the small-time gallery owner began his life as a big-time sex slave trader.

With an operation that was far more sophisticated than many people knew, Lopez-Garcia oversaw a loose network of scouts, smugglers, and buyers who brought girls to him from all over Central America and Mexico. Brazenly going by his own name in both legitimate and illegitimate business deals, Enrique figured that adopting a different name might cause people to wonder why. After all, many of his best art clients also enjoyed an occasional purchase from his 'reserve collection'.

Those clients and many others told The Broker what they were looking for – age, gender, race, build, beauty – and he contacted them when something arrived that he thought would interest them. Every girl, or boy, coming through his warehouse was tested for disease and examined for 'relative degree of purity' before receiving a grade: Prime, Choice, Select, or Standard. Many of his high-end clients had spent time studying or working in the United States, and they appreciated the humor associated with giving the sex workers the same labels that the US Department of Agriculture used for meat. Prime buyers were usually specialty escort services or one-off purchases, while the second-highest, Choice, went to high-end brothels in big cities or elite ones in smaller markets. People labeled Select or lower were sold in bulk to secondary auction houses. The Broker refused to show his clients anything below Choice.

When a loud knock sounded on the door to his study, El Agente turned away from the mirror. He was vain, but he didn't want his employees to know it.

"Adelante," he said, signaling for the visitor to enter.

One of Enrique's best buyers, Orlando, walked into the room. "They're ready for you in the warehouse, sir."

"Excellent," The Broker replied. "How many did you bring me?"

"Eight, sir. And no throwaways. These will all command excellent prices for you."

Enrique nodded his head and followed the other man out the door toward the warehouse on the back of his property. "They better," he said. "For your sake more than mine."

Orlando heard his boss' threat but was wise enough to keep his mouth shut. He knew who he was working with and where he stood in the pecking order. For what Luisa and Josefina's three prior owners didn't know was that they were all part of a giant human trafficking pyramid, and The Broker was one of a handful of people who sat at the top.

The cartels ran their own operations as part of a larger illicit trade business, but the sex slave market in Mexico City – particularly the high-end sex slave market – belonged to none other than the former art history student, Enrique Lopez-Garcia.

****

Inside the warehouse, Luisa and Josefina sat on the hard concrete floor and linked their arms together, a subconscious effort to stay as close as possible for as long as possible. Especially after Bianca's warning about being sold to different places.

42

One of the outside doors swung open with a bang and a man strode in. Wearing designer jeans, a patterned red button-down shirt, and brown leather loafers, he oozed power and wealth.

He must be El Agente who Bianca mentioned earlier, Luisa thought.

The lone female guard in the warehouse, a middle-aged, heavyset woman with thin hair and even thinner patience, kicked and pushed the girls – old and new alike – until they were all huddled together on one side of the room.

The man clasped his hands behind his back and walked in a slow circle around the warehouse, his gaze roaming over every inch of every person there. When his eyes came to rest on Luisa, she shuddered. *I feel like I need to take a shower just from him looking at me*, she thought. *Gross.*

Inspection complete, El Agente cleared his throat.

"You'll stay here until I find buyers for you. The bathroom is through there," he said, pointing to the small side room. "There's no door and I won't add one. I don't need any of you getting any desperate ideas while unsupervised in there." The Broker paused and scanned his eyes down the line of girls, issuing a silent threat to each of them.

"This is Yolanda," he added, gesturing to the large, glaring woman standing beside him. "She'll be watching you while you're out here. Behave, do what you're told, and you'll fetch a good price from a good buyer. Misbehave and you'll be working a street corner for the rest of your life. Understand?"

The girls nodded their heads and a few mumbled a quiet "yes sir."

"I said *understand?*"

"Yes sir," the group answered in unison.

Enrique nodded. "Good. Now go to sleep. I can't have you looking tired when customers come tomorrow."

FOURTEEN

Early the next morning, the door to the warehouse swung open again and Luisa awoke with a start. She saw Yolanda walk in, accompanied by a spectacled older gentleman wearing a suit who carried a small brown briefcase in his hand.

"Wake up, putas," said Yolanda, walking down the aisle of cots and kicking anyone who was still asleep. "This is Dr. Arbeloa. He's going to examine all of the new girls. Take off your clothes and stand up in a straight line. He doesn't have all day."

The medical visit proceeded how Bianca said it would, with the doctor taking measurements and blood samples before poking and prodding all over their bodies. Luisa, her sister, and the rest of the new girls were then made to lie down on their backs and straddle their feet in the air.

Leaning down, Dr. Arbeloa examined the young ladies' nether regions while asking a series of questions.

"Have you ever had sex with a man?"

"How many times?"

"How many men?"

When the physician got to Luisa, she squeezed her eyes shut and gritted her teeth before lifting her legs into the air. Her entire body tensed as the man more than five times her age stared at parts of her that not even Luisa herself had seen.

"Have you ever had sex with a man?"

Luisa shook her head back and forth.

"Speak, child!" ordered the matron, Yolanda. She kicked Luisa in the ribs with the pointed tip of her shoe.

"No," Luisa managed to say while trying to hold back tears. Some of them were from the pain in her side, but most of them were from the pain in her soul.

Why God? she asked, her eyes still scrunched closed. *Why me?*

****

Luisa's question went unanswered, and for the next three days she and Josefina were paraded back and forth from the warehouse to a showroom that doubled as The Broker's living room. Client after client inspected the naked teen and pre-teen, men of all ages, sizes, and levels of creepiness. Some wore business suits and acted as if they were at any other work meeting. Others came in jeans, flashy shirts, and gold chains and had to be reminded to check their firearms at the door. But, regardless of their attitude and appearance, client after client chose to purchase different girls. A sliver of hope began to push its way into Luisa's mind. *Maybe no one will buy us. Maybe we'll be sent somewhere else. To do different work.* Luisa had learned enough over the past week and a half to know that she wouldn't be set free, but she dared to hope that she might not have to become a prostitute like El Agente wanted her to.

That hope died on Luisa's fourth day in Mexico City.

Late Monday afternoon, on the Dominguez's eleventh day as captives, they were marched into the showroom, otherwise known as The Broker's living room. True to his personality, the interior of El Agente's house was the latest in fashion: sleek, modern, with sharp lines and black and white furniture accented by bright, abstract art. A black, L-shaped leather couch lined two full walls of the room, and built-in bookshelves filled with never-opened classics sat on either side of the black marble fireplace. Two paintings of what Luisa thought were bizarre-looking women – with eyes, ears, and noses out of place and in strange colors – sat on the walls above the couch. Luisa's bare feet squished over the bleach-white carpet and she breathed in the scent of clean furniture, clean humans, and the distant aroma of El Agente's steak dinner wafting in from the kitchen.

Standing in the middle of the room were two men. Luisa recognized one as El Agente, while the person standing next to him and sipping coffee was a middle-aged man with silver hair and a posture that radiated confidence. He was also, Luisa noticed, very handsome and almost as well-dressed as her current owner. *Nobody is as well-dressed as him, though*, she thought.

Luisa knew the routine by that point, and as soon as the living room door closed behind her she began to take off her clothes.

"Customers want to see all of the merchandise, not just the window dressing," Yolanda liked to say.

"Stand up straight," The Broker commanded. "Shoulders back, chin up."

45

The silver fox of a customer put his coffee cup down on the fireplace mantel and walked around the five girls who were on display. After he finished making a circle, the man turned to The Broker and nodded. "Good work. I like them. Except the one on the end," he added, pointing to a shy, mousy girl named Fiona. "She's too old."

Luisa glanced down the line at Fiona and saw the young woman's face turn pale. That morning, she told Luisa that her birthday was in a week. She would be turning seventeen.

"Okay," El Agente replied. "Four it is. Yolanda, take them back to the warehouse and get them ready to leave while my friend and I talk prices."

Luisa and the rest of the girls pulled their clothes out of a pile in the corner, dressed, and followed their guard the short distance back across the courtyard. Tears were already streaming down Luisa's face.

"What's wrong?" asked Bianca, who had been in the showroom with her.

"It's my sister, Josefina. She . . . s-she isn't going with me."

FIFTEEN

It took four guards, two per girl, to separate the Dominguez sisters. After a protracted struggle, the men holding on to Luisa decided to pick her up and carry her out of the warehouse. The young girl kicked and screamed and squirmed the whole way to the windowless van waiting for her in the service driveway. Luisa could hear similar screams coming from inside.

Both sisters were hysterical, and The Broker considered calling Dr. Arbeloa to administer a sedative before a better idea crossed his mind. Entering the warehouse, Lopez-Garcia grabbed a large metal baton from the grasp of the matron, Yolanda, and stormed over to the spot where little Josefina was being pinned down by two guards.

"Sit her up," he barked.

Once Josefina was upright, with her feet hogtied together and a man holding each of her arms, The Broker lifted the baton over his shoulder and swung it into the side of her face.

The guards dropped Josefina's arms as she crumbled into an unconscious heap on the floor. Blood dripped down out of her mouth, leaving little red dots on the concrete beneath her.

Turning to face the rest of his human merchandise, Enrique raised the baton in the air again and rocked it back and forth with his wrist while he spoke. "That punishment was mild compared to what I'll do if any of you whores ever try to pull a stunt like that again."

Meanwhile, in the van, Luisa's hands and feet were tied together and a piece of gray duct tape was slapped over her mouth.

"Shut the fuck up and calm the fuck down," a guard told her. Lowering his voice, he added: "they'll kill you if you don't."

****

After several hours traveling in the back of the van, the group was given a reprieve when they had to stop for gas. The duct tape was ripped off of Luisa's mouth and her hands and feet were untied.

"I'm watching you, puta," the van's driver hissed as he loosened the ropes. "One wrong move and I won't wait until Monterrey to get

47

rid of you. I'll shoot you right here in the middle of broad daylight. And guess what? Nobody will care."

By that point, Luisa was used to threats on her life. She knew he meant it, but she wasn't shocked like she had been before. *Antonio was right*, she thought. *Shit wasn't real on the train. But it is now.* Rather than the threat, her mind focused on the new information that the man had provided her. *We're going to Monterrey.*

Bathroom and gas break complete, the four girls were loaded back into the van to finish the remainder of their ten hour trip. Woman's intuition told Luisa that Monterrey would be the final stop on her long journey north.

"Psst, Bianca," she whispered, not wanting the two men in the front of the van to hear her.

"What?"

"Do you know anything about this guy who bought us?"

Bianca shook her head. "Never seen him before. That's the thing about pimps . . . there are way more of them than you'd think."

"Will you two shut up?" another girl hissed. Luisa recognized her as Ximena, a gruff fifteen year old with a large mane of brown ringlet curls.

"Seriously," the fourth passenger added. "He'll beat us all if you don't be quiet."

Lowering her voice even further, Luisa leaned closer to the unknown rider. "I'm Luisa," she said, extending her arm to shake hands.

The other girl looked down at Luisa's hand and back up at her face. A small huff of laughter escaped her lips. "Viviana," she said, then turned so her back was to her fellow passengers.

Geez, there's no need to be rude, Luisa thought. *We're all in this together.*

On the other side of the van, Ximena continued to shoot lasers at the two chatty girls sitting across from her. This wasn't a school bus, they weren't in a sorority, and Ximena hated when people acted like they were. *Everything will not be okay*, she thought as she ground her teeth back and forth. Ximena's mother was one of those happy people . . . the kind of woman who saw family bonding instead of cramped quarters, fashionable dieting instead of malnutrition, and love pats instead of bruises. A woman with the kind of head-in-the-sand blindness that caused her teenage daughter to lash out in anger and leave home in search of a different reality. *Mom was just like little miss sunshine over there*, Ximena thought, *trying to make friends with me. There are no friends in this life. There is no sunshine. The sooner she learns that, the better.*

****

A few hours later, with the northern Mexican sun beginning to rise, the slave owner, his driver, and his four new purchases rolled into Monterrey. A highly developed, 'Americanized' city, Monterrey was the second wealthiest urban area in Mexico and the home to many international corporations.

The van's brakes squeaked as it pulled to a stop in front of a nondescript building on one of the nicer streets in the Independencia neighborhood. Built on the city's hillside and resembling the favelas that border Rio de Janeiro, Independencia was originally developed as a residential area for cheap, unskilled laborers during Monterrey's industrial boom. Although the work dried up, the people stayed, and the Independencia neighborhood remained one of the poorest in the city with high unemployment and even higher levels of gang activity.

When the van's door slid open, it took a minute for Luisa's eyes to adjust to the early-morning sun. She and the rest of the girls were herded out of the vehicle onto the road.

"Get inside," the driver barked, waving them through a door with the same hand that held a pistol. "Hurry up, move it."

Despite his commands, Luisa managed to catch a glimpse of the street before she went inside. It was narrow compared to modern roads, with potholes and cracked gutters that spoke of better days in the past. The buildings were older too, most of them two or three story concrete structures with bars on the windows and doors. Looking to her right, Luisa saw that the houses climbed the hillside and disappeared into a mountain that dominated the sky above the city. Informed residents of Monterrey knew that it was called *Cerro de la Silla*, or Saddle Mountain, and that it was an official natural monument in Mexico. Turning around, Luisa saw the metropolis of Monterrey below her, a sprawling modern city with skyscrapers and over one million residents.

"I said get inside!" the man with the gun repeated before shoving Luisa in the back.

The pinching pain between her shoulders propelled the young woman forward, through an unmarked door into the single-story building that was her new home.

SIXTEEN

Luisa and the three other new acquisitions were marched at gunpoint down a long, straight hallway past a series of doors. It was dark, with only a single row of lights running down the middle and filling the space with an eerie yellow glow. The floors were concrete, freshly scrubbed, and the walls were made of dark slats of wood arranged in vertical rows. The doors, Luisa noticed, slid on tracks rather than swinging on hinges. When the group reached the second door on the left, Ximena was shoved inside and the sliding door slammed closed behind her. Third left belonged to Viviana. Bianca was placed at the fifth door on the right, and when Luisa and the armed guard reached the sixth and final door on the right-hand side, he flung it open and pushed her inside.

"Welcome home, chiquita," he said with a laugh, then slid the door closed with a thud.

Luisa landed in a heap on the hard floor of her new room. Brown stains dotted the concrete, and dents and cracks revealed years of disrepair. Even the parts of the floor that weren't stained with God-knows-what were starting to yellow, and a thin layer of dust covered everything in the room.

Including the bed, Luisa thought, looking over to see a full-sized mattress, complete with box springs and bed frame, filling nearly one half of the small room. The teenager had never slept on a proper bed before, but now that she had the chance she didn't think she wanted to. What Luisa wanted, though, was the least of anyone's concerns.

The young woman continued to sit on the concrete floor and survey her new surroundings. Plaster of some sort that looked like it might once have been white covered the walls. The original color was now gone, though, replaced by dirt, mold, and red stains that Luisa prayed weren't blood. A single light bulb dangled on a wire from the ceiling.

And that was it. Four walls, a ceiling, a floor, and a bed. No windows. No mirror, no dresser, no closet. No chair or desk. No sink or toilet. *The bathroom must be somewhere else*, Luisa thought. Knowing that gave her a slight bit of comfort, since it meant that she would be allowed to leave the eight-by-eight prison cell at some point. *Well, hopefully. Everybody else has made us go on the floor or in our pants.*

Speaking of urine, Luisa couldn't smell any . . . which was a welcome change from the past two weeks. Her room smelled like dust, mold, cigarette smoke, sweaty men, and something else she couldn't quite put her finger on. Whatever it was, it reminded Luisa of what her mother used to smell like after returning from her boyfriend's house.

The air was drier than she was used to, but Luisa was also much farther north than she had ever been before. Unlike her tropical homeland of Honduras, Monterrey was a subtropical oasis located a mere one hundred fifty miles from the US border.

Without warning, the door to Luisa's room slid open and the driver of the van who brought her there stood in the doorway.

"Still on the floor, eh? Like the dog that you are. Bark for me, mija," he said, grinning.

Luisa kept her eyes trained on the concrete floor in front of her and didn't respond.

Two seconds later, the man was standing over her. Grabbing a chunk of Luisa's hair, he pulled it back so she was forced to look up at him. With his free hand, he placed the muzzle of his gun underneath her chin. "I said bark, bitch!"

Luisa's lower lip began to quiver and tears pooled in her large, black eyes.

"W-w-woof," she managed to say before her eyes overflowed and warm, wet tears streamed down her face.

The man with the gun laughed. "That's better. Now get up," he added, pulling Luisa onto her feet by her hair. "Emilio wants to inspect the new girls."

****

Emilio, Luisa soon learned, was the manager of the brothel. Middle-aged with a receding hairline, massive beer belly, and pock marks covering his face, Emilio was the mano derecho to the brothel's owner, the silver fox who selected Luisa in Mexico City and who Emilio referred to as simply 'Señor'.

Emilio ran a tight ship for Señor, with twelve prostitutes working at all times. He was assisted by one full-time, in-residence matron named Silvia and three security guards who split their time between the brothel and Señor's other business interests in the city. Horatio, the oldest of the guards, was a short, fat man in his mid-forties who smoked like a chimney and was willing to smuggle in certain items to the captives . . . for a price. Silvia, la matrona, cooked meals for the house's residents and managed the girls with a combination of emotional and physical abuse. Emilio took care of the business side of the operation. Male visitors to the brothel paid him up front. Twelve hundred pesos, approximately $80 US, for forty-five minutes to do whatever he wanted with whichever prostitute he wanted. Most of the clients had a favorite who they would visit over and over again.

Prices weren't cheap at Señor's establishment, but the clients knew that they were getting quality. Drug-free, disease-free, with armed guards stationed at the front entrance to prevent an outbreak of the kind of ruffian violence that often plagued less reputable brothels.

La Casa Feliz, or 'Happy House' as it was known, was in the perfect location for its purpose. Far enough away from city center to avoid public scrutiny, yet not so far into the desolate Independencia neighborhood that clients felt unsafe traveling there. A person had to know what he was looking for in order to find the place, and even then some men still complained that they had trouble finding it. Which was exactly what the owner wanted.

The building itself was a former stable that was bought in the mid-twentieth century and converted into a tourist hostel. Each stall became a room, with the stable office up front turned into a reception area and the tack room in the back becoming a serviceable kitchen. There was also a small courtyard between the rooms and the kitchen that was once used to hot-walk the horses and now served as the one area where the girls could go for fresh air.

Carlos Perrera, better known as Señor, bought the house in the 1990s – one of his first big business ventures – and kept it registered with the government as a hostel so they wouldn't wonder why so many people kept coming and going.

La Casa Feliz was a cash cow for Señor Perrera, and Luisa and her three fellow newcomers formed part of the engine that kept the money flowing.

SEVENTEEN

Later that day, after inspections by Emilio and yet another doctor (Señor didn't trust the physician in Mexico City), Luisa and the eleven other prostitutes were allowed to congregate in the open air courtyard at the back of the house. Clients weren't permitted past the hall of bedrooms, so the courtyard was a safe space for the young women. Free of memories of what took place in the bedrooms.

Looking around, Luisa saw a group that was very different and very similar at the same time. Different ages, backgrounds, levels of experience, and levels of despair. But they were all young, even though most appeared to be a few years older than Luisa. At thirteen, she was the youngest in the house. They all had dark hair and pale to medium complexions, since clients preferred a more 'European'-looking girl. All of them were on the skinny side, some more so than others, and all of them were wearing sundresses and other cute outfits that Luisa had only ever dreamed of wearing. Despite the conditions and the nature of the business, Señor wanted his sex slaves to at least look like they were more than pieces of meat. Even if that's exactly how they were treated.

The teenagers also all looked clean, as in sober, which was another surprise for Luisa. The first prostitute she ever met, her mother, was strung out on something every chance she got. Many of the women that Luisa met or saw along her journey north from Honduras looked like they were currently or had recently been doing drugs. Every young woman in the courtyard with her, though, was sober.

It was a conscious decision on the part of her owner: he didn't want them doing drugs. That in itself was a rarity in the commercial sex business . . . pimps were notorious for getting girls hooked on drugs as a way to make them stay. And many of the women chose to smoke, snort, or shoot in an effort to numb the pain from their daily lives. But Señor didn't want drugs around the brothel because he didn't want the penalties associated with it if they got caught in a raid. Recent crackdowns by the Mexican government meant that illegal drug distribution was being taken more seriously, with heavy prison time attached to convictions.

Señor still dealt with drug dealers, and his shipping company's 'don't ask don't tell' policy all but guaranteed that his trucks were carrying weapons and narcotics for the cartels, but that's not what it said on the packing invoices. And if Señor Perrera learned anything during his time as a student in the United States, it was the value of 'plausible deniability'. *Given the shitty state of the Mexican court system*, he often thought, *plausible deniability is all I need.*

The slave owner wasn't at the brothel at that particular moment, though, and Luisa couldn't see any guards either. *I'm sure they're around here somewhere*, she thought.

Luisa felt a nudge in her arm and turned to see Bianca sitting down beside her. Glad to find a familiar face, Luisa flashed a small grin.

"Hey."

"Hey yourself," her friend replied. "How's your room?"

"Crappy."

Bianca nodded her head. "Yeah, mine too. And that bed . . ." the young woman shuddered. "Could they make it any more obvious what we're here for?"

Luisa knew the answer to the question but didn't want to say it. At thirteen, she had yet to even hold hands with a boy – let alone do anything else.

"What happens now?" she whispered, afraid to know but needing the information anyway.

"Now? We wait. Some tricks like to stop by during their lunch break, but most will come late afternoon after work or late evening after dinner."

"Tricks?" asked Luisa.

"Clients. Men," Bianca explained.

"Oh," she replied, lowering her gaze and slumping her shoulders. *Why God?* Luisa repeated her common prayer. *Why me?*

"We give them different names than that," said another girl, having overheard the conversation. "Labels based on how they behave."

"What do you mean?"

"Well, what you want is what we call a vaquero, or a cowboy." The young woman speaking looked much older than Luisa and had a rough, lifeless gaze that spoke of years of experience in the underworld of prostitution. Over the course of the next several days,

Luisa would learn that the woman's name was Roxana and that she was twenty-two years old – a seasoned professional, if one could call it that. The younger residents of the house looked to the tall, dark-haired siren for advice on how to survive. Since the law didn't exist in their world, and the men treated them like property, one wrong move could cost a girl her beauty or her life. To have made it as long as Roxana had – nine years – meant that she had to know a lot about the system. And, to her credit, she was willing to pass along her knowledge to anyone who would listen.

"A vaquero," Roxana continued after a long drag from her cigarette, "will treat you well enough. He knows what he wants and – don't be mistaken – he views you as a means to an end, but he'll be nice about it. Business-like. And might even give you a small tip. Keep your tips hidden," she added, "and never tell anybody about them."

Luisa sat mesmerized in front of her older housemate, soaking in all of the information. "What other kinds of guys are there?"

Roxana smiled, but Luisa noticed that the smile stopped at her cheek bones and didn't reach her eyes. It was a sad smile. That was another similarity – everyone in the house seemed to have that smile.

"How old are you, honey?"

"Thirteen."

"And this is your first house, no?"

The young girl nodded her head yes.

"Then I hope you get only vaqueros here," Roxana replied before taking in another puff of smoke. "Luckily, even though we're in Independencia, this place is on the higher end so we don't see many peones. They usually can't afford to come here, which is good because a peon, you know a farmhand or campesino or whatever, is dirty and sweaty and definitely doesn't have enough money for a tip."

"What's a caballero? asked Bianca, rejoining the conversation. "There was a girl at the last place where we were who was talking about caballeros."

Roxana sighed, and one of the other house veterans laughed.

"Caballeros don't come around here either, kiddo," Roxana said, with sadness in her eyes starting to spread until it enveloped her whole body.

"Urban legend," another girl added. It was Viviana, one of Señor's new acquisitions. She had wild black hair with eyes to match and might as well have stamped 'fuck off' across her forehead. *I wouldn't want to run into her in a dark alley*, Luisa thought.

"The caballero is the knight," Roxana explained. "The one who saves you from this place. Who sets you up in an apartment in some other part of the city and keeps you as his mistress."

"Why wouldn't a knight marry you?" Luisa asked, and the whole courtyard burst into laughter.

"Marry you?!" Viviana exclaimed, laughing so hard that a tear rolled down her cheek. "Not even a caballero is going to marry yeguas like us," she added, calling all of them by the name that Emilio used earlier that morning. For him, they were all female horses: yeguas. The brothel manager found some sick humor in that . . . probably because the girls were kept in a converted barn. But they were horses and the clients were jockeys – "they ride us, get it?" Ximena explained.

Bianca wasn't ready to give up on the knight idea, though. "The girl at the last place where we were, El Agente's warehouse, said that somebody from her old house found a caballero. He didn't move her to an apartment, but he paid extra so she didn't sleep with any other clients. Only him."

Roxana blew a cloud of smoke into the air and shook her head. "Forget anything you heard about caballeros or rescues or romance or anything else like that. Romance is for the rich. Love is for ladies, and we're no ladies. Not by any stretch of the imagination. Focus on the vaqueros, stay away from the peones, and don't be stupid."

EIGHTEEN

After a short moment of rest in the courtyard, the twelve young women were ushered back into their respective rooms to await the arrival of clients. Looking around the eight-by-eight cell, Luisa noticed some details that she missed earlier that morning. Stains on the ceiling. *Is that dirt? Blood?* She couldn't tell . . . and didn't really want to know. There were scratches and scrapes on the concrete floor; brown patchy stains there too. The bed was of a decent size and had a fairly comfortable mattress, but Luisa knew that was driven more by client expectations than any concern or care for the girls.

Turning in a slow circle, Luisa sighed. Except for the lack of windows, it wasn't really all that different from the apartment she shared with her mom and sister in Honduras.

I wonder where they took Josefina, the older sister thought, tears welling up in her eyes. She plopped down on the bed and pulled her feet up under her legs to sit crisscross. *Is she in a place like this?* Luisa wondered, her eyes tracing in the crack lines in the ceiling. *Somewhere better?* She shuddered. *Somewhere worse?*

A small smile crossed the girl's face as she thought back to the many conversations she and Josefina had over the years about boys. First dates, first kisses, and first loves had yet to arrive for the twelve and thirteen year old sisters, but that didn't mean they didn't talk about what they might be like. Luisa, an old soul, said she wanted to marry someone nice and smart with a good job.

"A police officer?" Josefina had asked, and the older sister shook her head.

"No. They're too corrupt. Maybe a teacher," she added with a smile.

"I want to marry somebody fun and beautiful," Josefina had declared, sounding like the girls' mother. "Somebody daring and brave who makes a lot of money and can buy me a house and clothes and jewelry."

"The only guys who make that kind of money are narcos," Luisa cautioned, but Josefina hadn't cared.

She had too much of Mami in her, Luisa thought while sitting on her bed in the brothel in Monterrey. *Has*, she corrected herself. *Josefina has too much of Mami in her.*

A knock at the door made Luisa jump. She leapt out of bed and darted across the room to the far back corner. Wrapping her arms around her waist, she began to tremble.

The door to the former horse stall slid open and Señora Silvia walked in, followed by a man who looked about forty years old. He wore brown loafers on his feet, khaki pants that were a size too big, and a navy blue golf shirt that did nothing to hide the massive gut of a stomach hanging over his cinched-tight belt.

"Here she is," the señora said, stepping aside and motioning to Luisa. "Just like Emilio promised. Young, untouched."

The man scanned his eyes over, up, and down Luisa's body, inspecting and admiring every square inch. Luisa's trembling intensified to shaking. The client nodded. "Good enough. Or at least she better be for what I'm paying you for her."

I'm being sold again? Luisa thought.

"Specialty girls cost more," the older woman responded. "You should know that by now, sir."

"I know, I know," he said, never taking his eyes off Luisa. "What's your name, sweetheart?"

Luisa's shaking had graduated to near-seizure levels, and she couldn't bring herself to even look at the man . . . let alone speak to him.

"Tell her to answer me. And to stop shaking like a fucking retard."

Señora Silvia strode across the small room and slapped Luisa's face. A ring on her middle finger drew a stinging line of blood on the Hondureña's cheek. Undeterred, the señora stood inches away from Luisa. "Answer him," she hissed. "Do what he wants. And smile, dammit."

The matron then spun on her heel and returned to stand beside the sweaty, balding client. "She's all yours. You have forty-five minutes."

****

60

Luisa's first client, her first everything, used his full allotment of time to rape, pillage, and destroy every last ounce of the young girl's innocence. Her screams of terror and pain, her wailing cries for help rang out into the night – boomeranging off the walls of her room and slapping her in the face with her own unending horror.

After the man left, she crawled out of the blood-stained bed, across the floor, and into the back corner of the room. Pulling her knees to her chest, Luisa collapsed on the ground and cried – a river of tears washing over the concrete floor. She could still smell him, feel him, hear him. The physical pain in her child-sized body from the assault by the much larger man was nothing compared to the pain in her heart and her soul. Luisa felt dirty, but a dirty that couldn't be cleaned. Dirty from the inside out. A part of her felt missing too, as if the man with the hairy back and enormous stomach cut a hole into her that could never be filled. Luisa had often heard her mother talk about how sleeping with a man for the first time would 'turn her into a woman', but after what Luisa just experienced, she didn't feel like a woman. She didn't feel like a person. Luisa felt like a piece of meat – chewed up and discarded in a heap on the floor.

What did I do wrong? the little girl thought as she remained huddled in a fetal position, her arms wrapped around knees that wouldn't stop shaking. *Maybe if I had been nicer to Mami. Gotten a job to help pay the bills. Maybe I should've run away . . . taken Josefina, disappeared, and started a new life somewhere else. I could've taken care of her. I could've taken care of us. But I didn't.*

I failed, Luisa thought, triggering a fresh wave of tears to roll down her cheeks. Some of them got trapped in the red valley that Señora's slap created – a stinging pain that radiated out over Luisa's entire face. She welcomed that pain, though. Immediate physical pain was a distraction from other, deeper wounds that would never scab over and heal. *I failed*, she repeated in her mind.

Her bedroom door slid open.

Oh my God. Not again.

NINETEEN

Eight hours and ten clients passed through Luisa's life during her first night in the brothel. Each man the same, yet different, using and abusing the tiny Hondureña until exhaustion overtook pain and she collapsed on the floor and fell asleep.

The next morning, Luisa awoke to the sound of her door sliding open and footsteps entering the room.

Oh please, God. Not again.

"It's okay," a female voice whispered. "It's me . . . Roxana."

Luisa's eyes fluttered open and she saw the older woman, still only twenty-two herself, squatting on the floor next to the rookie housemate.

"The first night is the worst," Roxana said, not bothering to ask if Luisa was okay. She knew the answer to that question.

Running her hand through Luisa's hair, Roxana soothed the young girl like her great-grandmother used to.

"Where are you from, niña?" asked Roxana, trying to take her mind off the night before.

"Honduras."

"What? You're not Mexican? You're an extranjera?"

Luisa shook her head. "No. I mean yes. Ugh . . . I'm a foreigner, yes."

"Oh, honey," Roxana replied, continuing to run her fingers through Luisa's long black hair. "Don't tell anybody that."

"Why not?"

"Clients won't like it, for starters. It's one thing to have Mexican prostitutes running around, but they can get weirdly moral and ethical about foreigners. Much more likely to call the police, and the police would be much more likely to do something."

"Like what?"

"Send you back to Honduras, probably."

"I can't go back there. My mom wouldn't let me come back."

Roxana shrugged her shoulders. "So make up a new place to be from. And do it fast, because the other girls won't like it either if they find out you're not Mexican. They don't want people from other countries coming in and stealing their jobs."

Surprise flashed through Luisa's mind. "You mean they actually want to be doing this?"

Her mentor nodded. "Some of them. Not anybody here, but other people in other places, sure. Fastest, most reliable way for a woman to make a somewhat decent wage. Especially if you can get a job at a government-run brothel." She paused. "It's better than begging on the street."

Luisa shook her head in disagreement. "I'd rather beg on the street than sell my body. Besides," she said with a sigh, "I didn't choose this life. It's different if you have a choice. I would've at least liked to have that."

The young girl's voice trailed off at the end of the sentence and Roxana felt a pang of sadness for Luisa. Although she herself now belonged to Señor, several years earlier Roxana did make the decision to do sex work. She was still a human trafficking victim – the moment her old boss took away her ability to leave, she became a slave. But Roxana was self-aware enough to know that she was part of a larger scheme, and that there was a day, what now seemed like three lifetimes ago, when she made that fateful choice. From what she was hearing, Luisa couldn't say that.

It's both helpful and hurtful for her, Roxana thought. *Helpful because she doesn't have to face the guilt of thinking she brought it on herself, but hurtful because she has no answer to the question 'why me?'*

Roxana shook her head to clear away her thoughts. It wasn't good to dig that deeply into feelings and philosophy. Wasn't healthy. Too dangerous. Too painful.

She took a deep breath and wrapped her arm around Luisa's waist in a side-hug. "Come up with a new story, okay? Be Mexican. Trust me."

After Roxana left her alone in her room, Luisa remained huddled in the corner and thought about what her new friend and mentor told her. Even though Roxana advised Luisa to make up a new story, and even though it was halfway tempting to leave the past behind and become someone new, Luisa couldn't do it. For all its troubles and heartache, her past was still light-years better than her present and any foreseeable future. It was also her last remaining tie to her sister and her beloved abuela. *I can't do it*, Luisa thought, shaking her head. *They may not like that I'm from Honduras, but I*

63

am. And so is my sister, and so were my great-grandparents. Honduras treated me way better than Mexico has so far. I won't do it.

TWENTY

Luisa stayed in her room the whole morning, ignoring visits from her other housemates and avoiding the gaze of the guards who passed by. At midday, though, Señora Silvia had had enough.

"Let's go," she said. "Out of the room. You have to eat something so you don't pass out when clients come tonight. They pay good money for you to be conscious."

Luisa was ushered out of her room and into the nearby courtyard where the rest of the young women were gathered. She found a seat next to Bianca and the señora dropped a plate of rice and beans on the table in front of her.

"Eat."

"Listen to her," Roxana recommended. "She can be an ally here."

Luisa looked back at the older girl with a detached sense of disbelief. Another emotion, anger, bubbled under the surface. Even though Luisa had watched over the past two weeks as a series of men bought and sold her like cattle, she was still young and inexperienced enough to believe that her life was her own. They hadn't broken her . . . yet.

"Don't look at me like that," Roxana said, reading Luisa's expression. "I'm just trying to help. You're no better than me and you'll think like the rest of us do soon enough." She paused. "Believe it or not, this place is a step up for me. Yeah, I'm a prostitute. And yeah, sometimes I get beat up or whatever. But at least here I get a roof over my head and food every day. Before Señor came along, I didn't even get that much."

A sense of sadness filled the room and Luisa wondered how many of her housemates agreed with what Roxana was saying. She didn't. She vowed she never would. Her bright black eyes retained a shine that spoke of freedom. Of escape. Of a life not lived in a former stable. *One day*, the Hondureña thought. *One day*.

****

65

Lunchtime came and went, but the sharp tone remained in the air. Unable to take out their frustrations on clients or guards, the girls' only recourse was their fellow sufferers.

"The springs in my mattress broke last night," complained a girl named Elena, hoping to elicit sympathy, "and now the metal parts poke up into my back."

"Still better than the cot I had at the last place where I worked," replied Ximena.

Viviana snorted. "You're lucky you had a bed at all. Try working the streets – back alleys and backseats. No gracias."

Elena eyed Viviana from across the room. As a daughter of privilege who was lured away from home by an older boyfriend, Elena was better educated than the rest of the girls and never afraid to speak her mind. "Lucky? You're telling me that you think we're *lucky* to be here? Are you serious?"

Viviana nodded, then repeated the same lines they heard every day from their captor and his goons. "It could be a lot worse, chiquita. A lot worse. Are we free? No. Are we whores? Yes. But we're whores who have a non-leaking roof over our heads, clothes to wear, and food to eat. Be grateful for what you have."

Elena rolled her eyes and shook her head in disgust. "You sound like *him*. Grateful? To be his slave? Never."

TWENTY-ONE

Luisa learned within a few days how the majority of clients wanted her to behave during their 'sessions'. After all, she hit the century mark after a week and had the bruises to prove it. The thirteen year old's eyes, cheeks, lips, and chin were all various shades of black and purple, with some transitioning to greenish-brown and a few, the ones from her first day, were solid yellow. More the color of urine than the color of the sun. *Which is appropriate*, Luisa thought as she inspected herself in the small mirror in the bathroom. *My life is more piss than sunshine anyway . . . makes sense that my bruises would match.*

The scratch from Señora Silvia's slap on the first day was red and infected, and Luisa figured that at some point someone would have to do something to fix it. Clients were beginning to notice.

Luisa's once vibrant black eyes had lost their shine, and long, black hair that used to cascade over her shoulders like a waterfall was now ratty and tangled. Her hair needed to be cut, it had gotten way too long, but Luisa doubted that a stylist would be visiting anytime soon.

Maybe Bianca or Ximena can cut it for me. If I can convince Señora Silvia or one of the guards to give me some scissors.

A pair of scissors was once used as a weapon in an attempted escape from the whorehouse so they were now banned. As were knives, forks, pens, and pencils. Hair dryers and curling irons were still permitted – the girls needed to look somewhat presentable – but Señora Silvia kept them in a locked crate and only took them out each morning before the house opened for the day. Food was eaten with a spoon.

Maybe the señora will cut my hair for me. That way she can't say I want to turn them into a weapon. Although, Luisa thought as she walked back to her room and ran her hands over her black and blue stomach, *people can do a lot of damage without any extra weapons.*

"Stop crying, bitch!" her first client had yelled, bringing his arm across his chest and slamming the back of his hand into the side of

67

her face, causing her ears to ring and black spots to fill the space in front of her eyes.

An hour later, when she didn't move quickly enough for her second client, the man grabbed her shoulders with his hands, picked her up in the air, and threw her onto the bed. He then climbed on top of her, pinning her down with his knee under her rib cage while he undressed. He weighed more than twice what Luisa did, and the pressure from his leg grew and grew in her chest – spreading through her ribs and lungs up into her throat until she could barely breathe.

Luisa had tried to cough to relieve the pressure, but he interpreted it as her wanting him to climb off of her. Grabbing a fistful of her hair, the client had leaned down until his face was inches away from Luisa's. The disastrous combination of tequila and cigarette smoke seeped from his pores and made it that much harder for her to breathe. "Not so fast, puta," he had sneered. "I paid good money for you."

Every client on that first night – and nearly every other night – hit, kicked, or otherwise physically hurt Luisa . . . to say nothing of the damage done when they raped her. A rainbow of pain covered the young woman's torso, and large male handprints wrapped themselves around her wrists and upper arms like shackles. Visible reminders that her body was no longer her own. That she was no longer free.

The bruises were beginning to fade, though, and lessened in number as Luisa continued her crash course in prostitution.

Never look them in the eye, she learned. Luisa had yet to have a client who wanted that.

Don't close your eyes either. They want to at least have the illusion that you want to be there.

Don't watch 'it' actually happening. That's "fucked up," as Luisa was soon informed.

The ceiling was a good place to look. Or his neck/upper chest area. Usually safe with that one too. Luisa often passed the time by reading the tattoos on her clients' bodies. Spider webs were popular. As were metal chains. Names. Numbers. Five-pointed crowns. Playing cards. Crosses. Praying hands. Our Lady of Guadalupe.

It was the religious tattoos that stood out to her the most. Praying hands asking for forgiveness but still committing the crimes.

Asking the Virgin Mary for protection when the biggest danger they faced was themselves.

I don't get it, Luisa often thought. But she dared not ask. The young girl grimaced as she touched her right cheekbone. *I only made that mistake once.*

"Why do you have so many tattoos?" Luisa had asked on her second night in Monterrey. The man was the first client she had with full-body tattoos, and it was a question she always wanted to ask before but never had the opportunity to.

"Shut the fuck up!" the client yelled in reply, slapping her hard on the face in the same spot where Señora Silvia got her the night before. The scab on Luisa's cheek ripped open, causing blood to pour out over her skin.

"Nobody gave you permission to talk!" the man said, continuing his angry response. He shoved the tiny teenager into the back wall, adding her blood stain to that of an untold number of women who came before her. When Luisa bent over and grabbed her elbow in pain, the gang member used the opportunity to kick her square in the stomach . . . the steel toe of his boot landing just above her belly button.

Luisa collapsed on the floor, coughing and spitting up blood.

Her male visitor growled and shook his head. "Fucking disaster," he pronounced before storming out of her room and down the hall to demand a refund.

Emilio and a young security guard named Raúl soon returned . . . each taking turns hitting, kicking, and slapping Luisa as she lay crumpled on the dirty concrete floor. "What the hell do you think this is – some kind of dating service?" Emilio bellowed as he landed another kick into Luisa's right side. "You don't get to ask them questions!"

"You don't get to do anything at all unless they tell you to!" Raúl added, the pointed toe of his cowboy boot piercing the middle of Luisa's chest. "You're a whore. Whores don't speak!"

Luisa didn't service any more clients that night. Her bloodied, bruised, and swollen body wouldn't allow for it.

Luisa never asked questions after that, either. She learned not to talk at all unless the men told her to . . . *and most don't tell you to.*

Don't smile too much – that makes them think you enjoy it and encourages them to be even rougher.

And, for the love of God and all things holy, don't cry. Don't ever, ever cry.

Luisa had always been good at school when she was little. She liked learning. But these were lessons she wished she never had.

TWENTY-TWO

On the morning of Luisa's two week anniversary at La Casa Feliz, the teenager made her way from her room into the courtyard and sat in one of several wooden chairs that were huddled around small tables. Any chance they got, Luisa and her housemates escaped their cells and spent time on the patio. Even when it rained, a couple of girls could still be found in the courtyard. It was their only place of peace in the house they were never allowed to leave.

Luisa knew all of her fellow prostitutes by that point: their names, ages, voices, and stories. Many were tricked into 'the life' by abusive boyfriends who became pimps. Other girls were runaways and turned to sex work as the only way to survive on the streets. A couple had been kidnapped, but as far as Luisa knew she was the only one who was sold by her family.

The young women had even started to form cliques like any other group of females would do.

There was Bianca, Luisa's best friend in the house.

Ximena and Viviana – Luisa's fellow newbies – were the resident mean girls. The only person they couldn't get away with bullying was Roxana, the house veteran and Luisa's mentor.

Elena, the fair-haired, fair-skinned, smart-mouthed former rich girl, tended to keep to herself . . . except for when she saw an opportunity to act superior to someone else.

María didn't belong to any particular clique and, despite the circumstances, retained a bright, sunny disposition. Luisa suspected that it was an act – that on the inside María was hurting just as much as the rest of them. But she didn't pry. Everyone did what they had to do to survive. *If it helps her to act happy, then she can act happy.*

Luisa didn't know much about the girls they called 'the two G's': Gabriela and Guadalupe. Friends from a stint at a prior brothel, the two G's kept to themselves. Susana was also quiet most of the time, except for when the devout Catholic was praying. Despite everything that had happened to her, Susana's faith was stronger than ever.

Cristina filled the eleventh spot in the house. On the first day, she told Luisa that she was from Acapulco, but when she later found out that Luisa was Honduran, the tiny sixteen year old changed her story.

"I was born in Guatemala," she whispered to Luisa so no one else could hear. "But Roxana said I should pretend to be Mexican, so I tell people I'm from Acapulco. I don't know what I'm going to do if we ever get a girl who is actually from there."

"Maybe it's a big enough city that you could both be from there and not know it?" Luisa suggested, despite knowing nothing of the beach haven in western Mexico.

"Yeah, hopefully," Cristina replied. Not even five feet tall, the Guatemalan immigrant looked both older and younger than the rest of the group. Born in a rural village, Luisa knew that Cristina's small stature was due to a shortage of food growing up. Malnourishment often began in the womb and continued through death in small towns like theirs. It was Cristina's face, though, that made her look older. A haunting, taut, leather-tanned face with big, round eyes that looked like they had seen enough for three lifetimes.

The two girls were huddled together at a corner table in the courtyard, away from any interested observers.

"My husband left me when I was thirteen," Cristina admitted over her cup of coffee.

Luisa choked on her drink.

"Did you say . . . your husband?"

Cristina nodded.

"How old were you when you got married?" Luisa asked.

"Eleven," her housemate answered. She saw the horrified expression on Luisa's face and shrugged her shoulders in response. "That's what happens where I come from. The law says you can marry at age fourteen, but my husband asked my parents for my hand in marriage and they said yes. So we got married."

"When you were eleven."

"Mmm hmm."

Luisa had seen a lot in her own thirteen years and knew that she shouldn't have been so surprised – after all, her own sister Josefina was only twelve when their mother sold them. But the idea of being married at eleven seemed . . . crazy.

"My daughter was born when I was twelve," Cristina continued, either unaware or uninterested in Luisa's shock. "My husband was mad. He said he wanted a boy. That a girl didn't do him any good."

72

The young Guatemalan sighed. "He stayed for a little while, but then he left."

"What about your daughter? Where is she?"

"Juana? She's with my parents." Cristina paused and looked around, wanting to make sure that there was still no one listening to their conversation. "A few months after Marco left, I met a woman who said she was looking for people to work for her in Mexico. She promised me great money and said it would be enough to send home to support my daughter. So I went with her. I thought I was going to work in a factory, and I guess it kinda was. A sex factory. Then the lady made a deal with Señor and here I am." She sighed. "I never had enough money to send any home. My daughter probably doesn't even know who I am anymore."

There was a sadness in Cristina's voice that Luisa often heard from the other girls, but Cristina's was also laced with anger. Vengeful, fierce anger that flashed especially bright in her eyes whenever the guards were nearby. Luisa knew that if Cristina ever got the chance, she would grab one of their guns and kill every male in sight.

"But what I don't understand in it all," Cristina added, "is how that lady could betray me. Men will be men, but for a *woman* to trick me like that and take me away from my daughter? She was the worst of all. A traitor." The girl paused, anger receding to make room for the return of sadness. "My daughter will be four next month."

"Cristina," Emilio barked as he walked into the courtyard. "Back to your room. You have a client."

The young mother sighed and stood up from her chair, shuffling her feet across the concrete, out of the bright courtyard, and into the darkness that awaited her.

After Cristina and Emilio were gone, Luisa left the corner and joined Bianca and another housemate, Esperanza, at a larger table in the center of the room.

Esperanza was talking, but the older girl was so lost in her thoughts that she didn't notice when Luisa sat down beside her.

"I was a good person," Esperanza said, twisting her coffee mug back and forth between her hands. "I had a job working as a receptionist at a hotel. I worked the late shift so I could be home with my son during the day." She took a long sip from her cup and

73

sighed. "One night, when I was waiting for the bus after work, the police came and arrested me."

"I was caught up in an operativo," Esperanza continued. "A raid. The police accused me of being a hooker. I had no way to prove that I wasn't. Other girls who were prostitutes had their pimps waiting for them at the police station to bail them out of jail. I didn't have a pimp, I didn't want a pimp, so I had to stay. By the time I got out, I had lost my home, my job, and my son. Social services took him away. They said I was 'unfit' to be his mother." The young woman buried her face in her hands and broke down sobbing.

After a few minutes, when the crying subsided, Esperanza looked back up through bloodshot eyes. "I tried to find another job to prove that I was a good mom and could take care of my baby, but nobody wants to hire a convicted ex-prostitute. Eventually, after being homeless for a while, I had no choice but to become what everybody already thought I was. It was the only way that I could afford to eat." Esperanza paused and looked down at her feet, scraping her toe across the concrete floor. "All I was doing was waiting for the bus."

TWENTY-THREE

The brothel's owner, Señor Carlos Perrera, didn't visit often. The well-respected businessman's home and office were on the other side of town where a man like him would be expected to reside. Trips to the hills of Independencia were limited to about once a month, except when he had to make a slave purchase or his deputy, Emilio, called and told him something was wrong. It didn't happen often. La Casa Feliz – named that way because clients always left happy – was a well-oiled machine.

On this particular day, though, a Saturday, the millionaire zipped his sports car through Monterrey traffic and into the rough part of town that housed his brothel. Señor Perrera was making an unannounced visit.

Pulling his car to a stop in front of the entrance to the converted barn, the business tycoon climbed out of the Audi coupe and tossed his keys to the young guard who came running outside. Perrera didn't worry about leaving his car parked there on the street, even though it was worth more money than the neighborhood residents would make in a lifetime. His security team was well-armed and well-trained, and people living in close proximity to the brothel knew better than to mess with any of the fancy cars that frequented La Casa Feliz.

Walking inside, Perrera was greeted by two large German Shepherds who patrolled the house day and night. "Hello boys," he cooed, petting them both on the head. "Are you keeping everyone in line?"

Standing up, the brothel owner drew in a deep breath and cringed at the smell filling the air.

"Emilio!" he called out, and a minute later his second-in-command came jogging down the main hall.

"¿Sí Señor?"

"What the hell is that smell? Dios mio, don't you ever clean this shithole? How can you expect clients to want to come into a place that smells like this?"

"I'm sorry, sir. We'll get it cleaned right away. It won't happen again," Emilio promised. Having grown up just a few blocks away,

75

the mano derecho to the millionaire didn't have the same exacting hygiene standards as his boss.

"It better not," Carlos Perrera replied. Walking down the hall of bedrooms, with the two guard dogs trotting behind him, he said: "where are all of the girls?"

"In the courtyard, sir. The doctor was just here for their monthly drug and disease tests."

"Ah, good. I can't have this place turning into any more a cesspool than it already is."

Emilio ignored the verbal jab and followed his boss down the hallway toward the back of the brothel. Walking into the courtyard, he saw all twelve prostitutes engaged in idle chatter and conversation. An uninformed visitor might have guessed that the place was some sort of sorority house.

"What the fuck are you whores doing sitting around here like you own the place?" Señor bellowed. All of the girls jumped to their feet, causing several coffee cups to fall and shatter on the concrete floor. "*I* own La Casa Feliz. *You* work here. If you aren't with a client, you should be cleaning this shithole until it stops smelling like one." Turning to the side, Señor gestured toward the manager, Emilio. "This is your fault for letting them be like this. I better never see them taking advantage of the situation like this again."

"Yes sir," Emilio replied. "Won't happen again, sir."

"Good." The slave owner put his hands in the pockets of his bespoke gray suit and walked around the room inspecting his property. "Did they all pass their disease tests?" he asked.

"Results will be back in a couple of days, sir," said Emilio.

Perrera nodded. "Get rid of anyone who doesn't pass." He paused in front of Luisa and let his eyes roam up and down her body. "I can't have any of you spreading some disease to a client. If news like that got out, this place would be finished."

"It'd be worth catching gonorrhea to make that happen," Ximena mumbled under her breath.

A few of the teenagers struggled to contain giggles of laughter.

"And what the hell is so funny, hmm?" their owner snapped, glaring at the group.

"Nothing, sir. Nothing is funny."

Perrera looked back and forth between the young women before letting out a deep breath and shaking his head. "Pinches putas," he

76

said and turned and walked out of the room. Emilio and the other guards followed him.

As soon as the courtyard's door slammed shut, María put her hands up beside her head with her thumbs touching her temples, wiggled her fingers, and stuck out her tongue. "Desgraciado."

"Who does he think would give us those diseases, anyway?" said Elena, factual as always. "Clients. Clients *he* brings here."

"No kidding," Bianca replied. "We all tested clean before we came here. He acts like it would be our fault for catching a disease from a man that he forced us to have sex with."

"Like I said: desgraciado," María quipped.

"Monstrúo," added Luisa.

"Imbecil."

"Puto."

The last description caused all of the girls to double over in laughter. The idea that their owner would live a double life as a gay male prostitute was too funny to ignore.

"Wait wait wait," Ximena said, still laughing. "I've got it: travesti!"

More laughter filled the room, and Luisa couldn't remember the last time she had been in that good of a mood. She was still a sex slave and her laughter was directed at the man who controlled every aspect of her daily life, but Luisa nonetheless found comfort in the shared experience with her housemates. *We may not always like each other and we may not always get along*, she thought, *but there is one thing we can agree on: we hate him.*

****

After giving Emilio further instructions and warning him to prepare in case of a police raid, Señor Perrera walked out into the late morning sunshine and drew in a deep breath of fresh air. "Good Lord that place stinks."

Grabbing the keys from the security guard, the businessman climbed back into his car and sped away from the brothel. The only good thing about the half hour visit, as usual, was seeing his two dogs.

Carlos Perrera loved dogs. He never had one when he was a kid, but when his parents sent him away to the US for boarding school, there were dogs everywhere. The housemom in his dorm had a Shih Tzu named Muffin. The headmaster had a huge, gorgeous Golden Retriever named Otis. Everywhere he went during high school, Perrera saw dogs. He loved it.

Carlos thought about getting a dog in college, but it seemed like a lot of work and a lot of money. Money he didn't have on the meager allowance his parents gave him every month. One day, while home for the holidays, an old friend asked if he might be interested in making some easy cash. The friend, Perrera was told, had contacts in the drug trade. What he needed was somebody in the US who they could trust to make sales.

Luckily, when the campus police showed up at his apartment, Carlos had just finished several sales and hadn't yet restocked. He was booked for simple possession and put on probation at the university. Perrera's parents made him come home, though, and that was the true beginning of his life of crime . . . and dog ownership.

After building a trucking empire from scratch, the millionaire magnate now had two Labrador Retrievers at his home – sweet, energetic family pets who slept at the foot of his daughter's bed every night. And then there were his other dogs. A trio of Dobermans lived at his warehouse, guarding whatever merchandise he was storing that day. And two German Shepherds made their home at the brothel. Nasty, vicious creatures who flunked police dog school but still learned enough to be able to terrify the prostitutes and make sure that no one entered or exited the building without proper authorization.

Yes, Señor Perrera loved dogs. They were the best security guards he ever had.

Perrera leaned his head back against the seat as he drove through Monterrey's busy streets on his way home. Going to the brothel was a tiresome trip. The building was a cash cow – Carlos made more money from his prostitution ring than any of his other businesses – but it was also a major headache. None of his other products caused him that much trouble. He shook his head. *Stupid bitches*.

Today had been particularly difficult after a close call with the police. Local cops usually turned a blind eye to his brothel, even

78

though they didn't believe for one second that he was running a hostel for tourists in one of the most dangerous parts of the city. But, early that morning, Perrera was summoned to the courthouse to speak with the police. The feds were in town checking up on things and had heard rumor of an illegal brothel with underage girls. While Carlos wasn't afraid of a raid by the local police, who would arrest the girls and then let Emilio pay their bail, federal agents wouldn't be as kind. *And might bring a military unit with them, given the location*, he thought. *I need a federal raid like I need a hole in the head.* Señor Perrera gritted his teeth and let out a small growl. The fact that he was singled out meant that someone had betrayed him. A client, maybe. Or an employee. *He'll be a dead employee soon if that's the case.* The whole situation made Carlos angry. *Damn brothel is getting to be a pain in the ass.*

Perrera sighed and flipped on his blinker as he turned onto his quiet, residential street. "And to top it all off, I had to go up to that rat-hole on a Saturday to make sure Emilio and his crew were ready in case of any raids," he said aloud. Exits to the building were limited in order to prevent the slaves from escaping, but there were a few doors only visible from the inside and an abandoned house several blocks away where the girls and the guards would wait until trucks could come from Carlos' warehouse to pick them up. Perrera drew up the plan himself and Emilio could recite it by heart, but knowledge and execution were two separate things. *And nobody ever accused Emilio of being smart.* He sighed. *What a fucking pain in the ass.*

Señor pulled his car to a stop inside the gates of his two-story mansion. It was ten times the size of the house he grew up in as a kid, and he was extremely proud of the business empire he built from the ground up. Proud and protective. *And willing to do whatever it takes to keep it running smoothly.*

Walking inside, Carlos was greeted with kisses from his wife, daughter, and dogs. An outside observer would've labelled the Perreras as the perfect family. Close, caring, successful. Fine upstanding citizens representing the best of Monterrey and Mexico. Indeed, that's exactly what *Clase* magazine said when it profiled the family earlier that year. Carlos' wife had a framed copy of the issue in the living room.

No one – not even his wife or daughter – suspected that most of the clients for Perrera's trucking business were members of drug cartels. Drug cartels who paid a premium for 'don't ask don't tell' shipping. No respectable person knew that the hostel he owned was, in truth, a brothel. And not even the police would've believed that the night before his meeting at the station, Carlos was at his warehouse swinging a baseball bat at the knees of an employee caught trying to steal money from his office safe.

TWENTY-FOUR

A couple of weeks after Señor's surprise visit, Luisa heard a commotion in the hall and stepped out of her room to see Ximena waving something in the air. Susana was jumping up trying to snatch the item from her hand.

"Give it back!" Susana screamed, and Ximena laughed.

"I'm serious, Ximena. Give me back my Bible!"

When the door to the kitchen swung open and Señora Silvia started to march toward the girls, bloody meat cleaver in hand, Ximena lowered her arm and passed the holy book back to its owner.

Susana grabbed it and scurried away to her room, hoping to avoid punishment from la matrona. Ximena, for her part, lowered her eyes and stepped to the side of the bedroom hallway but didn't leave.

"If you pull shit like that again," the supervisor said, "I'll cut off your arm and serve it to you for dinner."

Ximena nodded her head in response.

After the señora returned to the kitchen, Ximena looked up and saw Luisa watching her from her doorway. Nodding in the direction of Susana's room, she said:

"I was just trying to stop her from embarrassing herself. She's prays all the time. Like *all* the time," Ximena added. "She even told me once that she prays while with the clients. You know, like what do you think about during that, right? I usually try to not think, or I get distracted and can't stop thinking about how bad he smells or how sweaty or fat he is, but Susana *prays* the whole time. I mean, seriously. Who does that?"

Viviana emerged from her room and giggled. "Imagine if the men knew!"

Luisa gave a half smile in return, a little bit amused by the idea of any of the girls telling their clients that they were praying for them. *It's not as funny as Ximena is making it out to be, though*, she thought.

Luisa's great-grandmother had been a very religious woman, attending mass at least once a week and carrying a rosary with her everywhere she went. Luisa didn't have that level of devotion – *what kind of God would give me a life like this?* she often thought – but she wasn't one to mock the faith of others. And, from a practical perspective, she figured that the smarter bet was to believe in God than the other way around.

"If I believe and he doesn't exist, I lose nothing," a young Luisa told her sister one day after returning from church with their abuela. "But if I don't believe and he does exist, then I'm screwed."

Luisa remembered her sister shaking her head. "I don't think it works that way," Josefina had countered. "If you only believe because it's a safe bet, you're not really believing."

The older of the two Dominguez sisters had been struck by the beyond-her-years wisdom of little Josefina. It wasn't always evident, and most people who didn't know her very well thought that she was an airhead. But every once in a while a gem would pop out of Josefina's mouth like it did on that day. Luisa smiled at the memory.

Ximena mistook her smile for agreement. "See, even Luisa thinks it's funny to pray like Susana does."

Luisa shook her head. "No, I wasn't smiling about that. And I don't think it's funny. We all do what we have to do survive here and not go crazy. I sing sometimes, Bianca reads books that she gets Horatio to smuggle in, you make fun of everybody, and Susana has her faith. Good for her."

****

Down the hall in the reception room of the brothel, Horatio sat on one of the couches and scribbled in a small, handheld notebook. The security guard was writing in code so it couldn't be deciphered by any of his co-workers or, God forbid, his boss. If Señor Perrera ever found out about the black market business that Horatio ran with the prostitutes, the guard had no doubt that he would be strung up by his toenails and fed to Señor's dogs.

Using a miniature pencil, Horatio made note of that day's orders.

Ximena was out of cigarettes and asked him to bring her three packs. *So that's 15 . . . S . . . 3.* The brothel's rooms were numbered 5 through 50, counting in fives, alternating sides of the hall. Ximena was in the second room on the left, so she was fifteen. 'S' stood for smoking, and three for the number of items requested.

The religious one, Susana, asked Horatio to look for a 'daily devotional' to help her study her Bible. *Room 25 . . . J for Jesus . . . and quantity is one.* Horatio thought about Susana's request and shook his head. *God love her*, he thought, *because nobody else will.* If he knew how, if it wouldn't mean risking his and his family's lives, Horatio might have considered helping Susana escape to a convent. She could hide out there, start over, and he had no doubt that she'd love being a nun. But it wasn't good to get involved in the lives of the whores who came in and out of La Casa Feliz. Guarding them was his job; selling them contraband was his livelihood. Helping them escape would ruin both.

Bianca, the nice one, had read her current romance novel ten times and complained to Horatio that she knew every word by heart. "I need a new one. Something long. And good!" *Of all the things to spend her hard-earned money on.* Girls had asked Horatio to buy some strange things over the years, but Bianca's book requests topped the list. *Not just books*, he thought. *Romance novels. Imagine wanting to read love stories in a place like this.* The long-time employee at La Casa Feliz shrugged his shoulders and made note of the illicit order in his ledger. *Room 50 . . . R for reading . . . quantity one.*

Hearing footsteps in the hall, he snapped the notebook shut and stuffed it into the front pocket of his jeans. Señora Silvia poked her head into the parlor.

"Any clients yet?" she asked.

"Nope. Nobody so far." Horatio glanced at his watch. "They should start trickling in soon."

Silvia nodded her head and left, her stiletto heels click-clacking back down the hall toward the kitchen.

Horatio breathed a sigh of relief. He always took orders and made deliveries on Mondays – Emilio's day off. But between talking one-on-one to his customers, writing down the orders, and then delivering the merchandise to the rooms undetected, the black market business was almost more trouble than it was worth.

Almost, he thought with a smile. Pulling his cell phone out of his back pocket, Horatio swiped the screen to unlock it and reveal a background photo of two smiling children. With black curly hair and eyes that couldn't decide if they wanted to be amber or brown, Horatio's nine-year-old twin daughters were the center of their father's universe. His own dad abandoned his family when he was a young boy, causing little Horatio to have to drop out of school to help support his mother and younger siblings. Because of that, on the day his wife first told him she was pregnant, Horatio vowed to give his children everything he never had in life: a home, food, clothes, a father, and a proper education. He could cover the first four with his salary from Señor Perrera, but a proper education in his neighborhood meant private school. Expensive private school. That was where the contraband came into play.

Horatio nodded his head. *Between the money I get from the girls for bringing them this stuff and the night security job I have at the jewelry store downtown, I have barely enough to pay tuition each semester.*

A client walked in to the room and stirred Horatio from his thoughts. After taking the man's money and directing him back to the last door on the right, Luisa's room, Horatio sighed and shook his head. *I'd run twenty more illegal businesses and even sell drugs myself if it meant keeping my kids from ever having to work in a hell hole like this one.*

TWENTY-FIVE

Early that afternoon, after the lunch rush and before the brothel re-opened for the evening, the girls met in the courtyard to talk. Despite his promise to Señor, Emilio still allowed the impromptu gatherings. He didn't see the harm in it, provided there weren't any clients in the house.

From a distance, a bystander wouldn't have been able to differentiate their conversation from that of any other group of teenage girls.

Clothes were a popular topic. Who wore what and when. Can I borrow that? Will you lend me this?

Makeup as well. Which foundations did the best job hiding bruises. What color eyeshadow went best with which outfit. Is that a new lipstick? Can I use it?

They all liked to talk about music, too. The most popular songs, their all-time favorites, the bands they loved, and the singers they hated.

Señor let them play music in their rooms, but only because many clients liked it that way. The actual radio wasn't allowed, and neither was any kind of online streaming service. Those could be reconfigured to play the news or send messages asking for help. CD's were permitted, though, and, in an effort to make the clients happy, Emilio kept the house stocked with classic favorites like Carlos Santana as well as modern Top-40 from both Mexico and the United States. With Monterrey being so close to the border, the cultural influence from the north was impossible to ignore.

Señor was also relatively generous with clothes and makeup – again as part of showcasing his merchandise. His brothel was known for being affordable yet upscale, which meant that the young women couldn't be dressed in rags.

"We have to look nice," Roxana had explained to Luisa on her first day in the house. "The clients don't care very much – I mean a prostitute is a prostitute – but Señor cares. Emilio cares. If they care, Señora Silvia cares. And if she cares, we care. Got it?"

Luisa had nodded her head and made a mental note to keep closer watch on what the other residents wore and how they did their hair and makeup. She never thought about any of that stuff while she was in Honduras . . . she was lucky to have any clothes at all. Makeup was a luxury they couldn't afford, and her mom wouldn't have let her wear it anyway. "Too young for that," she always said.

But I'm not too young for this? Luisa thought, looking around at the barn-turned-brothel. *That makes a whole lot of sense, Mom.*

Luisa's time in the Happy House was teaching her a lot, and not only things a sex worker would be expected to learn. She now knew fashion, how to put on makeup without looking like a clown, how to walk in high heels without falling over (a life skill if there ever was one), and she had even gotten pretty good at nail art. Some of the girls would use their meager tips to pay Luisa to draw intricate designs on their fingernails.

Yes, Luisa thought as she sat in the courtyard that afternoon, *I like these group chats.* It was the school of life and class was in session. *I don't like today's topic, though.*

Luisa was sitting off to the side, picking at some chipped polish on her fingernails, trying to both listen to the conversation and avoid being drug into it. The others were talking about the future: hopes, dreams, goals, plans. Plans they knew would never come true, and dreams they dreamed anyway.

"If I ever make it out of here," María said, "I'm going to move to Mexico City. I'll get a job at one of the big, fancy stores and help ladies find the best things to wear. Then maybe one day I'll have my own clothes store."

Luisa smiled but kept her eyes downcast. *That makes sense. María is always talking about clothes and fashion.*

"Nice," said Cristina in response to María's plan. "If I ever make it out of here, I'm moving to the beach. I'll be a waitress or a bartender or whatever else, but I want to be near the water every day."

Several of the girls nodded their heads in approval, despite the fact that most had never seen the ocean.

"What about you, Luisa?" Cristina asked. "You're mighty quiet over there. What will you do if you ever get out of here?"

Luisa's head shot up and her black eyes grew wide. "Me?"

"Yeah, you. What's your dream?"

"I, uh . . . I, I don't know."

"What do you mean you don't know? Everybody's got a dream. That one secret thing they wish for that keeps them from stealing one of Señora's knives and stabbing themselves in the chest."

Luisa shrugged her shoulders and looked back down at her fingernails. "I don't." Taking a deep breath, she explained: "in my hometown, I never thought past the next day. Where dinner would come from or if my mom would have enough money to pay the rent. When my abuela was alive and I lived with her, things were a little better, but we were still really poor. Abuela always said that you can't change the past and you can't control the future, so focus on the present. Then my mom sold me when I was thirteen." Luisa shrugged again. "My future got taken away from me before I had a chance to make plans for it." She paused, then added: "My dream is freedom. I don't need to be rich. I just need to be free."

A hushed silence filled the courtyard. Luisa's words spoiled the fun of the moment.

María, the fashionista, wasn't ready to give up the game. "What would you *like* to do, though? If you could do anything?"

Luisa thought about it for a minute. "A nail salon, maybe. I like doing people's nails."

The rest of her housemates smiled and voiced their approval of the idea.

"Perfect," María said with a nod. "You'd be perfect at that."

Luisa understood why the house's other residents liked to talk about their hopes and dreams. It provided an escape from the present. A way of leaving their current miserable conditions, even if only for a few minutes and only in their minds.

Luisa understood it. But she couldn't do it herself. Happiness to her meant a roof over her head, clothes on her back, food in her stomach, and not having to have sex with strange men to get those things. It meant a day without violence. Luisa couldn't think beyond that because she'd never experienced beyond that. To even piggy-back on the dreams of another girl and see where they might lead was a step too far for Luisa. *Because as soon as the story ends, as soon as I wake up from the dream, I realize I'm still stuck here. All it does is remind me how far away things like that are, and how I'll never get them for myself.*

Luisa shook her head and stood up from her chair to return to her room. She didn't feel like talking anymore.

Client by client. Day by day, she thought. *Nada más. Nothing more.*

****

A few minutes later, there was a knock on Luisa's door. Susana's head poked through a small opening.

"Hi. Can I come in?"

"Sure," Luisa nodded. "What's up?" she asked as Susana took a seat beside her on the bed. There were no chairs or other furniture that could provide seating, so the girls were forced to use the mattress as not only a bed but also a workstation, table, and couch.

"I heard you talking in the courtyard," Susana said, her soft voice reminding Luisa more of her great-grandmother than a teenager. "About your life plans and freedom. When you said you don't need to be rich, you just need to be free?"

"Yeah," Luisa said. "What about it?"

"Well, I had also heard you say before how you used to go to mass when you were a little girl, so I thought I would bring you some Bible verses about freedom."

Luisa looked down at the piece of paper that Susana was handing to her. The whole thing, top to bottom, was covered in scribbled handwriting.

"In my anguish I cried to the Lord," Luisa read aloud, "and he answered by setting me free."

"Psalm 118:5," added Susana.

"Now the Lord is the Spirit, and where the Spirit of the Lord is, there is freedom."

"Second Corinthians 3:17."

"I don't understand," Luisa said, still looking at the paper. "What am I supposed to do with this?"

"Keep it," her visitor replied. "Read it whenever you need encouragement or reassurance that God can give you the freedom you want."

Luisa shook her head and handed the Bible verses back to Susana. "Look, I appreciate the effort. It was really nice of you and I hate that you wasted a piece of paper on something I won't keep. But I'm just . . . that's not the kind of freedom that I was talking about."

"It's the only kind of freedom that truly matters," Susana countered.

"Geez, you don't give up do you? What are you – a spy from the local parish or something?"

Luisa stood up from the bed and began to pace the room, her voice rising with each step. "If God loved me, if God gave freedom like those quotes say, then he'd get me the hell out of this place. He wouldn't make a world where people are forced to have lives like mine."

Susana sighed, nodded her head, and folded the piece of paper before putting it back in her pocket. She stood up and walked to the door.

"By the way, Luisa," she added, "he didn't."

"Excuse me?"

"He didn't make the world like this. The world that God created was perfect, beautiful, and free from sin, hurt, and pain. Humans chose to ruin that. We don't live in the world that God created. We live in what remains after the Original Sin and the Fall. It's not going to be pretty or fair or safe or fun, because it isn't what God intended. Humans chose this," she repeated. "Not God."

Susana then turned and left, leaving Luisa standing in the middle of her bedroom in silence.

TWENTY-SIX

Hours, days, and weeks passed by Luisa in slow motion, and the young woman felt like she had been at the brothel for six years when in truth she had been there for six weeks.

The same twelve prostitutes occupied the house for that first month and a half, even though Roxana warned Luisa to expect a high turnover rate. Girls who didn't prove up to the task – who cried too much, fought with clients, or refused to perform – were 'removed'.

"The men know they're coming to a whorehouse. It's no secret. But they don't want to be reminded of that fact while they're here," Señora Silvia always said.

"Sometimes people will disappear in the middle of the night," Cristina explained. "We all go to sleep after the brothel closes, and by the time we wake up the next morning one girl is gone and a new one has replaced her."

The first time Luisa saw it happen was at her six week mark in Monterrey. One of the nicest – and prettiest – girls in the house, Roxana, had befriended the young Honduran immigrant and taken Luisa under her wing. Roxana taught Luisa how to interact with clients, how to avoid the wrath of the guards, and had held her when she cried. Which happened a lot in the beginning.

Then, one morning, Roxana was gone.

Luisa woke up about nine, which was typical after entertaining clients until closing time at 1am. Roxana had promised to teach Luisa how to French braid her hair, so after putting on jeans and a pink fitted t-shirt, she walked down the hall to Roxana's room and knocked on the door.

"One second!" a voice called out.

When the door slid open, Luisa took a step back in surprise. Whereas Roxana had been tall and curvy with wavy brown hair, the girl standing in front of her was short, rail-thin, and had straight black hair. Her eyes were the color of coal.

"Where's Roxana?" Luisa blurted out.

"Who?" asked the imposter.

"Roxana. This is her room."

"Umm . . . I don't know who that is, but when I got here the señora told me this was my room."

"Did she say where Roxana went?" Luisa asked, concern mixing with panic in her voice. Roxana had become like a big sister to her – her confidant and support system. Luisa didn't know how she would survive without her.

The new girl shook her head. "Like I said, I've never heard of Roxana. I just got here a couple of hours ago."

Steam flew out of Luisa's ears and it felt like a giant fist was squeezed around her heart. She hadn't been this panicked since they took Josefina away from her in Mexico City.

Without thinking, Luisa spun on her heel and stormed down the hall, through the courtyard, and into the kitchen where Señora Silvia was preparing breakfast.

"Where is Roxana?" Luisa asked, her voice at near-screaming volume.

The señora didn't look up to acknowledge Luisa. She kept stirring the eggs and replied: "not here."

"I figured out that much," Luisa shot back. "Where is she?"

"Not here," Silvia repeated. When Luisa didn't leave, the older woman sighed and stopped working on the breakfast food. "You are still somewhat new, so I will forgive this outburst. But if it ever happens again, you'll find yourself disappearing in the middle of the night like your friend Roxana. And another thing," the señora added as she resumed cooking, "don't make any more friends. It's not good for you in a place like this. Every single one of you will die or be resold. There are no happy endings and no lasting friendships. The sooner you realize that the better. Now go do your chores and quit bothering me."

****

Despite the señora's warning about staying emotionally detached, Luisa wouldn't stop until she found out what happened to her missing housemate.

Exiting the kitchen, she found several of the other girls beginning to gather in the courtyard with a cup of morning coffee. It was one of their few moments of peace before the men – both guards and clients – began to take over their day.

"Where's Roxana?" Luisa asked, wasting no time with pleasantries.

"Didn't you hear?" Bianca whispered. "She got pregnant."

"Yeah, I know that. We all know that. I meant where is she this morning? She wasn't in her room when I walked by. The señora said she's gone but wouldn't tell me where."

Ximena sighed and Viviana shook her head.

"It's amazing that you still see the world through such innocent eyes," added Elena, the snobby one.

"Oh, leave her alone," said Esperanza, the former hotel clerk. "You keep that innocence as long as you can, querida."

"What are you talking about?" Luisa asked.

"Señora Silvia is right. Roxana is gone. She won't be coming back. Pregnant girls are bad for business," Elena explained. "They remind clients that there can be consequences for their actions."

"They give you two options," Cristina continued. "Kill the baby or kill you. Sometimes, for girls that are really popular with the clients, they do the abortion whether you want to or not. That happened once while I've been here. But she was so screwed up in the head afterward that I think they figured it's cheaper and easier to replace you."

"Why don't they kick you out?" Luisa asked. "Turn you out on the streets?"

Viviana laughed. "Give you your freedom?" She shook her head. "If that was all it took to get out of these shit holes then I would've gotten knocked up years ago." Viviana paused. "No, honey, nobody leaves here free. You get sold somewhere else or you die."

Luisa lowered her gaze to the floor. "That's what the señora told me," she said in a whisper.

"She's right," Elena added. "And I can't believe she didn't slap you with the frying pan for storming into the kitchen like you did."

"Yeah . . . I know that was dumb. I guess I was just really surprised when Roxana was gone."

"I'm surprised that you're still surprised," said Elena. "How long have you been here?"

"Six weeks."

"Give it another six, and nothing will surprise you anymore. You'll have seen – and done – it all by then."

There was one more question that Luisa needed answered. "So Roxana is . . . she's . . . dead?"

Esperanza, now the oldest remaining prostitute in the house, walked across the courtyard and sat down in a chair next to Luisa. She placed her hand on the younger girl's knee like Luisa's abuela used to. "Roxana might have gone back home . . . we don't know for sure. She was smart, and tough, so maybe she talked them into letting her go home. But it's more likely that they killed her."

Luisa's eyes grew wide and filled with tears. "Oh my God," she whispered, bringing her hand up to cover her mouth. *That poor girl,* she thought. *That poor baby.* "Oh my God," she repeated. *I've got to get out of here.*

TWENTY-SEVEN

Ana, Roxana's replacement, was a quiet sixteen year old who showed no interest in joining the more chatty girls in the house. Which was fine with Luisa. She didn't want to get to know Ana anyway. Luisa knew that the new girl had nothing to do with her mentor's disappearance, but she couldn't help feeling like befriending Ana would be betraying Roxana.

The one thing that Ana was good for, Luisa acknowledged, was cooking. She often helped Señora Silvia in the kitchen, making meals based on rice, tortillas, dried fruit, and more meat and cheese than Luisa had ever eaten before. Whatever could be bought cheaply and cooked easily in mass quantities. Señor wanted the young women to be at least borderline healthy, so he ensured that they were well fed. Better fed than many of them ever were before they became his slaves.

That was a point that Emilio and the rest of the guards often made to the teenagers when trying to convince them that they had a wonderful life at La Casa Feliz.

"You have a roof over your head, don't you?" Emilio said. "Do you pay for that? No. You get food and clothes and clean water and aren't out on the streets where the gangs and the perverts would get you. Señor protects you. He provides for you. You should be *grateful.*"

After a while, many of the girls started to believe him.

****

Three months into Luisa's time in Monterrey, Señora Silvia caught pneumonia. The middle-aged woman tried to hide the illness but, after several days, the former prostitute who now called herself a 'Talent Manager' collapsed on the floor of the kitchen and was taken to the hospital.

Cooking duties fell to her assistant, Ana.

On Ana's first day as head chef, she raided the pantry and found the combination of ingredients that she was looking for. Chicken, chili peppers, cabbage, salsa, lemons, and hominy rice.

94

"Why are you making pozole for lunch?" Bianca asked after joining Ana in the kitchen. "That's for celebrations. Parties. Happy times. What could we possibly have to celebrate?"

"No Señora here tonight to yell at us?" Ana shrugged her shoulders. "I figured it would be nice to have a good meal for once. My mom taught me how to make pozole and the pantry had all of the ingredients, so why not?"

"Yeah," Luisa chimed in as she popped a piece of chicken into her mouth. "Why not?"

Ana slapped the thief's hand away with a towel. "No taste-testing! It'll be ready soon enough."

Twenty minutes later, the twelve prostitutes pushed tables together in the courtyard to make one big eating space.

"This is nice," Ximena commented, a rare admission from the house's resident cynic.

Luisa nodded. "It is. We should do this more often."

Viviana shook her head. "The señora wouldn't let us. Anytime we find something that we actually enjoy, she takes it away."

The other girls knew that Viviana was right and returned their focus to the food in front of them.

After a few moments of silence, Elena leaned over to Luisa. In a low voice, the runaway debutante said: "You know I once heard that, a long time ago, the meat that was used in pozole was human."

Eleven spoons clattered down on the table and eleven pairs of eyes stared at their chef, Ana.

"What?" she said. "This is made of chicken. *Chicken.*"

Elena nodded her head, enjoying the attention. "Yeah, back when the natives were still in charge of everything, they would sacrifice humans to the gods. Then they chopped up the dead body and cooked it in the soup, and everybody ate it like it was their Holy Communion."

Luisa's stomach began to roil and a tart taste gathered at the base of her jaw.

"That's not true," Bianca said.

"It is too," replied Elena. "After the Spanish came and made the natives stop human sacrifice, they switched the meat that went in the soup."

Luisa's hand flew over her mouth and she stood up so fast that her chair crashed backward onto the floor. She didn't stop to pick it

95

up, though, and instead ran as fast as she could down the hall to the community bathroom. Luisa kicked open the door and dove for the toilet, vomiting the entire contents of her stomach into the porcelain bowl.

Back in the courtyard, Bianca glared at Elena. "Way to go. You ruined a perfectly good meal for everybody with that lame ass story. And you made Luisa get sick. Nice one."

TWENTY-EIGHT

When the rumbling in Luisa's stomach settled to a low roar, she climbed up off the bathroom floor and washed her face in the sink.

I could kill Elena for telling that story, she thought.

Luisa turned off the water, wiped her skin dry with a towel, and exited the bathroom. The hallway was quiet except for a few muffled sounds coming from rooms that were occupied with early afternoon clients.

Passing by Viviana's room, Luisa saw that the other girl was squatting in the corner and scratching something into the floor.

"What are you doing?" asked Luisa as she stepped into the room.

Viviana jumped and a small piece of gray metal dropped to the ground. The black-haired teenager grabbed it in a flash and stood up, straightening her dress before turning around to face Luisa.

"What do you want?"

"What were you doing?" Luisa countered, pointing at the floor in the corner.

"None of your business," the house's 'mean girl' huffed in response.

Luisa crossed her arms over her chest. "It is my business if they find that piece of metal in your hand and we all get in trouble for it."

Viviana's black eyes grew wide and she darted across the room to close the door behind Luisa. "Shhh! They'll hear you!"

"Okay, okay," Luisa said, lowering her voice. "But seriously: what were you doing?"

Viviana sighed and walked back over to the far corner. "I was updating my number."

"Your number?"

She nodded. "Every day I mark down how many clients I had the night before. A way to keep track, you know?"

"Dios – why? Why in the world would you want to know that?"

Viviana shrugged her shoulders. "I dunno. I just do." She paused. "Back before I ran away, I used to watch TV every day before my mom got home from work. I liked 'Sex and The City' reruns. They made it all seem so glamorous, you know?"

"I've never seen it." *Or heard of it*, Luisa thought, but kept that to herself. She didn't want the other girls in the house to know how poor she had been in Honduras.

"Oh," Viviana continued. "Well, it's about these four women who live in New York City and sleep around with a bunch of men, but they choose to – it's not like it is for us here. They talk about their 'number' . . . how many men they've had sex with. When I first started working the streets, I kept track of how many guys I was with. And I guess it kinda became a habit."

Luisa followed the other girl's eyes as they traveled up and down the floor of her room. There, in the concrete, barely visible, were thousands of tiny scratch marks.

Luisa gasped. "All of these . . ."

Viviana nodded. "We may have come here together, but this isn't my first brothel. You're new. You're probably still in the triple digits. But you'll get here." She sighed. "We all do. The only way you don't is if you die first."

A knock on the door made both girls scream.

Emilio flung open the door and glared at his two young charges. "Doors stay open during business hours unless you're with a client. You putas both know that!"

Luisa jumped back in fear, which only angered him further.

"What are you afraid of, huh? You should be happy! We feed you, we dress you, we give you a place to live. All we ask is that you play nice with Señor's friends. In other countries, whores like you would pay him for the privilege of working here. You'd pay your own rent, buy your own food and clothes, and still pay Señor most of the money you earned. Do we make you do that, chiquita? Hmm? No, we don't. You are lucky." He paused and a familiar gleam entered his eyes, the one that the girls all knew screamed 'DANGER'.

Stepping closer, Emilio grabbed hold of Luisa's hair at the base of her neck. "It's about time you showed me some damn gratitude for everything I do for you! And if I catch you out of your room again you'll be scrubbing the floor with a toothbrush for a month – on top of your usual work."

TWENTY-NINE

The spring months came and went in Monterrey, with the weather warming and the world outside the Casa Feliz continuing on while the girls inside its walls remained stationary and stagnant . . . trapped in a cycle of sex and clients and chores with occasional interruptions of violence.

Luisa knew nothing of the news of the day, of the politics or the business being conducted in more reputable areas of their international city. Economic recession or recovery was beyond her realm, for hers was an industry that paid cash and never ran dry. Global terrorism, beheadings, and mass graves were never brought to her attention, either, but wouldn't have caused any surprise if they were. After all, beheadings and mass graves were nothing new to the victims of the many forgotten wars raging in Latin America, and terrorism was more a description for Luisa's everyday life than a topic for news discussion.

Susana made sure to let the other girls know when it was Semana Santa, or the Holy Week preceding Easter. But Luisa had already figured that one out. Before she left, Roxana told Luisa how she kept time in the calendar by paying attention to swells in client traffic around certain holidays.

Christmas Day itself would be slow, Roxana told her, with most clients guilted into spending the entire time with their families. But then the week between Christmas and New Year's would be very busy, since everyone who had been cooped up with those same family members wanted to get out and have some fun. Holy Week was also slow, and Easter itself was practically a holiday for the girls. "A strange Catholic guilt settles over the city during Semana Santa," Roxana had told her. "In this place in Spain, a long time ago, all of the prostitutes used to be kicked out of the city during Lent. The first day after Lent, all of the men threw a party to celebrate the prostitutes' return. I guess some of that carried over to Mexico, and Holy Week is always really slow. The day after Easter, though . . . girl get ready. It's a flood."

True to her word, Semana Santa passed slowly for Luisa and her housemates, while the day after Easter was the busiest Luisa had been since arriving in Monterrey.

Primero de Mayo and Cinco de Mayo also came and went with heavier traffic than usual, and Luisa couldn't help but think of the number of scratch marks that Viviana was accumulating in her room. *Would she start filling in the walls soon?* Luisa wondered. *Trace over the marks already on the floor?*

In June, though, Luisa received a gift. One of her regular clients, an office manager for a company in the San Pedro Garza García neighborhood, brought a newspaper with him to the Casa Feliz. It was hidden in his briefcase, which was the only way it got past Emilio and the other security guards. Clients weren't supposed to bring in newspapers or other 'outside world' items, but Luisa spotted the paper when the middle-aged man opened his briefcase to pull out a few pesos for a tip.

Luisa's breath caught in her throat and she licked her lips, almost like a child would when spotting an ice cream cone.

Her client followed her gaze to the newspaper.

"You want to read it?" he asked.

"Huh? What? Oh, I . . . um . . ."

"Here," he said, grabbing the ink stained item from his bag and tossing it onto Luisa's bed. "All yours. There's not much interesting in there, but feel free. I already finished it."

Luisa snatched the paper off her bed and opened it to see the front page.

"Is this today?"

"What?" the man asked as he buttoned his dress pants and looped his belt buckle into place.

"The paper – it's from today?"

"Yeah, that's today's paper. Here," he added, handing Luisa a two-peso coin. "I'll see you next week."

Luisa wrapped her hand around the coin, smiled, and nodded at the man. "Thank you. Yes, next time." As soon as he left the room, the young teenager's eyes returned to the newspaper resting in her lap.

"June 9th," she whispered. For the first time since leaving Honduras, Luisa knew what day it was. Her heart swelled with a level of comfort one wouldn't expect from such a trivial piece of knowledge. It wasn't the date itself that made her happy, but rather the ability to place herself in time and space. "June 9th," she repeated. "Today is June 9th."

****

After the fateful client visit in June when Luisa learned what day it was, she took Viviana's idea of scratch marks and modified it – keeping track of the date with a makeshift calendar on the floor under her bed. Luisa didn't dare make the marks out in the open like the other young woman did . . . she was too afraid that she would be caught.

When the sun rose on the 44th day of the calendar, Luisa smiled. She lay in bed longer than usual, relaxed more than typical, and smiled brighter than she had since she arrived in Monterrey.

The forty-fourth day of the calendar, July 23rd, was Luisa's fourteenth birthday.

Sitting in her room, Luisa's thoughts drifted to other birthdays at home in Honduras. The celebrations were never grand, and Luisa's thirteenth birthday came and went without notice from her mom. *Of all the people in the world who should remember the day, you'd think it'd be her.* Aurelia Dominguez often forgot things, though, and sometimes Luisa wished she had inherited that quality.

There were lots of things one wanted to forget after growing up near the city that was often called the Murder Capital of the World. But no matter how hard Luisa tried to forget, she couldn't. Indeed, it seemed like the harder she worked to forget San Pedro Sula, Honduras, the more she would remember.

Tattooed men and boys patrolling the streets that belonged to their gang – always armed, always angry, and always ready to kill anyone who dared go where they didn't belong.

Luisa's great-grandmother taught her to avoid eye contact and dress as plainly as possible to try to stay below the gangs' radars. Abuela even told the story once of a lady who started dressing as a nun, thinking that the majority of the low-level gang members who loitered on the streets would be afraid of doing anything bad to a woman of God. Abuela said that the gang leaders probably wouldn't care, but residents didn't interact with them much anyway. The street-level hustlers and foot soldiers, though, were young enough to still retain some of the Catholic values taught to them by their families, churches, and schools. So the lady dressed like a nun whenever she left her house.

"Why didn't she just become a nun?" young Luisa had asked.

Abuela responded by smiling and kissing her great-granddaughter on the forehead. "A wonderful question, mi amor. A wonderful question."

Luisa also remembered the women who didn't heed Abuela's advice – women like her mother who dressed to impress and sought out the attention of any men they could find. Those women were used and abused in much the same way that Luisa was now, trading their bodies for shelter, food, or drugs. Until one day when their bodies gave out on them and they ended up on the streets or dead . . . oftentimes both.

San Pedro Sula also implanted in Luisa's mind the sights and sounds of gunfire. Of empty schools because the children were all in gangs, dead, or on their way to other, safer cities and countries. Of gutters running red after particularly brutal nights.

But what Luisa remembered most, no matter how hard she tried to forget, was the stench of death that hung like a cloud over her hometown. Even on days when no one died, it still smelled like death. The kind of smell one can feel . . . the kind that creeps into a person's bones and takes root, haunting their dreams at night with the cackling laughter of a witch saying 'you'll never be rid of me now'.

A knock on her door woke Luisa from her thoughts and reminded her that she was no longer in Honduras. She was in Monterrey, Mexico, living a different kind of nightmare.

Luisa stood up from her bed and walked to the door, sliding it open. The man waiting on the other side was a regular who preferred mid-morning visits, and the young woman stepped aside to let him into the room. Closing the door behind her, Luisa thought: *a different kind of nightmare indeed.*

THIRTY

A major downside to living in a converted horse stable, Luisa learned over the course of her time there, was that there was not a lot of privacy between the stalls-turned-rooms. Full doors had replaced the half-latch variety from the old days, and the iron bars that used to provide vision into each stall were now fully-covered, dry-walled enclosures. But little to no effort had been put into insulation or soundproofing, meaning that Luisa and her housemates could hear almost everything within a three-room radius.

That lack of privacy was how Luisa came to witness to her own real-life romance story.

The first time that Luisa met Felipe, a house security guard, he punched her. She was daydreaming about a picnic that she took one time with Josefina and Abuela and didn't notice when a client switched his attention from Ximena to her. The client got mad and left, causing Felipe to punch Luisa in the face, kick her in the stomach, and lock her in her room for two days without food.

Despite that beginning, Felipe soon became Luisa's favorite of all of the guards at the casa de citas. She wasn't alone in that opinion – all of the young women liked Felipe. He was rough around the edges, sure, and he did what Señor and Emilio told him to. But he wasn't mean about it. Felipe did his job, the girls did theirs, and every once in a while there would be a pained look on his face that told the female slaves he didn't want to be there either. They didn't know what made their owner have so much control over Felipe, but it was clear that the handsome foot soldier with dimples and black, wavy hair was as much a captive as the girls were.

It was also clear that he was in love with Bianca.

That was confirmed early one Tuesday afternoon. Before the day's rush of clients arrived, Luisa heard a knock on the door next to her room. It was Bianca's door – Luisa's best friend who had been with her since The Broker's house in Mexico City. Luisa didn't pay much attention to the sound – she figured a random client strolled in during his lunch break – but then she heard a familiar voice that made her sit up and listen.

"Bianca, it's Felipe," the man whispered, and Luisa recognized the voice as belonging to the young security guard and errand boy.

The door creaked when it opened.

"Felipe," Bianca said, repeating his name. "What do you want?"

"Can I come in?"

Bianca laughed and Luisa imagined her friend rolling her eyes and shaking her head. "You know Señor doesn't let you do that. Paying clients only. You know the rules."

"No no, that's not it," Felipe replied, his voice in such a hushed tone that Luisa had to walk across her room and press her ear to the wall in order to hear him.

"I thought, well, it's just that . . . I heard you say once that you're from Parral," Felipe explained.

"So?"

"So I'm from there too. My family sent me away eight years ago and I haven't been able to go back. Not since I got involved with Señor Perrera anyway," he added.

Luisa gasped and heard her friend do the same. "What did you say?" Bianca asked.

"That we're both from Parral."

"No, not that. You said Señor's name."

"Huh? What . . . no. No, you must have heard me wrong."

"Perrera. You said you work for Señor Perrera."

A desperate quality entered Felipe's voice and he grabbed Bianca by the wrists. "Please, please do not repeat that. Forget I ever said it. Pretend you don't know, okay? If anybody finds out I told you, I'm dead. Please. I'm not even supposed to know myself."

"How do you know it?" Bianca asked.

"The other guard, Raúl, and I have known each other ever since I moved to Monterrey. Raúl is Señor's nephew."

"He is?" Bianca's eyes grew wide. "Woah. I wouldn't have guessed that."

Felipe sighed and it came across as almost a growl. "Shit, I wasn't supposed to tell you that either. Dammit, all I wanted was to talk about home for a few minutes. You know, with someone who's been there too."

It struck Luisa as strange to hear homesickness in Felipe's voice. Even though he didn't look all that much older than her, to Luisa he still seemed much wiser and more powerful. All of which

104

might have been true, despite the weakness he was now revealing to her friend.

"Don't worry, I won't tell anyone anything," Bianca replied. "I didn't know you were from Parral," she added, nervousness mixing with a twinge of restrained excitement in her voice. It wasn't good to get too excited about anything, as they had all learned. Excitement led to hope, hope led to expectation, and expectation led to disappointment.

After a few seconds, Bianca nodded her head. "We can talk. For a couple of minutes. But not now. And definitely not in my room."

"When?" Felipe asked, eagerness overcoming his anxiety.

"This time tomorrow. In the courtyard. Five minutes. And have an excuse ready in case anybody sees us."

Luisa heard the door squeak and then close with a thud. Bianca didn't even bother to say goodbye, but Luisa still envied her friend. For the first time in eight months, the other girl had something to do the next day that didn't involve brothel clients, medical exams, or getting yelled at by Señor (¡Perrera!) and his minions. Bianca had a date. With a boy.

Luisa sighed. *If only I could be that lucky.*

THIRTY-ONE

Felipe Osvaldo de León had a spring in his step and a smile on his face as he left work that evening. The twenty-three year old security guard never met anybody from his hometown . . . even though Parral had a population near 100,000, most people who grew up in the Chihuahua city never left it. Most people in Parral also tended to avoid the Osvaldo family – Felipe's father was a notorious drunk and his children's favorite pastimes were petty theft and vandalism.

When Felipe moved away at age fifteen in search of a job to help support his family, no one in town missed him. He hoped that Bianca wouldn't recognize his last name or was perhaps too young to know his background. Monterrey was supposed to be his fresh start, but he still liked the idea of having someone with whom he could share memories of home.

Passing by row after row of shoddily-constructed homes with whitewashed concrete walls and windows covered in bars, Felipe wondered if Monterrey had indeed been the fresh start he hoped for when leaving Parral eight years earlier.

I make more money here than I ever could there, he thought, *but I'm still on the wrong side of the law. Like father, like son.*

"You'll never make it out there," Felipe's dad had slurred at him after the boy announced he was leaving to find 'a respectable job with respectable people in a respectable city'. "They'll never accept you," he continued. "You can try to cover it up, but you'll never be any better than your old man."

Felipe thought he had hit the jackpot and proven his father wrong when he landed a job as a security guard at the warehouse of Monterrey shipping magnate Carlos Perrera. He was even sharing an apartment with Perrera's nephew. *Me*, the teenager thought, *roommates with the family of Monterrey's most respected businessman. Take that, Papi.*

But when the nephew, Raúl, learned of Felipe's shady past and extensive juvenile record, the boy from Parral was recruited to perform other 'special assignments' for Señor Perrera. Those special assignments ultimately led to a position on Señor's trusted security team, which led to the brothel in Independencia. *Right back into the slums . . . just like Papi said I would.*

Reaching the door of his apartment building, Felipe shook his head and turned his thoughts back to Bianca. She was pretty, and kind, and Felipe smiled as he thought about their date for the next day. It had been a long time since he got that excited about a first date with a girl, and the fact that she was a forced prostitute at Señor's brothel didn't bother him at all. Indeed, it yet was another thing they had in common. *She's stuck in this life just like I am.*

****

The courtship between Felipe and Bianca continued in secret for months. Well, it was a secret from Señor and the other guards – at least as far as the brothel residents could tell. They all knew about it, though. Ximena thought it was disgusting and that Bianca was a traitor for getting involved with one of her captors, but Cristina threatened to tell Señora Silvia about Ximena's deal to buy cigarettes from Hector if she ever said anything about the Happy House romance.

Felipe proved himself to be a true Casanova, leaving flowers and love notes hidden under her bed where other guards couldn't see. The pair weren't able to spend much time together, given the circumstances, but any chance they got they would huddle together in the courtyard, her room, or even the bathroom to talk to each other.

He told her his dream of owning a mechanic's garage one day, and she said she thought he would be fantastic at it. He talked about a new life together in the United States, and she spoke of a home and a garden and maybe even kids running around – happy, safe, and far, far away from men like Señor. He said he wanted a daughter to look like her, and she said she wanted a son to look like him. And next door, through the paper-thin wall, Luisa listened to their conversations with longing in her heart and tears in her eyes, wondering if it would ever be her turn for happily ever after.

****

"Oye," Luisa said one day when she and her friend were alone, "maybe he'll be your caballero, no?"

Bianca rolled her eyes, even though she was secretly hoping the same thing. "Caballeros don't exist, remember?"

"What?" Luisa asked in feigned shock. "This from the girl who pays Horatio to smuggle in romance novels whenever he can? Of course caballeros exist!"

"Maybe real caballeros, sí. The kind of man who loves and supports and protects his family. But that kind of man would never come to a place like this or spend time with a girl like me."

Luisa sighed. "Okay, so not a 'real' caballero," she replied, putting air quotes around the word. "But a caballero as we know it. Felipe could be that. And you'd have to be stupid to not agree to it."

"An escape from here? Of course I'd agree to it. But honestly, Felipe is no caballero, real world or this world," Bianca said, trying to convince herself as much as her friend. "He's too poor. And that's not his style, anyway. He only works here to make money to send back to his family in Parral."

"I don't know," Luisa said, enjoying living vicariously through her friend's romance. "I think he works here to be near you."

Bianca bit her lip and lowered her gaze to the floor. "Well . . . he made me promise not say anything, but I'm so happy I have to tell someone."

"What?!"

"Yesterday morning, when the señora was in the kitchen and before Emilio had gotten here for the day, Felipe came into my room and we, well, you know."

"You slept with him?"

Bianca nodded her head up and down and a smile spread across her face. "The first time I've ever made love." She sighed. "And I do, Luisa. I love him."

****

That same afternoon, after his shift at the brothel ended, Felipe returned home to his apartment in another section of the Independencia neighborhood. Smiling as he walked, the young man couldn't help but rejoice over how well his plans were going.

Felipe wanted to escape Monterrey and get to the United States, but he didn't want to only mow lawns, wash dishes, or build houses when he got there. He wanted a true life of his own. When he talked to Bianca about running a mechanic's garage, he wasn't lying. Felipe loved cars. Although he'd never had enough money to own one, he loved them nonetheless.

But the twenty-three year old barely made enough to pay rent, even with roommates, and he had been squirreling away money for years to have something to start with once he got to the US. Felipe was still young enough to think he could make it to the border without the help of an experienced guide, *and besides*, he often thought, *why would I pay somebody that much money when I haven't even tried to make it across myself?* The young man knew about the multitude of bribes he could be required to pay along the journey from Monterrey to the border, including up to $500 to Mexican immigration officials to get through a checkpoint, $300 to the cartels to pass through one of their checkpoints, and $100 to a boat driver to get him across the Rio Grande into Texas. Nine hundred dollars on his own sounded a lot better than $4,000 to someone else.

That was still a lot of money, though. *Which is where Bianca comes into the picture*, he thought with a greedy smile. The tips Bianca earned from working for Señor Perrera – albeit small and 'illegal' according to house rules – would help shorten the amount of time that it took for Felipe to save enough to travel north. Especially since, unlike him who had bills to pay, Bianca got to keep one hundred percent of her tips. And once the pair made it to The States, Bianca would be his ticket out of poverty and into the American Dream. *Once a whore, always a whore*, Felipe thought as he unlocked the door to his apartment. *Just this once, baby*, he added with a snicker, *until I can find a job.*

"She'll do it in a heartbeat," he said, shutting the door behind him. "She loves me too much to say no."

THIRTY-TWO

The next May, fifteen months after Luisa first arrived in Monterrey, the teenage girl was showing signs of her abusive life. Her once lush black hair had lost its shine and was beginning to thin. A youthful complexion was now covered in the perplexing combination of acne and wrinkles. Luisa was also missing two teeth . . . casualties of encounters with violent clients.

Men who slapped her were Luisa's favorite – a slap meant they retained some sense of recognition that she was a female and a lot smaller than them.

The missing teeth were the result of clients who liked to punch. A closed-hand slam to the jaw demonstrated that they didn't care if she was a girl or half their size . . . might made right and their fists of fury meant that the little Hondureña was always in the wrong.

One of her frequent clients, a taxi driver, liked to punch her. Even when she did everything he demanded, Luisa could count on receiving at least one or two blows during the course of a forty-five minute session.

One night, when Luisa had the dangerous misfortune of slight head cold, her nose made the mistake of itching. She tried to turn her head to the side to avoid sneezing onto her client's face, but the end result was the same: he was livid.

"Shit! You fucking sneezed all over me!"

Pushing himself up to where he was kneeling on the bed, the middle-aged man balled his hand into a fist, pulled back his arm, and let go – unleashing a wrecking ball into the side of Luisa's face.

Three months later, looking into the mirror in the bathroom, Luisa gingerly pressed her fingers to the bones surrounding her left eye. The well-aimed blow had knocked her out cold, crushed the bones in Luisa's eye socket, and left her partially blind. The teenager's eyesight was only now beginning to recover.

It was the kicks that bothered her the most, though. The clients who pushed her down and kicked her in the stomach, back, and sides broke Luisa's spirit as much as her body. They were treating her like a dog – just like the guard did on her first night in Monterrey.

Every attack was as terrible as anyone would expect, and it never got any better. Each time, each client, was its own unique violation of personal sovereignty and human dignity. "I thought at first that it might get better eventually, you know?" Luisa whispered one night. The brothel had closed for the day and she and Bianca were sitting on her friend's floor trying to unwind. Friday nights were always busy . . . payday meant that men had money to spend.

"I thought I would somehow get used to it, or at least grow numb to it, so it wouldn't be as bad." Luisa shook her head. "I was wrong."

"You've gotta zone out, you know?" Bianca replied. "Take yourself to another place in your mind."

"I can't. I just . . . I can't. It's like somebody breaking into your home over and over again. Stealing your stuff and beating you up. Every night. But you can't leave and you can't stop it. How am I supposed to zone out from that? Seriously – I want to know. How?" Luisa shook her head again, making her black hair whip around her shoulders. "I can't." In a lower voice, she added: "I wish they had killed me when they got the chance. Death would be better than this life."

Luisa knew now, had known for a long time, that she was on her own. No one was coming to save her. There would be no heroes to rescue her. The young woman's endless prayers – to not have to live with her mom, to not be sold, for her first owner's car to break down or wreck, for her and Josefina to stay together – all of those prayers went unanswered. She didn't see a point in trying anymore. Manuel was right: God wasn't listening.

Luisa had always believed in the kind of love her great-grandparents had. Bad things happened to bad people like her mother, but she believed that, if she was a good person like her abuela, she could find happiness, fulfillment, and the man of her dreams. But now, lying crumpled on the floor, her tears mixing with the dust to create a concrete plaster on her body, Luisa knew it didn't matter if she was good or not. It didn't matter if she was nice, well-behaved, well-spoken, or hard-working. *I don't get happiness. Or love. Or fulfillment. The man of my dreams was replaced by the life of my nightmares.*

The Hondureña could tell that her friend was worried about her. Most of the other girls accepted their fates and went about their daily work with dull eyes and even duller hearts. Bianca had Felipe, her secret boyfriend, to give her hope and love and dreams for the future. All Luisa had was her anger. *It keeps me warm at night*, she thought with a shrug.

"That anger is going to eat you alive," Bianca said as if reading Luisa's mind. "You've gotta do something with it."

Luisa let out a short, sarcastic laugh. "You sound more and more like my abuela every day."

"It's true. Do something. Change something."

"What the hell am I supposed to do? What can I change?"

"Shhh . . . not so loud. The señora will hear you."

"See?" exclaimed Luisa. "I can't even be mad without risking getting in trouble. I'm trapped here."

Bianca lowered her eyes to her lap and fiddled with the edge of her skirt. Quietly, she said, "maybe you should leave like I'm going to."

"What?!"

"Shhhh!"

"Sorry," Luisa whispered. "But – what? When?"

A small smile crossed Bianca's lips. "Felipe and I are going together. We don't have an exact day yet, but we're going to go to the United States. He wants us to get married. Start a new life together."

"How?"

"I don't know, I don't know," replied Bianca, her smile growing wider. "But I'm getting out of here. And if you start working on your exit too, that'll give you something to do aside from being mad all the time."

****

June came and went without any further mention of Bianca and Felipe's escape, but Luisa could tell when watching the couple that they were up to something. She hoped no one else noticed it.

July was also quiet, aside from a weeklong visit by a group of rowdy American men in town for a business convention. If they were any indication of what people in the United States were like, Luisa never wanted to go. *Maybe Mami was right about something*, she thought several times that week. *She always said that people from the US were snobby racists.*

Later that month, on the 409th day of Luisa's makeshift calendar, the young woman woke up with the same smile that she had on that day a year earlier. July 23rd was her birthday. And it was a big one: Luisa was turning fifteen.

The fifteenth birthday for Hispanic girls is comparable to the thirteenth for a Jewish child. Whereas young Jewish boys and girls celebrate a bar or bat mitzvah at that age, fifteen year old Latinas have their quinceañera. Similar to the American tradition of a debutante ball, the quinceañera traditionally includes a celebratory Catholic mass and a party afterward – complete with the young girl in a beautiful formal gown, parents and godparents presenting gifts, and a court of honor full of the birthday girl's friends.

Once, when Luisa was living in San Pedro Sula with her mother and sister, she caught a glimpse of a quinceañera group taking photos after leaving mass. From her apartment window, Luisa saw the young lady in her flowing white gown and tiara, smiling and laughing while surrounded by her friends and family. She also saw the teenage boys who were chosen to be chambelanes, or escorts, in the court of honor fidgeting with their tuxedos and flirting with their counterparts in the court, the damas.

From behind her, Luisa's mother had laughed. "Don't even think about it, mija. No way you'll get a quinceañera like that one. You'll be lucky to be alive on your fifteenth birthday."

Her mother's words echoed in Luisa's mind as she sat in the whorehouse that had been her home for almost a year and a half. Four hundred nine days since the start of the calendar, but that was nearly four months after she first arrived in Monterrey.

"You'll be lucky to be alive on your fifteenth birthday."

Luisa shook her head. *If this is lucky, I never want to see unlucky.*

THIRTY-THREE

In the middle of August, early one morning while the house was still asleep, Bianca knocked three times on the wall between her and Luisa's rooms. Three knocks was the signal to come over and talk. Two knocks, on the other hand, was the panic button. At first they said that the emergency alert should be one loud knock, but Luisa figured that they might accidentally hit the wall one time and trigger a false alarm. "Nobody hits the wall twice in a row like that unless they mean to," she said.

The newly-minted fifteen year old rolled open her door as quietly as she could, checked the hall to make sure no one was watching, and darted the few feet over to Bianca's room. Walking inside, she saw that her friend wasn't alone.

"Hey Luisa," Felipe said, sitting on Bianca's bed.

"Umm, hey." Luisa looked back and forth between the room's other occupants. "What's going on?"

"We're leaving," Bianca announced with a smile. "This time tomorrow."

Luisa's chest tightened with a combination of fear, excitement, and jealousy. "How?" she asked. "What are you going to do?"

"We've been saving money for almost a year now," her friend explained, "and Felipe bought bus tickets to take us to Nuevo Laredo. If the bus doesn't work, we'll walk. We've got a map marked with how to get there."

"And then what? How will you get past the border?"

Felipe shrugged his shoulders. "The same way everybody else does. Sneak across. I heard about a guy with a boat who will take people across the Rio Grande, and there are people waiting on the other side who will drive you up past the immigration checkpoints to San Antonio. It's not cheap, but we've got enough. We'll make it," he added with a smile, squeezing Bianca's hand with his own.

Another pang of jealousy hit Luisa's chest. "Wow. That's . . . that's amazing. I wish I could go with you!"

"I know," Bianca responded. "I wish you could too."

Felipe reached into the back pocket of his jeans and handed Luisa a folded piece of paper. "Here," he said. "B wanted me to make this for you. A second map. For when you make your own escape. There are two routes," he explained, unfolding the paper to show her. "The red one takes you to Nuevo Laredo. The green one goes to Reynosa. Both towns are right on the border."

Luisa looked down at the map and shook her head. "It would take me forever to save enough money to pay for boat rides and cars driving me to San Antonio."

"No, chica," Felipe replied. "You don't have to worry about any of that. If it's just you, a girl who is – how old are you?"

"Fifteen."

"Yeah, if you're traveling alone you can walk across the border. Don't even try to hide. Get caught on purpose and then you get to stay."

Luisa's eyes grew wide and her jaw dropped in surprise. "They let you stay?"

Felipe nodded. "Basically. What I heard is that if you're not eighteen yet, they have to take you in front of a judge and he decides if you stay or get deported. But there are so many people that it takes a while to get an appointment for your court date, and you get to stay until then." He paused. "Do you have any relatives in the US?"

Luisa shook her head. "No. I don't have any relatives anywhere. Except my little sister, but I don't know where she is." The teenager didn't count her mother anymore. Not after what she did.

"Hmm, well, I heard that if you have family in the United States then you go live with them until it's time to have your immigration hearing. I don't know what happens if you don't have relatives there. But really, could it be any worse than living here?"

Bianca looked over to the door to make sure no one was listening, then leaned forward close to Luisa. "Listen, tell them what you told me about your hometown. About the gangs and the violence and all that. How you have no family left. You'll be fine. Besides," she added, reclining back against the wall, "what happens once you're in the US is the least of your problems. Getting out of here and up to the border . . . that's what you have to worry about."

The trio heard a noise coming from the front of the building, causing Felipe and Luisa to jump off of Bianca's bed.

"Hurry," the room's regular occupant said. "If anybody finds you in here then the whole thing is ruined!"

Felipe slid open the door to his girlfriend's room and slipped out into the hall to make his escape. Luisa, at less of a risk of punishment if caught in Bianca's room, turned to face the young woman who had become like a sister to her.

Luisa wrapped her arms around Bianca and hugged her tight. "I don't know if I'll get another chance to say goodbye."

Tears welled in the eyes of both girls.

"Be careful," Luisa added. "Don't leave here just to let something bad happen to you out there."

"I won't," said Bianca, shaking her head. "Plus, Felipe will take care of me."

The teenagers hugged again and then Luisa left, tip-toeing the short distance back to her room.

Sitting down on the bed (she had long since stopped caring enough to sleep on the floor), Luisa was overwhelmed by a sense of loneliness. There were still ten other girls in the brothel with her, eleven once Bianca was replaced, but none of them would be like her best friend.

I hope she makes it, Luisa prayed. *God, help her make it.*

THIRTY-FOUR

Twenty-four hours later, when Bianca was missing at morning bed check, Monterrey's most profitable brothel was put on lockdown. No one in, no one out until the sex slave was located. There had never been a successful escape from La Casa Feliz, and Señor Perrera and his guards were determined to keep it that way.

But when one of those men didn't respond to the emergency call in to work, Señor knew the streak was over. Carlos Perrera didn't believe in coincidences. A guard and a girl going missing on the same morning? He shook his head and growled, running a frustrated hand through his white hair. "Fuck!"

Emilio and Horatio walked back in the front door after searching every street within ten blocks of the brothel.

"No sign of them, sir," Emilio said, stepping into the building's front parlor. "The last client left the house at 12:45am and we did a final bed check at 1am. She was still here then."

"But Felipe wasn't," the boss replied.

"That's correct, sir. He works the day shift."

"Which means," Señor continued, "sometime after the final bed check, Felipe came back inside the house and helped the whore – what's her name?"

"Bianca."

"Helped Bianca escape." The brothel's owner let out another growl and glared in the direction of the two night guards: Silvia and Raúl. "What the hell were you two doing when all of that happened?"

"I was in the back in the kitchen, sir," Señora Silvia responded. Security wasn't part of her technical job description, so she knew she was slightly less in the warpath. "If they went in and out the front door, I wouldn't have heard it."

"And you?" Señor asked, turning his attention to his nephew. "What the fuck were you doing?"

The younger man fumbled for a response. "I . . . ugh . . ."

"You . . . ugh . . . weren't doing a damn thing! You work the night shift, for fuck's sake. Your *entire job* is to guard the front door

117

and make sure shit like this doesn't happen. I swear, if your mother wasn't my sister I would put a bullet in your skull right now."

"Where are the rest of the whores?" Perrera bellowed, turning away from his disappointment of a nephew.

"They're locked in their rooms, sir."

"Bring them in here," their owner commanded. "I've had about enough of this shit."

****

Luisa and the ten other remaining prostitutes were drug out of their rooms at gunpoint and herded down the hall into the front parlor. They didn't go in that room often . . . it was usually reserved for business transactions between Emilio and the clients. Occasionally there was a large group or party of some sort, though, and a collection of the 'merchandise' would be put on display for the visitors to see.

Walking into the parlor, Luisa surveyed the room and saw that it hadn't changed any since her last visit. Beige carpet covered the floor, light blue paint decorated the walls, and an assortment of couches and chairs filled the otherwise empty space. Two barred windows were on the front wall, guarded on either side by floor-length navy blue drapes.

Luisa's gaze settled on Señor. *Uh oh*, she thought. *He's even more pissed than I thought he would be.*

Luisa was in a precarious position as the only person in the house with advance knowledge of Bianca and Felipe's escape. She did her best to hide that fact by appearing as shocked and bewildered as the rest of the group.

"Line up," Emilio barked, and the eleven young women complied. Forming a straight line in the center of the room, Luisa was the next to last girl on the right.

To everyone's surprise, Señor's first words weren't said in anger. He sighed, put his hands in his pockets, and scanned the row of teenagers with more curiosity than rage.

"I'm only going to ask this once," he said, speaking in a soft voice, "and I want you ladies to tell me the truth. If you tell me the truth, nobody gets hurt." Señor shrugged his shoulders. "I replace

118

people all the time. Not a big deal. A cost of doing business. But I want to know," he added, "if any of you knew that Bianca and Felipe were going to leave."

Silence covered the room and eleven pairs of eyes filled with fear. All but one didn't know about the escape, but all of them did know about the illicit romance.

"Hmm?" their owner pressed, walking up and down the line. "Anybody? I promise: tell me the truth and you can all go back to your rooms."

Silence filled the air.

Perrera nodded his head and stepped away from the group. "Okay, I see how it's going to be," he said in a new, harsh tone. "Because I know . . . I know that there's no fucking way those two escaped without somebody hearing something. You knew, and you didn't tell. You lied then and you're lying now."

Señor's eyes switched from curiosity to fury, and his shock white hair would have been spitting flames of fire if it were possible.

"You know, I heard a story once about Saddam Hussein." Señor paused. "Do you even know who that is?"

Most of the girls, Luisa included, shook their heads no. Elena was the sole exception.

Their owner laughed, but it was a sound that came across like more of a witch's cackle than a humorous noise. "What a bunch of idiots I have working here. It is a good thing you don't need to be smart to be a whore."

"Saddam Hussein," Señor explained, "was the president of Iraq for a long time. Iraq is a country on the other side of the world, for the idiots in the room. Saddam was all-powerful. Many say he was a bad man, but I'm not one to judge. What I heard, though, and what I like about him, is that he made sure everyone around him knew that they owed their lives to him."

As he spoke, Señor pointed his finger at each person in the room, prostitutes and guards alike.

"Now," the boss continued, "I heard that one day at a meeting Saddam killed many of his top advisors. They hadn't done anything wrong, but he wanted everyone who survived to know that their lives were in Saddam's hands. And that he could take those lives away at any moment if they did not obey him."

The señor paused and a harsh, manic look entered his eyes. "You see, putas, I am your Saddam Hussein. I am your all-powerful ruler. Except I'm not stupid enough to get caught by the United States like he did. But anyway, you owe your lives to me. For instance," he said, reaching behind his back and pulling a gun out of the waistband of his pants, "let's use one of you as an example. Come here," he ordered, pointing at the girl in the middle of the line.

Gabriela, terrified, didn't move.

"I said come here, dammit!"

Emilio walked over and shoved Gabriela in front of their boss.

Perrera nodded. "Good. What's your name, yegua?"

"G . . . g . . . gabri . . . ela."

Her owner smiled. "Gabriela here is a good enough worker, right Emilio?"

"Sí Señor."

"She's not all that pretty," Perrera continued, "and she has gotten fatter since I bought her . . . I remember that much. But she's a decent enough earner for me. She's done nothing to make me angry, right chiquita?"

By that point, Gabriela was shaking so badly from fear that she barely had to do anything at all to make her head nod up and down.

"S . . . s . . . sí, Señor. I . . . I haven't d-done anyt-thing wrong."

"Good girl," the man said, petting her on the head like a dog. "Good girl."

Perrera then raised the gun in his other hand and shot Gabriela square between the eyes.

THIRTY-FIVE

Bone-chilling screams filled the air as the group of young women watched their housemate's body fall lifeless to the floor. Blood and brain matter pooled out of Gabriela's head onto the carpet, and several of the girls vomited upon realizing that they too were covered in human debris.

Their owner, on the other hand, wiped the splattered blood off his face like it was nothing more than a bead of sweat. El Señor had no interest in everyone's hysterics.

"¡Cállense! Shut up!" he yelled, firing a gunshot into the plaster ceiling.

Luisa and the other girls stopped screaming and struggled to contain their choked tears.

Oh my God, Luisa thought. *He's going to kill us all. He's gone crazy. We're all going to die. Oh God, we're all going to die!*

The madman in the center of the room nodded when it was quiet enough to satisfy his tastes.

"Gabriela was a decent earner. A solid worker. If I will do that to her for no reason, imagine what I will do to any of you who disobey me. Imagine what I will do if another one of you even thinks about trying to escape! You belong to me. You can never leave. Ever! Do you understand?"

A few of the teenagers nodded their heads up and down, but most were still in too much shock to register a response.

"I asked you a question!" Perrera bellowed. He pointed his gun at Luisa's head. "Or do you need another example?"

A chorus of "we understand", "sí señor", and "don't shoot her" reverberated around the room.

"Good. That's what I thought. Now clean up this mess. I can't have clients seeing blood and a body when they come in here tonight."

****

Driving away from the scene and back to his office across town, anger seeped out of Carlos Perrera's pores and into the expensive leather seats of his car.

No matter what happened that afternoon, his day was ruined. The first escape – ever – from his brothel. *And the fact that she took Felipe with her?* Carlos gritted his teeth and let out a small growl. His hands gripped the steering wheel so tightly that his knuckles turned white. The betrayal of one of his best young guards was what really made him angry. Prostitutes could be replaced. Hardworking, capable, smart employees? Those were harder to find.

Although he couldn't have been too smart. Piece of shit threw it all away for a woman. A whore. Perrera sighed and flipped on his blinker as he turned onto his office's street. *What a fucking idiot. And because of him, I have to replace one guard and two prostitutes. Such a pain in the ass.*

Carlos hadn't wanted to kill the other one. She seemed pretty enough and wasn't causing anyone any trouble. *Or so I had been told*, he thought, shaking his head. *But somebody's gotta lay down the law. Put the fear of God into them.*

It wasn't the escape that bothered him the most, though. Bianca, Felipe, and Gabriela could all be replaced. What worried Señor Perrera was what the two runaways might do once they were free. Away from the clutches of his empire, they could go to the federal police and file a denuncia against him and the brothel. Bianca was the victim, and Felipe knew his boss' real name and how the business worked.

"¡Mierda!" Carlos cursed, slamming his hands against the steering wheel. A police complaint like that could bring down his entire house of cards. *And I have no way to stop it.* "Shit shit shit!"

In what was becoming a common occurrence, Perrera thought seriously about selling the brothel and getting out of the sex slave trade altogether. It was starting to get way too risky for his liking.

THIRTY-SIX

Three days after they left – one by bus and one by hearse – the first of Bianca and Gabriela's replacements arrived at La Casa Feliz.

Walking past Bianca's old room that morning, Luisa noticed that the door was closed for the first time since her friend left. It was official: Bianca had been replaced. The new person's name was Sara, Luisa would learn, and she was older than Señor's typical purchases. She was chosen for precisely that reason. Being older, Sara had more years in the life and less spirit remaining. Ximena also noted that Sara was 'lower on the attractive ladder'. Señor didn't want to have to deal with another pretty, spirited young worker running off with a guard. So he picked Sara . . . a wallflower devoid of hope, confidence, or social skills. Luisa said hi to her once, but that was the extent of their interactions. The house's new resident didn't want to chat; wasn't interested in commiserating with the others. She just wanted to make it through each day alive – which was exactly why Señor picked her.

Luisa didn't mind that her next-door neighbor wanted to keep to herself. She didn't want another friend anyway. After losing Josefina, Roxana, and Bianca, the young woman came to the conclusion that Señora Silvia was right after all. There were no lasting friendships and no happy endings in her world.

She did hope that Bianca and Felipe had a happy ending, though. If all went according to plan, they should've reached the Mexico-US border on the same day of their escape. Luisa didn't know how long people had to wait for the boats to drive them across the Rio Grande, but she figured it couldn't be more than a day or two. After all, she and her sister were shipped over 1400 miles through three countries in the span of twelve days. *Surely they can make it 150 miles and one country in three days*, Luisa thought.

****

Gabriela's replacement, the twelfth and final prostitute to bring the brothel back to full capacity, was of a different sort than shy Sara. Not finding what he was looking for in The Broker's merchandise and not wanting to lose revenue while he waited, Señor had driven to another part of Mexico City and bought the first drug- and disease-free prostitute that he could find.

Rafaela was beautiful – the kind of beautiful that not even five years in the life could hide. As 'the pretty one', she soon became the Happy Girl who clients preferred. Her housemates found it strange, though, because Rafaela seemed to prefer the men too. There was something about the way she walked, a vibe she gave off, that lured men wherever she went. Whereas Luisa and many of the other sex workers averted their eyes and slunk to the corner of whatever room they were in, Rafaela took center stage. Smiling, flirting, laughing. And being the only girl in the house who was disappointed when business was slow.

"Do you think she actually *likes* it?" Elena whispered to Luisa, not wanting Rafaela to hear her.

"I dunno. Maybe." Thinking for a minute, Luisa added: "My mom was the same way. Craving attention from guys. Almost like she was addicted to it. That's kinda what Rafaela reminds me of."

"What about me?" the other girl asked after hearing her name.

"Umm, I said I like your hair pulled back like that. Very classy and pretty."

Rafaela preened. "If you ever want any beauty tips, just ask. I know what the men like."

"Don't ask her for clothing advice, though," said María, the fashionista, as she walked into the room. "For that, you must come to me."

The teenager spun in a circle to show off a navy blue dress that she was wearing. In a world like theirs, living lives like theirs, the young women took solace in whatever small joys they could find. For Ana, it was cooking. For María, it was clothes. Luisa was pretty sure the remaining member of The Two G's, Guadalupe, was cutting herself when no one was watching. But she didn't ask and had no room to judge. *We all do what we must to survive*, Luisa told herself.

"Oooh, that's such a pretty dress!" Elena exclaimed, bringing Luisa's thoughts back to the present. Elena ran her hands over the fabric on María's clothes and asked: "where in the world did you get that? The señora never gives me anything that cute."

María cast her eyes downward and lowered her voice. "Promise you won't say anything to the guards?" It was a standard question

124

following their owner's 'tell us everything or else' outburst after Bianca's escape.

Elena nodded her head up and down. "I promise."

"I made it."

"But how?"

"Well, Señora Silvia was replacing the drapes in the front room. Emilio said it needed to be done after . . . well, after Gabriela got shot." A somber look crossed María's face as she remembered her fallen housemate.

"The drapes didn't get dirty from that, though," Elena countered. "I would know because I had to clean the room, and everything up front by the windows and drapes was fine."

María nodded her head. "I know. We all helped in the clean-up. But Emilio wanted the drapes replaced anyway, so they were. I asked the señora if I could have the fabric."

"You need more than fabric to make a dress," Elena replied, never missing a moment to try to make herself seem smarter than the rest of the group.

"Señora has a sewing machine in her room. She let me use it."

A look of jealousy entered Elena's eyes. "What? How? Why?"

María laughed. "Don't look so surprised. Señora is kinda nice when you get to know her. She used to be like us. Did you know that? When she got too old, she moved to the kitchen. And Señor likes having a woman watching over the girls. He thinks we will try to seduce and trick the male guards . . . I guess he was right when you look at Bianca and Felipe. But anyway, Señora does cooking and 'talent management' as she calls it."

Elena shook her head. "I can't believe you're friends with her. And wearing a dress made from drapes."

"We're not friends," María said. "And I'm like the von Trapp kids in 'The Sound of Music'."

"Who?" Elena asked.

"It's a movie. During one part, the characters wear clothes made out of drapes. When I was a domestic in Mexico City, my boss' kids used to watch it all the time. It's actually pretty good."

"What's pretty good?" Luisa asked.

"'The Sound of Music'. It's a movie."

"I've never seen it," Elena said.

Luisa sighed. "I've never seen any movies before."

125

"What? You've never seen a movie? Ever?"

Luisa shook her head and shrugged her shoulders. "We didn't have TVs in my great-grandma's house. Or in the apartment building where my mom, sister, and I lived in the city. I never had enough money to go to the theater. And we definitely don't get to watch any movies here."

"How sad," Rafaela said, rejoining the conversation. "I love movies."

"Me too," added María. "One day," she said with a smile, "we're going to get out of this place and we'll all go to the movies together."

The other girls smiled and nodded their heads in agreement, even though all four knew they were far more likely to end up like Gabriela, splattered against the curtains, than they were to ever sit together in a movie theater.

THIRTY-SEVEN

Two months shy of two years in Monterrey, Luisa decided enough was enough. She knew that her odds of surviving an escape attempt were low, especially without the help of a guard, but she had to try it anyway. *I'd rather die trying to escape than live in this hell hole any longer*, she thought.

Luisa had already memorized the map that Felipe gave her. She knew the name and location of every road and town leading north, south, east, and west from Monterrey. Mostly the northern ones, though. Despite her mother's warnings about the kind of people who lived in the United States, Luisa decided she had to at least give it a shot. *Tens of thousands of people try to get to the US every year . . . they must be going there for something.*

After saving her tip money for twenty-two months, the Hondureña knew that she almost had enough to make it through the official and unofficial checkpoints on her journey north. The government ran the official checks, looking for either proper identification or a bribe. Drug cartels patrolled the narcobloqueos, and they also wanted to see travelers' paperwork. "Foreigners get charged more," Felipe explained to her. "Mexicans pay the least, Central Americans pay more, and people from Europe or Asia pay the most."

"What happens if you don't pay?" Luisa asked.

Felipe had laughed in response. "Everybody pays the cartels. Everybody."

Based on what Felipe told her, Luisa didn't think she would need any money to get over the actual border itself. As far as what she would do once she got to the United States? Luisa shook her head. *I don't know and I don't care.*

Needing someone to cover for her in case something went wrong, Luisa enlisted the help of Cristina in planning her escape. The two girls sat in the courtyard one morning talking.

"You can't just walk up to the border and say 'let me in'," Cristina cautioned. "It doesn't work that way."

"There's no other option," replied Luisa. "I'd have to work the rest of my life to save enough money to pay a coyote. I can't do that.

And I can't stay here." Tears filled her eyes and her voice crumbled. "I . . . I c-can't do this anym-more."

"Okay, okay. Tranquila. Calm down. It's okay." Cristina ran her hand through her thick black hair. "Maybe you can be one of those – what are they – you know, you say you can't go back or they'll kill you?"

"Refugee," Luisa said, then shook her head. "I heard people talk about them on the train to Oaxaca. You have to have something super special about you. Like you're Jewish and the Muslims hate you or you're gay or a communist or something. 'Hello, I'm a whore' doesn't sound like a good enough reason."

"You're not a whore."

Luisa didn't reply, and instead looked over at her friend and raised one eyebrow.

Cristina sighed. "You can't be a whore if it was never your choice."

Luisa considered the other girl's words for a minute, then shook her head. "Doesn't matter," she said, shifting in her chair to cross one leg over the other. "Choice or no choice, it's still not a good enough reason. I'll have to try to sneak in on my own and take my chances after that."

****

Two weeks shy of two years in Monterrey, months after Bianca and Felipe made their own daring escape, Luisa's moment came. She had saved enough money to make a run for it. After the brothel closed that night, Luisa sat on the concrete floor of her room and counted her cash. Paper money and coins, all earned in the worst way imaginable. During the course of her life as a sex slave, Luisa averaged seventy clients per week. Twenty-three and a half months, or ninety-four weeks, totaled up to be slightly more than 6,500 tricks in two years. Most clients didn't tip at all – house rules said they weren't supposed to – but every once in a while a man would toss Luisa a peso or two on his way out. Her regular clients, like the man who gave her the newspaper, sometimes tipped up to five pesos. Five peso days were good days. Once, a businessman from the United States came to La Casa Feliz while he was in town for a convention. After his forty-five minutes ended, he pressed a $20 bill into Luisa's hand. *Twenty dollars*, Luisa remembered, shaking her head. Whereas most of the men didn't give her any tip at all, that client handed her the equivalent of three hundred pesos. *Like it was nothing*, she recalled. After he left the room, Luisa broke down crying.

Including that one extremely generous client, two years' work earned Luisa just shy of 1,500 pesos. Which was, consequently, only 300 pesos more than the cost of one session with her. *Two years to save what they spend for forty-five minutes. Increíble.*

The pain that came with her work in the beginning was now dull, as were Luisa's once vibrant black eyes. Despite that bone-crushing despair, Luisa refused to accept that her life would never change. She refused to believe him when Emilio declared that she was lucky to be there and should feel grateful to belong to Señor. *No*, Luisa thought, shaking her head. *No more.*

When she heard whispers and shuffled steps in the hallway, Luisa shoved her money back into the hole in her mattress and slid open her door to see what was happening.

"Come on," whispered Cristina, waving Luisa out into the hall. "We're all going to the courtyard."

"Why?"

"María said that the moon is going to turn red tonight. Want to see?"

"Yeah," Luisa replied, joining the other captives in the one open-air section of their prison.

"What are we looking for?" Esperanza whispered.

"The moon."

"There it is!" Susana exclaimed, and the rest of the group hushed her into silence.

"What's so special about the moon? Looks normal to me."

"My client told me about it," answered María. "He said the moon will turn red tonight, like blood."

"What?"

"No way."

"That's what he said," María countered. "That the moon goes behind the sun or the sun behind the moon or something like that. And then it turns red."

"What is he some kind of science teacher?"

129

María giggled. "I think he is, yeah. At a local high school."

"Ooooh," Susana gasped. "You like him!"

María shook her head back and forth. "No I don't."

"Look," Ximena said with a laugh. "No need for a red moon. We can look at María's red face!"

Everyone in the courtyard burst into muffled laughter.

"Hey, no, look. For real," Luisa said, pointing at the sky. "Look at the moon. It really is turning red!"

Twelve pairs of eyes gazed northward to the stars and watched in awe as the gray moon transitioned to brown, then copper, then a true blood red.

"Oh my gosh," Susana said. "It's so beautiful." Her housemates nodded their agreement, too mesmerized for words.

In that moment, even though they didn't realize it, the teenagers were more connected to the outside world than they had ever been before at the Casa Feliz. All over the earth, billions of people were looking skyward as the galaxy put on an art show for the humans to see.

****

Four hundred miles north of Monterrey, near the small Texas town of El Dorado, an American named Max Jacobbsen was also up late watching the lunar eclipse. The son of Scandinavian immigrants and himself a native of Dallas, Texas, Max had gone to Stanford University for college and remained in northern California after graduation. An engineering student and self-professed nerd, Max worked for several different companies before landing a gig as Chief of Design for an internet start-up. When the business went public, Max's bank account went through the roof. Jacobbsen retired before the dot-com bubble busted, and he and his wife, a fellow Stanford grad named Esmerelda, bought a ranch in West Texas where they could live out their golden years. He did some consulting and speech-making on the side in order to fend off cabin fever, but most of Max's time was spent on his ranch. He loved it there.

A door creaked open behind him and Max turned around to see his wife walking out onto the porch.

"Honey, it's almost two in the morning. What are you doing out here?"

"Waiting to see the blood moon," he replied, glancing up to the sky.

Esmerelda sighed. "I thought you had to leave for DC at eight tomorrow."

"I do."

Esmerelda, a licensed psychologist who grew up in Guadalajara, Mexico, shook her head at her college sweetheart. "You're going to be exhausted."

"Nah, estaré bien," Max replied in Spanish. His childhood nanny was from Mexico, which meant he was able to speak his wife's native language with only a slight accent. "Besides, I can always grab a power nap at my hotel before my speech tomorrow night."

"Fine," Esmerelda said, knowing when to pick her battles. "But don't stay out here too much longer."

"I won't," promised Max, before turning his eyes back to the sky. The eclipse was at its full height, filling the night air with a hazy red glow.

****

Back in Monterrey, Luisa Dominguez was enjoying the blood moon for more reasons than her housemates knew. As of that afternoon, after her fourth client gave her a tip that was larger than usual, Luisa had the money she needed to make her escape. She knew enough about the stars to know that eclipses like this one only happened on a full moon, and a full moon meant that in two short weeks she would be leaving her current world behind and escaping into freedom. Luisa's instinct was to run that night – that afternoon really, as soon as she got the money – but she knew that the full moon would make it too easy to see her. *If I wait two weeks*, Luisa thought, *the moon will be small and I'll have the cover of darkness to help me get away.*

THIRTY-EIGHT

In early March, Luisa made her move. She had dreamt of escaping so often, had thought and planned and prayed and planned some more – accounting for every possible obstacle she could think of – that when the day finally came, Luisa almost couldn't believe it.

Following Bianca and Felipe's idea, she waited until the brothel closed for the night and the final bed check was performed. The click-clack of Señora Silvia's stiletto heels could be heard crossing the floor of the courtyard, and then the kitchen door slammed closed with a thud. Luisa knew that the señora slept on a cot in the food pantry.

Without a watch to help her keep time, Luisa counted to 3,000 before getting out of bed. *She should be asleep by now*, the teenager thought.

Wrapping up all of her money in a plastic bag and taping it to her stomach, Luisa pulled her door open inch by inch to make sure it didn't squeak. She peered the top of her head out into the hallway.

It was empty.

Luisa squeezed through the small opening and tip-toed out into the hall, pushing the door to her room closed behind her. Wearing skinny jeans and a white tank top, she carried her shoes in her hand and darted across the courtyard as fast as her bare feet could carry her.

Upon reaching the kitchen, Luisa pressed her back against the wall and checked again to make sure no one was watching her. The night before, in a dream, Luisa made it this far only to be caught by a guard who had seen the whole thing. "I was waiting for you to make it to the window," he sneered. "That way I could prove to Señor that you were trying to escape and not just looking for a glass of water or something."

But there were no guards around now . . . at least none that Luisa could see. Taking a deep breath, Luisa crossed herself in prayer and slowly, ever so slowly, crept past the open door to the pantry. She could see the señora's feet and hear her snoring. *Please don't wake up. Please don't wake up.*

On the other end of the kitchen, away from the pantry, there was a second storage room. It housed cleaning supplies, a first-aid kit, and extra sets of things the ladies might need like underwear and sheets.

Luisa's heart was pounding and sweat beaded on her forehead as she twisted the knob on the handle and began to pull the door open. Then, Luisa's worst nightmare: it squeaked. It wasn't a loud noise, more like a peep from a mouse, but it was enough to alert the señora if she happened to be awake.

Luisa's chest heaved up and down and she closed her eyes, waiting to be caught. There was no legitimate excuse to be in the kitchen opening the storage closet at 2:30 in the morning. If Señora Silvia came out of the pantry, Luisa was a dead woman.

Seconds turned into minutes and still the kitchen remained quiet. By that point, despite the night's cool temperature, Luisa's jet black hair was damp with sweat and plastered against her forehead and the back of her neck.

It's now or never, she thought.

Luisa resumed her attempt to open the closet and this time, to her immense relief, the door made no sounds as it swung toward the teenage escapee. Stepping inside the small, dark room, Luisa pulled the door closed behind her. To her right, just below the ceiling, was her ticket to freedom. It was a tiny slit of a window and the only one in the entire brothel that wasn't covered by metal bars. Luisa knew . . . she checked them all.

She took a deep breath, placed her hands on one of the built-in shelves, and began to climb. When Luisa got high enough to reach the window, she flipped the lever on the outdated lock and pushed the glass open. Her head went through first, followed by an arm, a shoulder, another arm, and another shoulder. Luisa had never been big-chested, and that night marked the first time in her life that she was glad of that fact.

When it came time for the teenager to pull her hips through the window, the last step before an inevitable fall to the concrete ground below her, Luisa got stuck. No matter how much she pushed, no matter how hard she struggled, the young woman couldn't get the lower half of her body out the window.

"No, no," she whispered to herself as tears filled her eyes. "Not now . . . not when I'm so close!"

A few minutes later, Luisa quit fighting. It was dangerous for her to stay there like that, dangling half inside the building and half outside. If anyone happened to walk by on the street, they might alert the guards. After all, everyone in that section of Independencia knew that the building Luisa was climbing out of was a brothel.

Inch by inch, body part by body part, Luisa pushed herself back inside the former barn that was now her prison. Fighting back tears, she retraced her steps out of the closet, through the kitchen, across the courtyard, and into her room.

After closing her door behind her, Luisa collapsed in the corner and cried.

****

When Luisa walked into the courtyard the next morning, Cristina was shocked. Rushing over, eyes wide, she whispered: "what are you still doing here?"

"I got stuck in the window."

"You?" Cristina replied, looking at the skinny girl standing in front of her. "That's impossible."

Luisa shook her head. "No, getting out of that window is impossible. It's way smaller than I expected."

"So what are you going to do now?"

"Wait a month," Luisa said, "and try again. In the meantime, I won't eat."

THIRTY-NINE

In April, twenty-three months after she arrived at the Casa Feliz, Luisa left it. Thirty days of crash dieting brought the always-thin teenager down to an almost skeletal weight, but it was worth it. Because that time, when she slipped undetected through the whorehouse and into the storage closet, Luisa was able to shimmy her hips out of the window with ease.

Not wanting to waste time or get caught with her body halfway outside, Luisa forged ahead without giving any thought to what lay on the other side of the window. Fortunately and unfortunately, there was nothing.

No guards waiting to capture her and drag her back inside.

No neighbors watching who might knock on the door and tell Emilio what happened.

No padding to break her fall.

Luisa tumbled head first out the rectangular window and did a half somersault down nine feet before landing with a thud on her back.

"Oouumphhh," she coughed, the air whooshing out of her lungs. "Ay Dios. Oww," Luisa added, closing her eyes.

Luisa heard a bird chirping and her eyes flew open. She scrambled to her feet, forgetting about the bruises from her fall. A feeling much more powerful than pain was coursing through the young woman's body: freedom.

Using the map she had memorized, Luisa weaved her way through the neighborhood's convoluted streets – always careful to avoid any passersby. Luisa crossed a bridge over the Santa Caterina, a river that separated Independencia from the majority of the city. The teenager then continued her march, past the Monumento al Sol and the Contemporary Art Museum, to the left of the massive Metropolitan Cathedral, and into the Macroplaza . . . home to many of Monterrey's iconic buildings. Similar to the National Mall in Washington, DC, the plaza had the art museum on one end and the city and state government buildings on the other end, with a large greenspace in between. In the middle of the park was Luisa's objective: the Estación Zaragosa transit stop.

Much to Luisa's dismay, the trains weren't running when she arrived. Not much was at three o'clock in the morning, but the escaped slave didn't know that. She didn't know anything about transit schedules . . . especially since the only train she had ever ridden on was La Bestia. Sitting down in the plaza near the station entrance, Luisa shuddered when she remembered her death-defying ride through the jungles of southern Mexico. It seemed like two lifetimes rather than two years had passed since she and Josefina sat huddled together on the top of the boxcars with their third owner, Antonio. *I wonder what he's doing now*, Luisa thought as she leaned her head back against a wall. *He was the nicest of all of them.*

With that, an exhausted Luisa drifted off to sleep. The best sleep she'd ever had in Mexico.

****

Three hours later, the bone-thin Hondureña woke up to the feeling of a boot nudging into her ribs. Remembering where she was, Luisa's eyes flew open and she stared at the uniformed police officer standing above her.

"Let's go, get out of here," the man said, nudging her again. "No sleeping in the parks. You know the rules."

Luisa didn't know the rules – she didn't know anything about life outside the brothel – but she didn't tell the police officer that. The only uniform that had ever been kind to the teenage girl was that of her village priest. Her abuela told her that not all police were bad, *but now is not the time to test that theory*, Luisa thought.

"I'm sorry," she said to the officer, standing up and brushing off her jeans. "I'm leaving."

After the constable walked away, Luisa looked around to see dozens of people streaming in and out of the public transit stop beside her. *The trains are running!* she thought with a smile.

Scurrying down the stairs into the underground station, Luisa at first tried to pass through a turn-style by paying with peso coins.

"You've gotta buy a pass," a man in a suit said before scanning his and continuing on his way.

Ten minutes later, a frustrated Luisa – with the help of an equally frustrated station attendant – bought her transit pass and made it through the turn-style onto the train platforms. Luisa kept her head on a swivel, always on the lookout for Señor, Emilio, or one of the other guards. Anyone who looked like they might be looking for her.

Luisa didn't think about what Señor might do to the girls who remained at the Casa Feliz. No one had blamed Bianca for escaping, despite what happened to Gabriela. And no one would blame Luisa. The housemates got along well enough given the circumstances, but each knew that at the end of the day they were alone in the world. Luisa would be applauded for making her way to freedom, not scorned for leaving others behind. *At least I hope so*, she thought before stepping onto a train and into her new life.

FORTY

Twelve stops later, Luisa found herself at the end of Line Two of the Metrorrey, Monterrey's two-line rail system. From there, the Sendero station, she caught the first of several buses which would take her north to the border town of Reynosa.

An hour into her trip along Route 40D, a few minutes after passing by the Sierra de Papagayos mountain range, the bus she was on came to an abrupt halt. Standing up, the driver turned around to face his passengers.

"I just got word that there's an immigration checkpoint five miles north of here. If any of you don't have papers, get off now. I'm not getting fined for transporting illegals. A couple of miles north of here there's a town called Los Ramones. You should be able to catch a different bus there. The checkpoints never stay in the same place for more than one or two days," he added in a rare gesture of support for the illegal immigrants.

Over half of the bus, Luisa included, got up from their seats and made their way to the exit. Their luck had run out.

At least I made it this far, Luisa thought to herself as she stepped out into the mid-morning sun. *A couple days spent in that town is better than a couple minutes back at Señor's place.*

What Luisa and her fellow travelers didn't know was that their bus driver had been told to send them to Los Ramones. The town of 6,000 was home to a small but notorious road gang that preyed on people making their way north to the United States. In order to supplement his meager income, the driver was paid cash to kick undocumented migrants off his bus, warn them of a fictitious checkpoint, and send them on their way to Los Ramones.

Before they even reached the city limits, a gang leader named Javier and his crew were waiting.

One by one, the muscle-bound criminal kicked, punched, slapped, and spit on the new arrivals before making them pay a fine of several hundred dollars for the privilege of passing through his town.

Standing at the back of the group, Luisa's body tensed as she prepared to face this new threat to her freedom. Not even twelve hours after escaping the brothel in Monterrey, the fifteen year old had a newfound confidence and was determined to never go back to that life.

"Well well well," Javier said when he reached Luisa. "What do we have here? Pretty little thing, aren't you?" he hissed, letting his eyes roam up and down her body.

Luisa stared straight ahead, no longer bothered by lecherous looks from lecherous men.

"I can think of a different kind of payment I'd like from you, sweet thing," the gang leader added.

"No."

"Excuse me?"

"No. I'll pay you a bribe like the other people did, but nothing else."

Javier pulled a gun out of the back of his waistband and pointed it at Luisa's head. The weapon clicked in her ear when Javier pulled off the safety. Sharp, cool metal planted itself on her forehead, with only skin and bone separating bullet and brain.

"Nobody says no to me," he replied, baring his crooked, yellow teeth like a snarling dog. "Give me one good reason why I shouldn't kill you right now."

"That's a nice shirt."

The dog stopped snarling and stared at Luisa. "What?"

The Hondureña closed her eyes and let out a deep breath, having half expected the man to shoot her midway through her sentence.

"That's a nice shirt you're wearing," Luisa repeated, "and if you kill me then you'll get blood on it and mess it up."

Javier furrowed his brow and narrowed his eyes, then glanced from Luisa to his shirt and back again.

A second click sounded and the metal drifted away from Luisa's forehead.

Deep, male laughter filled the air.

"This is a nice shirt," he said to his companions who joined in the laughter. "Don't kill me – it'll mess up your clothes." The roadside gangster continued to laugh. "I like this one," Javier said, waving his gun toward Luisa as if it were a giant foam finger. "She's funny. And pretty," he added.

The dog returns, thought Luisa, feeling every second of his long, lingering gaze up and down her body. Men staring was nothing new. *But they don't usually have a gun in their hand while they do.*

"Tie her up," her newest captor ordered. "Put her in the truck."

The dog's minion stepped forward and pulled a plastic zip-tie out of his back pocket.

How convenient.

The makeshift handcuffs were halfway around her wrists when the boy – *he can't be any older than me* – stopped.

"Umm . . . Javier?"

"What?"

"You should see this."

"Stop being dramatic and tell me."

"You can't keep her," the boy said, and Luisa heard what sounded almost like fear in his voice.

The leader, Javier, stomped back over to where his prisoner was standing. "What the hell do you mean I can't keep her?"

The boy grabbed Luisa's right arm and pulled it around in front of her. "See?" he said, pointing to her wrist.

The older man looked at Luisa's arm, then her face, then turned around and kicked the tire on his truck.

"¡Mierda! Shit!"

The dog started to pace, pant, and growl. When he turned back around to face Luisa, the snarling was worse than ever.

"Why the hell didn't you tell me you belong to the cartel?"

"What?"

"Don't play stupid, bitch," he said, pulling his gun back out of his waistband and waving at Luisa. "Why didn't you tell me?"

"I . . . I . . . I didn't know."

Javier stared at Luisa for a second, then laughed. He looked over at his henchmen with a smile. "She didn't know."

All of the men laughed.

I don't know why they think all of this is so funny. The teenager blinked her eyes, and in that split second the laughter stopped and the cold metal of the gang leader's gun returned to her forehead.

"Nobody belongs to a cartel but doesn't know it. You see this?" Javier said, lifting up Luisa's arm to show her the tattoo on her wrist. "Did you not ever wonder what this was?"

140

A single tear spilled out of Luisa's eye and rolled down her cheek. "It meant I belonged to Señor."

"Señor who?"

Luisa was about to say she didn't know, but her mind flashed back to the conversation she had with Felipe before he left. "Perrera," she answered. "Señor Perrera. He owns the prostíbulo in Monterrey and all of the girls who work there. But he said he was a businessman. He never said anything about the cartels."

The man in front of her drew in a deep breath and ran his tongue across his upper teeth, causing his lip to stick out in a wavelike motion. He sighed.

"What she knew or didn't know doesn't matter. She belongs to the narcos, and we can't steal from them. She goes back." Javier sighed again and shrugged his shoulders. "She's pretty enough . . . maybe we'll get a finder's fee."

Javier looked back over at the boy under his command. "Tie her up now. Put her in the truck. We've gotta go to Monterrey. The rest of you," he added, gesturing toward the bus riders, "got lucky today. Don't ever come back to my town, though. You won't be lucky twice."

Riding along in the back of the truck, being guarded by the boy who now held a semi-automatic rifle in his hands, Luisa looked down at her wrist and the tattoo that was a chain, pulling her back into the life she worked so hard to escape.

It was the one thing she hadn't accounted for in her plans. The black ink barcode was branded into her arm on her first day at the Casa Feliz and had been there so long that she forgot about it.

Luisa dropped her head into her cuffed hands and cried. It took a lot longer than most, but Señor had finally succeeded. Her spirit was broken. Slave or free, alive or dead . . . Luisa didn't care anymore. *It's not like my life matters anyway.*

FORTY-ONE

Luisa spent three days locked inside of the same storage closet that she used to escape, although by that point the window had been covered up with concrete. There would be no more unauthorized exits from La Casa Feliz.

There was also no food or water for the runaway slave. No light. No bathroom break. Just Luisa in the room in solitary confinement, guarded at the door by Señor's German Shepherds.

On the morning of the third day, Emilio dragged Luisa out of the closet and through the house to a car that was waiting outside the front of the building. Shoving her in the trunk, Emilio hogtied Luisa's feet and hands and wrapped a bandanna around her mouth as a muzzle.

"She's a pain in the ass," Señor commented from the sidewalk, "but she's still worth something. Make sure you get a decent price for her."

"Yes sir," the brothel manager replied. He slammed the trunk lid closed, climbed in the driver's seat, started the engine, and sped off in the direction of Mexico City.

****

After ten hours on the road, Emilio's car rolled to a stop and squeaky brakes announced their arrival. Seconds later, the trunk was lifted open and an exhausted, dehydrated Luisa was pulled out like a sack of potatoes.

Blinking her eyes to adjust to the light, Luisa looked at her surroundings.

Oh my God. This can't be happening. The girl's black eyes grew as wide as saucers and, as soon as Emilio removed the gag from her mouth, her jaw hung open in shock.

"What are you staring at? Go!" he commanded, having untied her hands and feet as well.

Emilio shoved Luisa in the back with his gun, forcing her to march forward through an open door into a dimly-lit warehouse. After the door shut behind her, the lights turned on.

Luisa closed her eyes. *Not again. Please God not again. I didn't go through all of that just to start all over again.*

A few minutes later, the warehouse door opened behind her and an impeccably dressed middle-aged man walked inside. He surveyed Luisa and the other new arrivals and nodded his head, liking the merchandise.

"You'll stay here until I find buyers for you," El Agente began, using what Luisa realized was a rehearsed speech. "The bathroom is through there. There's no door and I won't add one. I don't need any of you getting any desperate ideas while unsupervised in there."

The man paused, glaring at each of the girls. Walking over to stand in front of Luisa, he looked her up and down and smiled. "Especially you, bonita."

Luisa shivered. *Not the slightest bit of recognition,* she thought. *How many people have come through here? He's seen so many that he doesn't even recognize the repeats.*

"This is Yolanda," The Broker continued, gesturing to the same nasty woman as before. "She'll be watching you while you're out here. Behave, do what you're told, and you'll fetch a good price from a good buyer. Misbehave and you'll be working a street corner for the rest of your life. Understand?"

This group all answered loudly enough the first time.

His reputation must be growing, Luisa smirked.

"Good. Now settle in and get washed up. There might be some buyers coming over later tonight."

****

Luisa walked over to a cot in the far corner and laid down. She wasn't interested in meeting any of the other slaves awaiting sale. Wasn't interested in gossip or speculation. *None of it matters, anyway,* she thought with a sigh.

A few cots down, two girls who weren't yet broken sat talking. Luisa couldn't help but overhear their conversation.

"This is my second time at a place like this," one of the young women said. "The first time, I was at a broker's place for a week. That guy wasn't anywhere near as sophisticated as this one. But anyway, he knew that a certain buyer would like me, so he kept me off to the side while he dealt with other sales. I met a lot of new people that way," she continued. "Women who would arrive and stay in the back for a day or two and then move on. I kinda liked it, you know? Getting to share stories with people from all over the country who knew what you were going through." The young woman paused and lowered her voice. "I even met a vestida."

"A dress?" her companion asked.

"No, not a dress. A travesti. Transvestite."

The second prostitute's eyes grew large and she inched closer to her new friend, shooting questions at her in rapid fire succession.

"A travesti? At a broker's house? I thought they only worked the streets. What did he look like? Or she? Which one do we call them? What was he like? Was it weird?"

The more experienced of the pair put her hands up in front of her chest in self-defense. "Woah, woah. Calm down. I didn't know you would freak out like that."

"He was nice," she added. "Pretty. Very skinny. He told me that that broker had a handful of rich clients who were into that sort of thing but wouldn't be caught dead cruising La Merced in Mexico City looking for a hookup. So they used a specialty agent to get what they wanted."

Unable to ignore the conversation any longer, Luisa sat up in her cot. "Where did he – she? – end up going?" she asked. "Do you know?" *Maybe he's in the same place as Josefina and I could find her.*

The other girl shook her head. "The buyer never said anything during the inspection, so he didn't know. I asked him when he came back to get his duffel bag."

"How much did he cost?" the third member of the group asked.

Luisa was surprised as much by the question as by the fact that no one else was surprised. *I guess everything – and everyone – has a price.*

"20,000 pesos," was the answer.

"20,000?! Are you serious?"

The storyteller nodded. "A rich buyer with very particular tastes and the prettiest man I'd ever seen . . . you know that's gonna mean top dollar."

Luisa shook her head and laid back down. *A man dressed as a woman is worth more than me. Isn't that fabulous.*

FORTY-TWO

In a hotel about thirty minutes away from The Broker's establishment, the Texas millionaire named Max Jacobbsen was standing in the fifth-floor hallway talking to his employee, Jesús. Both men flew to Mexico City from San Antonio that afternoon.

"Based on what we got last time," Max said, "I think we have room for around ten. Maybe twelve."

Jesús raised his eyebrows. "That's a big class."

His boss nodded his clean-shaven head. "I know. But we want to have a well-rounded group, and I think we have some holes to fill in that regard. Especially with the middle-aged girls."

"That's true," Jesús nodded. "We're solid in the older, seventeen to nineteen age range, and also with the young ones at twelve to fourteen. But there's definite room to grow with the fifteen and sixteen year olds." He paused. "It might take this Enrique guy a little while to round up that many in that age range who would still fit our other qualifications."

"Hmm . . . you're right. I'll give him a call so he can go ahead and start working on it."

Max Jacobbsen had very strict requirements for the girls he wanted, and the dealers he worked with knew that. No older than eighteen when they got to him, no diseases, no pregnancies, no criminal records. They also had to show some signs of intelligence. *They don't have to be Mensa members*, Max thought, *but I don't want complete idiots either.*

That's why I like buying from Enrique. His art background means he knows how to work with discerning customers like me.

Max had just stepped in the door of his hotel room when his cell phone rang.

"Bueno."

"Hola Max, it's Enrique Lopez-Garcia. I got your message that you were going to be in town."

"Hey Enrique, I was about to call you. How are you man?"

"Good, good," The Broker replied. "You here yet?"

"Just got here. Haven't even unpacked yet."

145

"Well good, don't," said Enrique. "I have some new items that I think you might like. All lined up and ready for you to see."

"Oh yeah?" Max asked, flipping the lid closed on his suitcase.

"Yes sir. A new shipment came in today. Some high quality, Grade B stock. I think they would showcase very well for you."

"Excellent," Max said with a smile, causing wrinkles to form around his crystal blue eyes. "I have a few things to do today for some other business, but I can come by later tonight to take a look if that works for you."

"Tonight is great. I'll see you then."

Max pressed the red 'end' button on his phone and tossed it onto his hotel bed. *In and out in less than a day?* he thought. *That would be awesome. Enrique is outdoing himself this time.*

****

Six hours later, Max Jacobbsen and his Mexican-American assistant, Jesús Alcantera, hailed a taxi and gave the driver the street address for El Agente's home.

Max liked his new deputy. The young man was smart and tough and understood the business they were in. But he was still a little raw. A little too sympathetic.

"Remember," Max told him before the two men left their hotel to go to The Broker's house. "These girls aren't humans. They're objects. You go to the farmer's market to buy yourself some vegetables, right? Well, we're going to the market tonight to buy ourselves some women."

Jesús nodded and mumbled "yes sir", but Max could tell that it would take more time before his assistant had full control of his emotions during their shopping sprees.

Half an hour later, the Americans arrived at the home gallery of El Agente. Getting out of the taxi, the two men were greeted by Señora Lopez-Garcia – Enrique's wife and office manager.

"Right this way, gentlemen. My husband is waiting for you in the viewing room."

"Max!" The Broker said with a smile when one of his most loyal customers walked in. "Great to see you!"

146

"You too," replied Max. Turning to the side, he added: "I'd like to introduce you to my assistant, Jesús. He's still new to the business but he's starting to get it all figured out."

"Welcome," the proprietor said. "Nice to meet you."

"Thank you," Jesús replied in a quiet tone. "Nice to meet you too."

"You'll have to forgive him," Max said with a sigh and a pointed glance in the direction of his employee. "He worked with drugs for years in the Houston area but he's only been dealing in people for a few months."

"I understand. Takes a little getting used to. I was asked one time why I do this," The Broker said, running his hand through what remained of the hair on top of his head. "Why I don't stick to art. Why take the risk, right?"

Max smiled. "That's like asking the robber why he targets banks."

Enrique laughed. "Exactly, my friend. Exactly."

They both looked at Jesús and said: "because that's where the money is."

FORTY-THREE

While the three men were talking, El Agente's wife went out to the warehouse and gathered up the large group of girls who Max would be viewing.

Upon entering the parlor and seeing new buyers standing next to The Broker, Luisa's gaze rested on the shorter, older of the two. For some reason, he looked different than the six other men who had owned her. He dressed like them: a style Luisa learned was called 'business casual', with nice pants and a button-up shirt but no jacket and no tie. He looked like them, for the most part: skinny, bald, light-skinned but not super gringo-looking. He talked mostly to the man who seemed to be his assistant, a younger guy with black hair and a darker complexion.

Max and Jesús – Luisa heard them say their names – were just as inquisitive and just as business-like as the others, too. It didn't seem to bother them at all to be in a room full of naked women and inspecting them like cattle.

Jesús didn't speak as much as he grumbled, and he made the girls sit, stand, turn in circles, smile, and say things such as "what would you like tonight" and "the customer is always right."

All the while Max stood beside him, watching.

Yet despite all of that, despite every indication that he was the same as every other slave owner who had passed through her life, there was something different about Max. A feeling, a vibe, telling Luisa that there was more to him than met the eye. For the first time since exiting La Bestia in Oaxaca two years earlier, Luisa was terrified.

****

Max, the former computer systems engineer, finished inspecting the girls and walked back over to stand next to their current vendor.

"You have some good items here," Max said, crossing his arms over his chest and nodding his head in approval. "They don't look as old as the last batch I got . . . that's good," he added with a smile. "My patrons like them young."

"We do have a young crop this time, you're right," the slave trader said. "Oldest ones are barely sixteen. You should be able to get some solid years of work out of them."

Max uncrossed his arms and put his hands in his pockets before walking a slow circle around the 'merchandise'. "How much?"

"300,000 pesos for the group."

"300,000?! Come on, man. I wouldn't pay 300 grand for Grade A, and you said yourself these are Grade B. I'll give you 100."

"100,000?" The Broker laughed. "Are you trying to insult me? They may not be premium choice Grade A, but these girls are still solid buys. Disease free, not completely ugly, and young like you wanted." He paused. "I can do 200,000. No lower."

Max stopped walking and turned to face his dealer. "Equivalent of 150. Paid in US dollars." He pulled his cell phone out of his back pocket and started punching buttons. "That's $820 per item. We'll call it an even 850. Cash money. Now."

The Broker's eyes grew bigger – and greedier – upon hearing Max's latest counteroffer. "Deal."

Buyer and seller smiled and shared a laugh as Enrique walked over to a drink tray to pour all three men a shot of tequila. He handed Max and Jesús their glasses and raised his own in the air.

"To our continued good business relationship – and tourists at your brothel in Acapulco who pay in American dollars."

Max clinked his glass against El Agente's and smiled. "Salud."

While the men celebrated their new sale, Luisa and the rest of the items up for bid glared at them in contempt.

They talk about us like we're pieces of meat, Luisa thought with disgust. Her earlier despair had given way to a fresh wave of anger. *What I wouldn't give to be able to walk over there and kick them both in the cojones.*

"Tranquila, chica," the person next to her whispered. Luisa had only met her that morning but was struck by how nonchalant the girl was about the whole situation. She said she was being practical, but Luisa suspected that there was a missing part of her story.

"Getting mad won't change anything," she added.

"You're right, it won't," Luisa whispered back. "But sometimes it feels good to be pissed."

Luisa looked across the room at the person who now controlled her life. The skinny, bald man with striking blue eyes was her seventh owner, if she counted El Agente twice. First was Manuel, the jack-of-all-illegal-trades who bought her and Josefina from their mom and took them across the border to Guatemala. Rogelio was next, a career coyote who smoked like a chimney, drank like a fish, and took great pleasure in telling the girls that the only reason he wasn't 'having fun' with them was that they were worth so much more as virgins. Luisa's third owner was Antonio, perhaps her favorite of them all. Antonio was nice compared to the others, and despite his youth he was also very businesslike. Luisa got the impression that Antonio treated her no differently than he would have treated a shipment of cocaine. Protect it, move it, sell it for a profit.

The Hondureña's fourth owner was the only one to hold the title twice: El Agente. Luisa didn't know much about him personally, but the fact that he earned so much money buying and selling so many people made him seem like the Devil incarnate to her.

There was also Señor, of course, the man who owned her for the longest amount of time. He felt like her true owner, since the rest of them only held her life in passing.

But after Señor came El Agente again, and then this new guy. Max. With his creepy stare and lecherous smile that sent chills running down Luisa's spine.

For a brief second, which later grew into a minute and an hour and longer during her ride to her undisclosed new home, Luisa wished she was back in the converted barn in Monterrey. *At least there I had my own room. I was kept clean and fed and safe from the violence of the streets. Señor was violent, sure, but only if you did something you weren't supposed to.*

The fact that she was now echoing Viviana's words that she once rejected didn't cross Luisa's mind. The young woman didn't remember the time her former owner shot and killed her friend for no apparent reason. She didn't remember the argument she once witnessed between Viviana and Elena when the former was making those same kinds of 'we have it good' statements and Elena vehemently disagreed (with Luisa taking the side of the latter). She had blocked out those memories . . . buried them deep down where she hoped no one – including herself – would ever find them.

Señor Perrera was a businessman, Luisa's thoughts continued, praising the man she risked her life to escape. *He never crossed the line. He treated us like employees.*

The Hondureña shuddered when she remembered the carnal look on her new owner's face as he examined his 'property'. The way his eyes scanned her body from head to toe and back up again, and how he licked then bit his lower lip as a sign of his approval.

Luisa had been working as a sex slave for over two years and had been with an untold number of men, but she never felt dirtier, less important, or less human than she did at that moment with Señor Max.

She shuddered again, her whole body convulsing at the thought of working in a prostíbulo owned by that slimy creature.

I've heard about these places, Luisa thought. *Ximena told me about them. Where the rooms have whips and chains and the clients make you do all kinds of weird, nasty things.* She felt a wave of nausea rising up in her throat. *Oh my God. I never should've left Monterrey.*

FORTY-FOUR

Max Jacobbsen's twelve new acquisitions were herded out of the viewing room and into the courtyard where a van was waiting. Rental vehicles were yet another service offered by The Broker for buyers who needed a way to haul their property to its new location.

Jesús, Max's assistant, waved his handgun back and forth when motioning the girls toward the van.

"Be careful with that," El Agente cautioned. "As you can see, this is a nice part of town. Professionals live here. Doctors, lawyers, business executives. The narcos have their own flashy neighborhoods, but this is not one of them. If people around here see a guy with a gun, they'll call the police. And the police will actually respond. Understand?"

Jesús nodded. "Yeah, yeah, I understand. If they call the cops on me, they'll come investigate you and your whole little 'art' gallery will go up in smoke."

The Broker narrowed his eyes and crossed his arms in front of his chest. "Is that a threat?"

Jesús shook his head. "Nope. An observation. And maybe a suggestion, a reminder, that just because you live here doesn't make you any less of a criminal than the people you do business with."

"Jesús! Shut up and get in the van," Max yelled. "Sorry about him, Enrique. He speaks when he shouldn't."

The slave trader unfolded his arms and gave his customer a slight smile. "Not a problem. Unfortunately that's how it is these days . . . the help think they're entitled to their own opinions. It was good doing business with you again, Max," he said, reaching out to shake hands.

"You too. You've got some great merchandise this year. I think they'll do well at my place."

"Good. Glad to hear it. Let me know when you're ready for more."

Max nodded. "Will do."

The two men shook hands again before Max walked over to the van and climbed in the front passenger seat.

"Alright, Jesús. Let's get the hell out of here."

****

Not long after leaving The Broker's house, while the van was still making its way through traffic in the Greater Mexico City area – a space home to over twenty-one million people – the silence was broken with a question.

"So . . . how much were you?"

A passenger who appeared to be about the same age as Luisa was looking at her from the other side of the truck.

"Me?"

"Yeah, you," the girl replied with a nod, causing her black ringlet curls to bounce up and down. "What'd he pay for you?"

Luisa shrugged her shoulders. "You were standing there too. What was it, like $850 US?"

"No . . . how much did El Agente pay your previous owner to buy you?"

"I dunno. They didn't talk about it in front of me."

The other girl sighed. "Yeah, me neither."

She seems bothered by the fact that she doesn't know, Luisa thought. *How weird. I don't want to know.*

As if reading Luisa's mind, her road companion added: "I'm just curious is all. I like to know how much they think I'm worth."

"Whatever they think is wrong," Luisa countered. "You can't put a price on somebody's life."

"Sure you can," the girl shot back. Her name was Sofia, and personality-wise she was a near carbon copy of the mean one from Monterrey, Ximena. "They do it all the time. The first time I went through a sale, El Agente paid $700 to get me. Don't know this time, but I'm probably worth less now because I'm older. Used goods and all."

Luisa shook her head and found herself remembering all of the things that her great-grandmother and Susana had told her. The two religious figures preached to her that every life was precious because it came from God. "Those numbers and all that money have nothing to do with your true value and worth as a person."

Sofia laughed. "We've got ourselves a dreamer here, ladies."

153

"No. I don't have any dreams for my life. Any goals or plans. I know that I'm stuck in this world. I tried to escape once, but they brought me back in. I don't expect any more for my life," she said with a mix of sadness and defiance. "I'm just saying that it's my life. Not theirs. Mine."

The group fell silent after that conversation, with each passenger returning to her thoughts.

The rented van rumbled along out of the city and into the Mexican countryside, bouncing and jarring on a stretch of highway and a set of shocks that had both seen better days. Luisa closed her eyes to try to sleep, but the noise from the road and the constant movement kept her awake.

The young Miss Dominguez looked around the van at her travel companions. It was easy to tell who was new to 'the life' and who wasn't. The rookies were all wide-eyed, pale, and either sitting up straight or leaning forward with their heads on swivels and their hands balled up into fists, ready to pounce. None of them dared risk falling asleep.

The veterans, Luisa included, were more relaxed. Some were leaning back against the wall of the van. Others had turned to the side and were attempting to use the metal exterior as a pillow. Many of them were asleep, and all were experienced enough to know that the people in the back of the van with them were the least of their worries.

"Try to relax, yeah?" Luisa whispered to a little brunette sitting beside her. "This is free time. No work required. No clients. Enjoy it while it lasts."

The teenager furrowed her brow and cut her eyes sideways. "You expect me to enjoy this?"

"Are there any men back here with us?" another veteran replied after eavesdropping on the conversation.

"No."

"Are you being forced to have sex right now?"

The rookie cringed. "No."

"Then she's right. Enjoy the vacation while it lasts."

Luisa heard sniffling coming from the other side of her and turned to see a girl struggling to hold back tears. Luisa felt sorry for her, partly because she was so sad and partly because tears at this point didn't bode well for the future. *Tears show a lack of emotional strength, and a lack of emotional strength in this business will get you killed.* Luisa hadn't paid attention to much of what Señora Silvia said while she was in Monterrey, but those words stuck with her.

"If you're going to cry, cry now," Luisa told the bundle of sadness sitting next to her. "No one here will judge you for it, but the clients won't like it. And the owner won't allow it." Luisa shuddered when remembering the way that Señor Max inspected her like a piece of meat. "He definitely won't allow it."

"H-how can you b-be so calm?"

"Getting upset isn't going to change anything." Without realizing it, Luisa had adopted the same detached reserve as the girl who told her to calm down a couple of hours earlier. Surprise flooded Luisa's mind. *I'm the new Roxana.*

"How old are you?" she asked the person sitting next to her. "Fourteen."

"And how did you get caught up in all of this?"

The girl sniffed back tears and wiped her nose on her shirt sleeve. "I needed to work to help my family. I thought I was going to be a maid in a house in Mexico City."

Luisa nodded. "I know others like you. Same story. I was thirteen when my mom sold me and my sister into the life. I'm fifteen now. Two years from now, if you're alive, you'll know what I know and you'll only get upset about things that you can change."

The child nodded her head as if in agreement, but a few seconds later Luisa saw more tears begin to drop from her nose and chin onto the floor of the van.

Poor little thing, Luisa thought, then rested her head back against the wall. The metal bounced and buzzed with each bump in the road, and soon Luisa leaned forward again to keep from getting a headache.

"Do you believe in God?" her crying companion whispered.

"Do I believe in God?"

The girl nodded, sniffed, and wiped more tears off of her cheek.

"Well, yeah, of course. Why?"

"The priest in my hometown told us that prostitutes are sinners and God hates sin, but my grandma said that God loves us, and I guess I don't understand why he would make me be a prostitute if he loved me."

Luisa sighed and shook her head. "I don't know." She thought for a minute before adding: "my abuela always said God loved us too, but my mom told us church was a waste of time and just a bunch of people trying to make us give them money that we didn't have." Luisa flashed a rueful grin. "And the owner at the last place where I worked said that he was God." Luisa paused. "Of all of those people, the only one who was ever nice to me was my abuela, so I believe her. And I think maybe people see in God a reflection of themselves."

"What do you mean?"

"If you're a nasty, unfair, greedy person, then you'll only see the nasty, greedy, and unfair in the world and blame God for it. If you're a kind, loving person, then you'll see the kindness and love in the world and say that that's what God is like."

"So which one is real?" the younger passenger asked.

Luisa thought about her answer for a minute. "I think he's kind and loving."

"Why?" asked the brunette on the other side of her.

"Because it's easier to be mean and nasty and blame somebody else for everything than it is to be kind and loving and give somebody else the credit. And it seems to me that a God who is powerful enough to create the world and everything in it would be powerful enough to be kind and loving too."

"Well shit," Sofia said, breaking into the conversation. "Look who's a fucking philosopher now."

Sofia's friend, a bottle blonde named Victoria, laughed. "Yes, please tell us more, Sister Luisa."

"Sister Luisa! Ha – that's perfect!"

Half of the van burst into laughter while the other half busied themselves with looking at the floor, too afraid to admit that they agreed with what 'Sister Luisa' said.

"Sure, sure. Laugh your heads off," Luisa countered, dismissing her critics with a wave of her hand. "See if I care."

FORTY-FIVE

Six hours after leaving Mexico City, the windowless van rolled to a stop and the passengers heard the brakes squeak, hiss, and pop.

"Do you think we're there?" asked a girl named Lola. Luisa had learned a lot about her while riding together in the back of the truck. Mainly because Lola wouldn't stop talking.

How am I supposed to know if we're there or not? Luisa thought, irritated by her chatty companion. She tried to not let the irritation show, though, and shrugged her shoulders in response. "I dunno. Maybe."

Lola's question was answered when the side door of the van slid open and their new owner's henchman, Jesús, ordered them all to get out of the vehicle.

Luisa shielded her eyes from the bright sun and stepped out of the van onto a beautiful cobblestone driveway. She lowered her hand from her eyes and gasped. *It's a palace*, Luisa thought as she stood in awe of the two-story house in front of her. The outside walls had a medium pink hue to them – decorators would call it salmon stucco – with brown tile shingles on the roof that matched the cobblestone under Luisa's feet. Lush green grass filled the yard in front of the home, and the largest vases that Luisa had ever seen decorated the front porch with a rainbow of beautiful flowers. Reds, blues, yellows, and everything in between.

It's amazing, the girl thought, and she could hear the gasps and murmured aww of the other teenagers around her.

"Welcome," Jesús said, breaking their trance.

Luisa glared at him.

"Let's get you ladies inside the house, okay?" he added. "I'm sure you're tired from your trip." The man took a step to the side and extended his arm toward the front door. "This way."

Why is he acting so nice? thought Luisa. A quick glance behind her confirmed that the solid metal gates at the end of the driveway were already closed. That, combined with the high concrete wall around the property that matched the color of the house, meant that no one was escaping and no one on the outside of the compound could see inside.

"Different building, same prison," Lola whispered, and for once Luisa agreed with her.

All twelve teenagers were brought inside the house and made to line up in the center of a large two-story living room. Floor to ceiling windows on the back wall revealed a yard that was even more beautiful than the front, complete with a pool, Jacuzzi, and even more flowers.

What is this place? Luisa thought. *This must be a really high-end brothel. Does that mean the clients will be better? Or worse?*

A stone-faced Señor Max walked into the room and past the line of girls he purchased from The Broker. Taking a few steps back, he turned to face the group and clasped his hands together in front of him.

Luisa saw the golden flash of a wedding band. She knew that El Agente and Señor Perrera also had wives. *What kind of women could be married to monsters like them?*

Then, when she expected her new owner to launch into his own variation of El Agente's welcome speech, Max closed his eyes. He bowed his head. And he said, "let us pray."

An audible gasp filled the room and the women all looked around, unsure what to do. Every authority figure in the house – Max, Jesús, and a lady standing in the doorway – had their heads bowed and eyes closed.

"What do we do?" Lola whispered.

Luisa shrugged. "I guess we do what they do? I dunno."

Max's lips quivered and Luisa would've sworn it almost looked like a smile.

What in the world is going on? What kind of lunatic buys sex slaves and then prays with them?

"Heavenly Father," Max said, and the girls took that as their cue to bow their heads and close their eyes. "Heavenly Father, we thank you for today. We thank you for our safe journey from Mexico City to Guadalajara."

So that's where we are now.

"Thank you, Lord, for each and every young woman standing here in this room with me."

Sick bastard.

"Thank you, God, for providing me with the means to purchase them from El Agente."

Really sick bastard.

"Father God, I pray that you would wrap your arms around these young women and fill them with love, comfort, and joy as they begin the new stage of their lives in freedom."

Wait . . . what?

"Lord, I know they've been through so much pain and suffering, and I pray that in you they will find the strength to create new lives away from the horrors of the past."

Huh?

"In your name I pray. Amen."

Luisa opened her eyes and raised her head to look over at her new owner. He was smiling. The gleam that had been in his eyes was now a sparkle.

"It's true, ladies," Max said. "You don't have to work in brothels anymore." His smile grew wider and he laughed at the looks of shock on his young charges' faces. It was the same look the last group had. And the one before that.

"Why don't y'all take a seat here on the couches and I'll explain."

FORTY-SIX

Every time Max Jacobbsen purchased a group of girls from The Broker and brought them to the safe house in Guadalajara, and every time he sat down with all of the shocked young ladies to explain to them what was happening, his mind flashed back to when he and his wife first started their rescue program.

Esmerelda Gomez-Jacobbsen was born and raised in Guadalajara. As the youngest child and only daughter of a renowned surgeon, the striking beauty with black hair and caramel eyes never wanted for anything. She lived with both of her parents and her two older brothers in a house much like the one where Max was now. After attending the city's finest prep school, Esmerelda went to Stanford University for college. She stayed in Palo Alto after graduation, marrying her sweetheart – a Scandinavian gringo named Max – and earning her PhD in Psychology.

It was Dr. Gomez-Jacobbsen's idea to try to find a way to help victims of human trafficking.

Max, ever the overachiever, went far beyond what his wife expected by buying a ranch and starting a school where rescued teens could live, learn, and recover.

"Why don't you call the police?" Esmerelda had asked when Max told her about his plan to buy the girls direct from a slave trader. "Let them know where this guy, The Broker, lives, how they can pose as a buyer, and have them sweep in?"

"To what end?" her husband countered. "*If* the police showed up, *if* one of them didn't tip off The Broker, where would the girls go? They have no money, no true occupation, and in many cases no identity. They'll be back on the streets or back in another casa de citas before you can say 'prostitution'. And the auction houses won't go away. They'll move. Another gallery, another warehouse, another day. Not to mention that big raids like that would decrease supply, which would increase prices, which would lead to more girls being kidnapped and sold. It's simple economics." He paused. "Besides, The Broker is my only connection into that world. If his operation is shut down, I won't have a way to keep doing what we're doing." Max sighed, frustration lining his face. "Look, I know it's not enough. It'll never be enough. Not until everyone is free. But I can't rescue them all. What I can do – what we can do – is save as many as we can. Get them out. Permanently. Get them healthy and happy and headed toward a better life."

Max knew that some people would disagree with his methods. They would say he should call the police and shut down El Agente's business once and for all. But he wasn't interested in short-term fixes. His mission was long-term restoration. Looking at the group of young ladies sitting in front of him that day, Max knew he was doing the right thing. Taking a deep breath, he began to explain how everything would work.

"To start with," he said, "I want to reiterate that I'm so, so happy to have all of you here with me today. This house isn't a brothel . . . far from it. It belongs to some friends of mine, Señor and Señora Barrón. Señora Barrón has been friends with my wife since they were both kids . . . they even went to college together. Juan and Paloma are nice enough to let me stay here for a few weeks each year when I come to Mexico on rescue missions."

Gesturing to his right, Max said: "that woman there in the doorway is Paloma Barrón. In a day or two, after a doctor and dentist come and we get started on your travel visas, the señora is going to take you to a mall so you can get some new clothes. How does that sound?"

Twelve pairs of eyes stared back at Max, too stunned to respond.

He smiled. That reaction was typical. "We've got two rooms for you ladies here. There are bunk beds in them, so it'll be six to a room. Tight quarters, I know, but it's the best we can do in the short term. Now, I mentioned travel visas . . . that part is important. You won't be staying here at this house. I live in Texas, in the United States, and my wife and I run a special boarding school on our ranch. All of the students are teens who are like you: former sex workers who I bought from The Broker. We'll go to the Consulate here in Guadalajara, get you a student visa, and then, if all goes according to plan, a few weeks from now you'll be on a plane headed to the US."

His audience's frozen faces began to melt as Max's words sunk in.

"You're gonna take us to the United States?" Lola asked.

Max nodded and smiled. "I am."

"What's the catch?" said Sofia, asking the question on everyone's mind.

"No catch. In fact, you're free to leave here at any time. I do ask that you tell us you're leaving so we know that you left and aren't missing or something like that. But I can't stress this enough: you're free to go. I bought you, yes, but I don't own you. You're free. If you want to go home or go back to Mexico City or whatever the case may be, you can. I'm not your guardian, I'm not your boss, and I'm definitely not your owner. Does everybody understand?" Max asked. "I don't want anyone to feel like they're being forced to stay here."

The group of girls nodded their heads and mumbled "yes sir."

Max smiled. "Good. Now, that being said, I really do hope you stay. We're going to feed you good food, take you shopping for some new clothes, and have a doctor and a dentist come check you out. And the best part is: you get to relax. In the meantime, we'll be getting your paperwork together to go to the school I told you about in the United States. So," Max said, clapping his hands together, "who's hungry?"

****

Later that night, after dinner and several extended conversations with girls who said they wanted to leave to go back home to their families, Max closed the door of his room, walked over to the bed, and fell face-first onto the mattress. The former head of a technology start-up kicked off his loafers before Army-crawling up the bed and plopping his head down on the pillow. *What a day*, he thought with a sigh. *Heck, what a week.*

Forty-eight hours earlier, Max had been almost 900 miles away at the University of Texas at Austin giving a speech about human trafficking. Wanting to grab headlines and attendance at the end of the semester, the student group who sponsored the event titled it 'How Much Does a Person Cost? Slavery in the 21st Century'.

Max was asked to give a general overview of human trafficking around the world and to give some examples from his travels to Latin America. As the author of three books on the subject, Jacobbsen had made a second career out of researching modern slavery and helping raise awareness of the issue in the United States.

162

What his colleagues, readers, and event sponsors didn't know, though, was that he was actively involved in saving young women from the clutches of slavery. He wasn't doing anything illegal *per se*, unless one counted purchasing the girls under the guise of running his own brothel. Max knew that every time he went to a sale, he faced the risk of being arrested in a police raid. But he wasn't buying the young ladies to pimp them out for sex work. He was buying them to save them from it. "A ransom payment," he told his wife before every trip. "Those sick bastards are holding the girls hostage, and I'm paying ransom to set them free."

The 150 college students, staff, and professors seated in the auditorium that night didn't know about any of Max's efforts, though. They didn't know about his biannual trips to El Agente's sex slave brokerage house in Mexico City, or his contact at the US Consulate in Guadalajara who helped push through the student visa requests, or the 1,000-acre ranch he and his wife owned in West Texas with its fully-accredited private high school where the rescued girls went to live and learn.

No, these people know none of that. So don't slip up and tell them tonight, Max had said to himself while standing offstage and listening to a gangly college sophomore introduce him. It was a reminder that Max gave himself every day. If he blew his cover, he'd be blackballed from any future slave auctions. Sellers would be on the lookout for illegitimate buyers – even more than they already were. Not to mention the fact that he might get in trouble for participating in the sales (regardless of his motives), and the young consular officer in Guadalajara might face sanction for participating in the scheme without informing his supervisors.

So Resurrection Ranch and Wilberforce Academy remained secret. Max covered them up with a smile and a wave to the crowd as he took his place at the podium.

"Good afternoon. Well, I guess it's evening now. Good evening," Max said with a grin. "Thank you so much for that excellent introduction. It won't be too much longer until I start speaking to groups of students who weren't even alive yet when I – how did you put it? – sold my dot-com company and made bank?"

A gentle laughter filled the auditorium, and Max had a feeling that it was going to be a good event.

"I met a professor the other day," Jacobbsen said, jumping into his speech. "An older gentleman who beamed when telling me the story of how he once met a former slave. The professor was a young boy and the former slave was very old, but he said it was a fascinating experience to meet someone who survived being a slave in America before the Civil War." Max paused and looked around the auditorium, seeing heads nodding in agreement and a few mouths saying 'yeah, that'd be so cool'. He fought the urge to grin. *Gets 'em every time.*

"I told the professor that that was really neat and a unique experience for sure, but then I told him that I had talked with over one hundred former slaves . . . and ate dinner with one the night before."

Gasps of surprise and murmured disbelief rippled through the audience.

"I've met over one hundred former slaves," Max continued, "and I would venture to guess that many of you have met former slaves without knowing it."

The disbelief grew more audible.

"What if I were to tell you that there are upwards of thirty million slaves in the world today? Not former slaves. Nearly thirty million *current* slaves. People living and working in 2015 who do not own their own lives. What if I were to tell you," Max continued, "that the importation of slaves into the United States did not end in 1808, and the Thirteenth Amendment didn't abolish slavery like it says in the Constitution? It only abolished *legal* slavery. What if I were to tell you that slave traders today make over $150 billion each year . . . and that that's more than the gross domestic product of 134 countries?"

The auditorium was silent.

"More people are trafficked today, more people are slaves today, than ever before in history," Max told them. "Seventy-nine percent of human trafficking involves sexual exploitation. Mostly women and girls, but some men and boys too, bought and sold as sex slaves. The average age of entry into 'the life' as they call it? Eleven to fourteen years old."

The speaker paused for a minute, then changed directions. "My son recently graduated from this school with a degree in liberal arts. One semester of tuition for him, in-state, was right around $4,700.

164

Of course that didn't include room and board and everything else kids your age spend money on. Tuition alone, for one semester: $4,700." Max paused. "How much do you think a slave costs? Go ahead, throw out some numbers."

"Ten grand," a voice called out from the back of the auditorium. "Twenty."

"Dollars or thousand dollars?" Max asked.

A low, nervous laughter rippled across the room.

"Twenty thousand," the student clarified.

"Anybody else?"

"Five hundred," a young woman said, and sounds of surprise could be heard around her.

Max nodded. "Getting closer. The average cost of a slave today is $140. Think about that: you spend more on textbooks in one semester than a slave trader would spend to purchase someone's life."

"Now, not all slaves cost $140," Max explained to the stunned audience. "Depending on where you are in the world and how particular the buyer wants to be, a trafficked sex slave could cost upwards of $2,000. The Islamic State, ISIS, sells girls under the age of nine for around $170, but a woman over the age of forty is going to cost about a dollar per year she's been alive . . . approximately $45. And yet, one sex slave can earn her – or his – owner between $18,000 and $49,000 in their lifetime, depending on the location. What's that, like a 2000% return on investment?" He cleared his throat in disgust. "I'm not making up these numbers, folks. As my son would say, this shit is real."

Max took a sip of water from the glass on the podium. "How many of you would've guessed in the tens of thousands for the cost of a slave? Raise your hand if that was your guess."

A few people lifted their hands into the air, followed by more and more, with the risk of embarrassment decreasing as the number of hands increased.

"That would have been an accurate guess in the American South in 1850. Back then, a regular, average slave cost about the equivalent of $11,000. A prime working-age field hand ran about thirty-four grand, and a skilled slave – a blacksmith or something like that – could cost up to fifty-five or fifty-six thousand. Now don't get me wrong," Max said, putting his hands up in front of him, "I'm not in

165

any way defending the legalized slavery that used to exist in the United States. It was a horrific crime against nature and humanity and thank God it ended. But the economics behind legal slavery back then and illegal slavery today are interesting because they reveal the mindset of the slave owners. In the past," Max explained, "slaves were viewed as valuable property and an economic investment. That was reflected in the price. Now, slaves are cheaper to replace than to maintain. Use them up, get rid of them, and buy new ones. Not only the price of a life but also the value of a life has gone down, and all the while the slave trade grows."

Chairs in the auditorium started to squeak as the audience grew more and more uncomfortable by the facts being presented by their speaker.

"Surprised?" Max asked, knowing that they were. "Asking yourself 'how have I not heard about this?' Well, you probably have and didn't know it. Because we don't call it slavery anymore. Instead, we say it's 'human trafficking'," he explained, using air quotes around the phrase. "You all know about human trafficking, right? Seen rally posters about it in the student union, or maybe seen some classmates walking around with big red X's on their hands one day a year?"

When no one replied, Max smiled. "It's okay, you can answer. You've heard about human trafficking, right?"

Heads started nodding and mumbles of 'yes' and 'uh huh' spilled forward from the crowd.

"That sounds a lot nicer than slavery, doesn't it?" Max asked, knowing that he had the audience hooked now. "Slavery is such a bad, nasty word with such bad, nasty connotations, and if we use that word in 2015 then it might make us feel like bad, nasty people for not doing something to stop it. So we call it human trafficking, because we can say that at a dinner party without wanting to throw up our champagne and crab cakes. Because it sounds a lot like drug trafficking, and that helps us forget that the items being trafficked aren't marijuana or cocaine or meth, but people. Because it doesn't *bother us* to hear it."

Max took another sip of water and let his words sink in around the room.

"Slavery, ladies and gentlemen," he continued, "did not end in 1863 with the Emancipation Proclamation. It exists today – over 150 years later. Like I said earlier, more people are enslaved today than ever before. Think about that: *more people* are enslaved today than. ever. before."

"In Bangkok. In Buenos Aires. In Mauritania, which some call the slavery capital of the world. In Mexico City. In Los Angeles, New York, Atlanta . . . Austin. Yep, that's right. Here. Now."

"I want to challenge each of you today to do three things. First," Max said, holding up his index finger, "is to call a spade a spade. Human trafficking is a specific term with a specific meaning, but it is not a substitute for another term with another meaning: slavery. Let's start calling it what it is."

"Second," he said, adding his middle finger, "tell somebody. Your generation, with texting and blogging and social media, can raise more awareness in less time than ever before. So tell people what you've heard and learned here tonight."

"And third," said Max, raising his ring finger, "follow through. Don't tweet out 'hashtag end slavery' and feel like you've saved the world. Awareness is great, but it's meaningless unless you also take action. Raise money for victim assistance programs. Lobby the legislature here in Austin to change prostitution laws to criminalize the buying of sex, not the selling of it. Sweden did that and commercial sexual exploitation in that country is on its way to extinction. Volunteer for an organization dedicated to ending modern slavery. Work for the police or the FBI in their anti-trafficking divisions. It doesn't matter what it is, but *do something*."

"So that's three things. Call it what it is. Say something. Do something. And then maybe, just maybe, one day when I talk to people about having met former slaves, it truly will be as rare a thing as y'all thought it was at the beginning of my speech."

FORTY-SEVEN

The next several days in Guadalajara proceeded how Señor Max said they would. A doctor and dentist came to the house to perform health inspections on the girls. Paloma Barrón, the owner of the house, was also a licensed psychiatrist and got the young ladies started with some group therapy sessions. She didn't want to establish a true counseling connection with them since they would all be leaving after such a short period of time, but Paloma and her counterpart in America, Esmerelda, knew that they should try to begin the healing process as soon as possible. The teenagers were also given some basic lessons in English – a subject that would be mandatory at their new high school in the United States.

On Luisa's third day in Guadalajara, Señora Barrón took her and three other young ladies to the local mall for their shopping trip. The open-air Plaza del Sol was located southwest of the city center and was the first commercial mall in Latin America.

The stores were used to Señora Barrón's visits by then, and on the morning of every shopping excursion, Paloma would drive over to the mall and have the store employees sign non-disclosure agreements to keep their visits out of the press.

"The first time I did it," Señora Barrón once told her friend Esmerelda over the phone, "I just showed up with a group of girls. It was like I was Richard Gere in Pretty Woman and had six Julia Robertses with me. Total disaster. The girls were mortified and the shop workers almost called security. Now," Paloma explained, "I stop by ahead of time and let everyone know we're coming. Makes things go much more smoothly."

"What do the workers think?" Esmerelda had asked.

"I tell them it's a charity service for poor people from the country. We give them a day of pampering and buy them some new clothes. Nothing fancy . . . just nice, comfortable, and stylish. The mall employees think it's great. People like to think that they're being charitable, even if all they're really doing is their job – helping people buy clothes or get a haircut or a manicure."

Luisa received all of those things during her trip to Plaza del Sol: a haircut, a mani/pedi, and a brand new 'starter wardrobe' complete with two pairs of jeans, five shirts, three dresses, two pairs of shoes, a swimsuit, and the necessary undergarments.

Holding her shopping bags in her lap on the ride back to the Barróns' home, Luisa still couldn't believe what was happening to her. She thought she was having an extended dream, or maybe had died and was now in a bizarre state of Purgatory. *There's no way this is all real*, Luisa thought. *No way.*

****

Several miles away, on the tree-lined Calle Progreso in downtown Guadalajara, Max was hard at work trying to arrange student visas for the seven trafficking victims who remained under his care. The US Consulate General in Guadalajara was a large tan and white striped building protected by rows of concrete barriers and three layers of green metal fences, not to mention armed security guards stationed at each entrance checkpoint. The Consulate was a very busy place, since Western Mexico was home to 50,000 American citizens and another 100,000 American tourists, students, and businesspeople who were visiting the region on any given day.

It was there in the Visa Section that Max could be found that morning, sifting through piles of paperwork that needed to be filled out for each prospective student at his boarding school.

"You said you're down to seven now?" asked David Hargrove, the consular officer who helped Max expedite the visa applications. The son of an African-American dad and a Mexican-American mom, David grew up in Los Angeles as the third of five children. All of the women in his family were teachers, and all of the men were police officers . . . except for David. After working his way through college, David accepted a job with the State Department and requested consular duty in order to help people who were trying to immigrate 'the right way' like his mom did.

Hargrove was now the head of the Visa Section at the Consulate – a position that gave him enough power to help Max Jacobbsen and the teenagers he rescued.

"Yeah. We've had five leave. It's not all that unusual, unfortunately," Max said with a sigh. "What these girls are thinking and feeling is a lot like – almost identical to – what victims of

169

domestic violence are going through. Although they don't see themselves as victims at all. That word is almost never part of their vocabulary. But people always ask why women with abusive husbands or boyfriends keep going back, and it's the same question here. Why would the girls choose to go back to that life?"

"They haven't hit rock bottom yet," Max added, answering his own question. "Plus there's an overwhelming anxiety about entering into a life that's not 'the life'. What they're coming from is terrible and traumatic, but it's the only world they know. They know how to live in that environment. They know how to survive – and survival is really the farthest they get in the thought process. It's all instinct for many of them."

David nodded his head. "Better the devil you know than the devil you don't."

"Exactly. That's exactly it," replied Max. "Even when we come across people who have hit rock bottom, who do know that they need to get out of the life, oftentimes they don't have the desire to do it. They know, in their head, that they should go with us. Leave that world behind. But their heart-set isn't right. They have to want it. We can't force them to go."

"What happens to them if they leave?" David asked. "There's no formal foster care system in Mexico, so what do you do?"

Max let out a deep breath and sadness filled his eyes. "There's nothing we can do. You're right . . . there's no established government-run foster system in Mexico. It's not like in the US where the state Departments of Children and Family Services would step in. We can call the Church, if they're interested in that. But most of the time they say they're going to their families but head straight back to their pimps. Some of them tell us the truth, except of course he's not a pimp . . . 'he's my boyfriend', they'll say. But yeah," he shook his head. "It's a sad side of things; a devastating side of things. But it's part of it."

Max paused. "Have you heard of the Stages of Change model?" David shook his head no.

"It's something my wife and the other counselors use when working with the girls. It's this theory that people with addictive disorders, or any other major things in their life that they're trying to change, go through six stages. Precontemplation, contemplation, preparation, action, maintenance, and termination. A lot of the girls who don't stay are in that first stage. Precontemplation. They're not ready yet. And until they are, we can't help them."

FORTY-EIGHT

David Hargrove looked at the middle-aged man sitting on the other side of his desk and sighed. It was admirable what Mr. Jacobbsen was trying to do, but David could tell that the work was taking a toll on Max. *How could it not?* he thought. *All I'm doing is processing paperwork and I still get stressed out thinking about the horrors these young women have lived through.*

Hargrove could still remember the first day he met Max Jacobbsen. It was four years earlier, and David had just been promoted to the senior agent in his department.

A knock on the door of his new office had interrupted the consular official from his work.

"Hey David, got a minute?" asked Shannon, a pretty blonde who had been at the Consulate for eight months. She handled lower level work than David did and stood out like a sore thumb because of her hair and complexion. David hadn't quite gotten up the courage to ask her out on a date.

"Sure," he replied, looking away from his computer monitor and over at his colleague. "What's up?"

Shannon stepped through the doorway and sat on the arm of one of the chairs facing David's desk. After a lifetime of marching and orders and 'straight-back-stiff-lip' attitude, David loved the relaxed approach that Shannon had in life.

"There's a guy here – an American – who says he has questions about F-1 visas?" Shannon leaned forward, bit her lip, and lowered her voice. "I don't even know what those are."

David had responded with a smile. "Don't worry. There are way too many different combinations of letters and numbers." He pointed to a laminated piece of paper stuck to the outside of a file cabinet. "See that? It's my cheat sheet. I've been here long enough now that I know them all, but for over a year at least I would use that when one came along that I hadn't heard of."

Shannon breathed a sigh of relief and smiled. "Phew. Glad I'm not the only one. So what's an F-1 visa?"

"Students."

The young woman's brow furrowed and David caught himself staring, thinking about how adorable she looked rather than the task at hand. *Get a grip, dude!* he told himself.

"I thought student visas were M-1."

"M-1 is for vocational or non-academic schools. All of the other students – university, high school, etc. – need F-1."

David stood up from his desk and walked over to the corner of his office. Peeling the cheat sheet off the cabinet, he turned and handed it to Shannon. "Here, all yours. And go ahead and bring that guy back here."

A few minutes later, Shannon had returned with the visitor.

David Hargrove stood up from his chair and walked around to the front of his desk.

"Welcome," he said, shaking hands with the other man. "I'm David Hargrove, a foreign service officer here at the Consulate."

The visitor smiled. "David Hargrove doesn't sound like a name one would typically find working in Mexico."

"My mom is Mexican," David replied. "My dad is American. Technically, they call me a Blaxican." He grinned. "My parents wanted a name that could work well in both countries. So in the US, I'm David. And here, I'm Davíd. It works."

"Well . . . there you go," the other man replied. "I'm Max Jacobbsen." He looked to be around fifty or so, was on the short side, David noticed, and rail thin. His pressed khakis, boat shoes, and button-down shirt with the sleeves rolled up his forearms all spoke of a casual American wealth.

"Please, have a seat," David had said, gesturing toward an empty chair before returning to his own. "What can I do for you, Mr. Jacobbsen?"

"Max, please. And I'm hoping you can help me with some student visas."

"To study in Mexico?"

Max shook his head. "No, sorry. I guess I should've started at the beginning. I'm headmaster at a school for girls in Texas. There are some students here in Mexico who would like to attend my school, but I know they'll need visas for that."

David nodded. "They will. What you'll need to do first, though, is get your school accredited by the Student and Exchange Visitor

Program. Once you get that clearance – it's run through the Department of State – you'll be able to enroll foreign students."

"Already done."

"Oh, okay," David replied. "Well then, each student wishing to study in the United States will need an F-1 visa. Depending on their age, they might have to do an interview and they might not. They'll also need proper proof of identification," David had continued, "a Mexican passport, proof of acceptance at your school, and something demonstrating how they'll pay for the tuition, room, and board."

Hargrove spun in his chair and opened a filing cabinet drawer behind him. "Here," he said, spinning back around. "The F-1 visa checklist. It shows everything they'll need."

"Great, thanks," Max replied. "This will be a big help. Once we've gathered all of the documents and everything, can I bring it all back to you?"

"Sure, yeah. I'll probably be the one processing it."

"Okay, wonderful. Thanks. I should be in touch again within the next couple of days."

"My pleasure," David said with a smile. "Here, let me walk you out. This place can be a maze if you don't know where you're going."

****

It had taken Hargrove a grand total of two minutes to see that the visa applications Mr. Jacobbsen turned in were not of the normal variety. Red flags flared up all over the paperwork, and David called the American headmaster back into his office for a discussion. Suspecting trafficking of some sort, he made sure to have security waiting on standby.

"Please, take a seat," David said that afternoon as he shut the office door. "Thank you for coming in. I have some questions for you and I wanted to be able to walk through the paperwork together while we talked."

"Sure, no problem. What kind of questions?"

David shifted in his seat. He wasn't used to interrogating someone who he suspected might be a criminal.

"Well, I'll be honest with you. I noticed a few irregularities in the girls' applications."

"Irregularities?" Max had asked.

David nodded. "Mmm hmm. For starters, there are no school transcripts or records of standardized tests. How did your school . . . Wilberforce Academy, is it? . . . how did you make an admissions decision without knowing the student's academic capabilities?"

Max drew in a deep breath and a hardness overtook his tone of voice. "What other irregularities?" he asked.

"Pardon?"

"You said there were a few irregularities in the applications. What else?"

"Well, Wilberforce Academy has no website. That's very strange in the year 2007. And every applicant put that she'll be on full scholarship. Every single one."

"They will be," replied Max. "And I don't see what not having a website has to do with anything."

David hadn't liked the edge that took over Mr. Jacobbsen's voice. "Nothing, really, you're right," he said, putting his hands up in front of him in a protective gesture. "It's just that, well, as a consular officer I'm expected to keep an eye out for certain red flags that indicate everything might not be above board."

Jacobbsen leaned back in his chair and folded his arms over his chest. "What are you accusing me of?"

Oh God, David had thought, trying to hide the panic in his eyes. *I've pissed off a slave trading cartel member. I'm gonna die. Oh God.*

"I'm not accusing you of anything, sir," David said, scrambling to save his hide. "I'm merely pointing out that all of this information indicates to me that some kind of illegal activity may be involved. On the surface, to me, it looks like someone is trying to invent a school and a past for these girls in order to get them from Mexico to the US."

Max sighed and pursed his lips together. He ran his hand over his bald head and looked up at the ceiling.

"You aren't going to approve the visas until I explain things, are you?"

"No."

175

"Will you at least promise to keep this conversation private and confidential?" he asked, and David noticed that the edge was gone from his voice.

"No."

Max sighed again. "I guess I don't have any choice." He slid his fingers under his glasses and rubbed his eyes, then looked up at the consular officer. "You're right. There is illegal activity involved. But it's not what you think."

Shit. I knew it, David thought. "What is it then?"

"I really do have a boarding school in Texas called Wilberforce Academy. These six girls would be the first students. All of them, up until five days ago, were sex slaves at brothels around the country."

"What happened five days ago?" David asked, not sure if he should believe the story or not.

"I bought them from a broker in Mexico City. He thinks I bought them for my own brothel, but really I was buying their freedom. I want to take them to the US and get them medical care, counseling, and a solid education. Get them away from their former life."

David's suspicions had still remained. "Why not tell the police about this 'broker' as you called him?"

Max raised his eyebrows and tiled his head to the side. "The police? Really?"

"I'm sure if you, as an American, told the federal police about somebody selling humans then they'd raid the location."

"And somebody else would step in to take the old broker's place," Max said. "Plus all of the girls would get swept up in the raid and either wind up in jail or back on the streets. C'mon man, you know how it is. Sex workers are arrested while the pimps and johns go free."

David sighed. This Mr. Jacobbsen character had a point. And he admired the older man for what he was trying to do. *If he's telling the truth*, David cautioned himself.

"Why not set up the school here? Why go through all the hassle of taking them to the United States?"

"I can't guarantee their safety here like I can in America. The kinds of men who own these girls are brutal. Ruthless. They mark the women as their property in the same way that a rancher brands his cattle. Almost every girl has a tattoo on her body saying who she 'belongs' to. Usually the pimp's name. Sometimes it's an actual barcode on her wrist or her neck or even the inside of her lip."

"What happens if we're running the school here and one of the girls goes to the mall one day?" Max had asked. "She gets spotted by someone who recognizes the tattoo. Suddenly she's swept right back up in that life, and the safety of the rest of the students at the school might be at risk too. No," Max shook his head. "For this to work, we have to get them out of Mexico and away from their captors' sphere of influence."

"I admire what you're trying to do," David replied. "Or what you're telling me you're trying to do."

"You don't believe me."

"I'm gonna need some proof first."

"Such as?"

"Employment contracts for the school's teachers and counselors. Financials on where the scholarship money is coming from. Interviews with all of the applicants."

"And if you get all of that?" Max had asked him.

"Then . . . I'll consider issuing the visas."

Jacobbsen clapped his hands together and smiled. "Yes."

"I said I'll consider it."

"I know, I know. But it's all above board. You'll see." Max stood up from his chair. "I'll go get started on pulling all of that together. And let me know when you want to do the interviews."

"Where are the young ladies now, Mr. Jacobbsen?"

"A friend's house here in Guadalajara. They're safe and have already seen a doctor."

David nodded. "Okay."

"Oh, hey, Mr. Hargrove?" Max said, turning back from the door.

"Yes?"

"Maybe now you'll consider keeping this private? Walls have ears in Mexico, and if The Broker finds out what I'm up to, he'll never let me go back."

David had nodded his head in agreement. "You got it. Not a word to anybody."

FORTY-NINE

Four years later, Max Jacobbsen and David Hargrove were still working together. David's now-wife, Shannon, was also brought on board to make sure all of the paperwork and interviews could be turned around fast enough.

On the day of Luisa's visa interview, Señor Max drove her to the Consulate in Juan Barrón's car. The teenager wore one of her new outfits for the occasion . . . a pretty blue sundress with small pink flowers around the trim.

Shannon escorted the two visitors up to the conference room by David's office. Max stopped outside the door and looked at Luisa. "I have to stay here during the interview," he explained. "They want to make sure that you're telling them the truth without any influence from me. But don't worry, Ms. Shannon and Mr. David are both very nice."

"Ready?" David asked, exiting his office. He stood aside to let Luisa and Shannon enter the conference room before him and then shut the door. Walking over to the head of the table, David sat down and motioned for the two women to join him.

Turning to Luisa, he smiled. "I know you and Shannon introduced yourselves out in the lobby, but I thought we'd do it again to make sure you know everybody. I'm David Hargrove. I work here at the Consulate. And this is my associate, Shannon Stewart Hargrove. We're both Americans, but we live here in Guadalajara full time and work for the US government."

"Hi Luisa," Shannon added.

"Hi," she whispered back.

"There's no need to be afraid or worried or anything like that. I think Max explained what this interview is for, right?"

Luisa nodded her head.

"Good. Well, to clarify, it's my job to make sure that all of your paperwork and everything is in order and that you meet all of the requirements for the type of visa that you're applying for. Okay?"

Luisa's head bobbed up and down.

"Don't worry, Luisa. I'll be here the whole time and it's totally painless," Shannon said. Luisa's lips curved up into a small smile.

Having her in here for these interviews was a brilliant idea, David thought. In prior years, before Shannon joined the project, it took him hours or sometimes days to get the girls to open up and talk to him. Now, with another woman in the room, they were much more comfortable.

"Alright, you ready to get started?" asked David. "I will need you to say your answers out loud, not just nod your head."

"Okay," Luisa replied.

"Great. Alright. First question, super easy one, what's your full name?"

"Luisa Dominguez."

"No middle name or second family name?"

The girl shook her head. "Oh, sorry. No. Not that I know of."

David smiled. "No need to apologize. How old are you, Luisa?"

"Fifteen."

"And when is your birthday?"

"July 23rd."

"Great," David said, writing down the answers on the notepad in front of him. "You're doing great. Next question: where are you from?"

"San Pedro Sula."

David furrowed his brow and flipped back a couple of pages in his notebook. "I thought I had you listed as being from Monterrey."

"That's where I used to live, before Señor Max bought . . . err, rescued, me. But my hometown is San Pedro Sula."

"I'm not familiar with that city," David said.

"It's in Honduras," Shannon offered.

"Hold on. You're not Mexican?"

Luisa shook her head. "No sir. Hondureña."

David sighed and ran a hand through his hair. "That could complicate things. When and how did you come to Mexico?"

The confidence that was growing in Luisa's eyes faded and was replaced by pain. *And what looks like shame*, David thought.

"Two years ago, my mom, she . . . well, she couldn't take care of us anymore. So she sold us."

"Us?"

"Me and my little sister. Josefina. She sold us to a guy who sold us to a guy and on and on until we ended up at El Agente's house in

179

Mexico City. Josefina was bought by somebody else. I don't know where she is."

"And you went to Monterrey?" asked David.

"Mmm hmm. Yes sir."

The consular officer sighed. "I don't suppose you have any form of identification? A passport or anything like that?"

"No, I've never had a passport."

Shannon reached across the table and patted Luisa on the hand. "It's okay, sweetie. We'll get it all figured out. You're doing great." She turned to David. "Can't we skip ahead to some other questions and come back to these?"

"Sure. Good idea." David forced a smile back onto his face, even though he knew that getting Miss Dominguez into the United States was going to be a very difficult task.

"So, let's talk about the school you'll be attending in the US. Tell me about it."

"Me tell you about it?" Luisa asked.

"Yeah. What do you know about it, why do you want to go there, et cetera."

"Umm . . . well, I know it's in Texas. It's on a ranch with horses and a lot of land. It's only girls, and they're all like me."

"What do you mean: girls like me?"

Luisa cut her eyes over at her interviewer in surprise. *Does he not know?* she wondered. *Señor Max told us that he knows.* Taking a deep breath, Luisa plunged into her story.

"All of the girls are like me because they were all rescued by Señor Max. We all used to be prostitutes. El Agente thought he was selling us to Señor Max to work in his brothel, but really he was buying us so we wouldn't have to do that stuff anymore."

"That stuff being sex work?"

Luisa nodded. "Yeah."

David continued scribbling in his notebook. "I'm sorry, I know these questions are uncomfortable, but I have to ask them. Do you understand that, if we grant you the visa, it's only temporary and you'll have to leave the United States after you graduate high school?"

"Yes sir. Señor Max told us. He said we might get to stay if we study hard and get into a university, but when we're done with school we have to leave."

"Good. Okay. I have one more question for you and then you're done for the day. Why not go home? I've been helping Max with these visas for several years now and I know that he offers to help you girls go back to your families if that's what you want. Why not go back home to Honduras?" *That would make my life a lot easier,* David thought.

Luisa shrugged her shoulders and looked down at the conference table in front of her, using her finger to trace the circle of a water mark left by the drink a previous visitor. "There's nothing left for me there."

"What do you mean?"

"My hometown, San Pedro Sula, is called the Murder Capital of the World. They're proud of it, too. Nobody goes into a neighborhood or down a street that isn't their own. La Mara and Barrio 18 and all of the smaller gangs make sure of it. Nobody can get jobs or even go to school. They started recruiting there too. At first parents thought the schools would be safe, you know? Send the kids there to keep them away from the gangs." Luisa shook her head. "They're everywhere. On the playground, in the lunch room, and sitting next to you in class. Recruiting you to join up, pay up, or die. That's what they say. To eight year olds. Seven year olds. Anybody. Before I left, an eleven year old who lived down the street had his throat slit because he didn't pay a fifty cent extortion fee. Fifty cents."

"The gangs control everything," Luisa explained. "*Everything.* If you have a problem, you don't call the police. You call the gang. Or you pretend there isn't a problem. When the police find a dead body in a field," she added, "they're extra careful to *not* dig around it. They're afraid of how many other bodies they might find there." The young woman paused, then looked over at David. "In the United States, your bad guys wear masks. They don't want to be seen. Known. In my country, the good guys wear masks. That's how you can tell who has the power. Who is really in control."

David stopped writing halfway through Luisa's answer, and Shannon was on the verge of crying.

"All of that," Luisa added, tears filling her own eyes, "would mean nothing if my family was still there. I would go back to be with them. But my abuelos are dead, my sister is I don't know where, and my mom is the one who sold me in the first place. Why not go back home?" She shook her head. "That's not my home anymore. There's nothing left for me there."

FIFTY

David told Luisa to wait in the hall and invited Max to join him and Shannon in the conference room. At fifteen years old and worldlier than anyone her age ever should be, Luisa knew that the adults were talking about her and that it wasn't good. The consular officer shut the door so she couldn't hear their conversation, and every so often Max turned around and looked at Luisa through the window glass with a strange kind of despair in his eyes. *What is going on?*

Inside the conference room, David Hargrove pulled no punches.

"I want to help her," he told Max. "She's certainly been through enough, with the forced prostitution and then coming from where she did on top of that. San Pedro Sula is no joke. All of Honduras has a population of less than Los Angeles County, and it still averages twenty murders a day. Kids as young as seven are being tortured and killed, with gang recruiters infiltrating the schools so nowhere is safe."

Max nodded. "I've read articles about how advocacy organizations are urging the State Department to treat kids arriving at the border from Central America as refugees. Kind of like how children leaving Iraq and Haiti have their asylum claims evaluated there and those who are accepted can travel safely to their new country. Why can't you treat Luisa as a refugee? Surely no one would dispute that her hometown is a war zone."

David sighed. "Unfortunately, the State Department would dispute that. There's violence, sure, but no declared war. We have no apparatus for evaluating asylum or refugee petitions from Central Americans. To get her a student visa, I need valid Honduran identification. Even then, I'll probably have to route it through the US Embassy in Tegucigalpa since Luisa is in Mexico illegally."

"But she was brought here against her will. That must count for something."

The consular official shook his head. "Mexico offers one-year humanitarian visas to foreign victims of human trafficking. Luisa could apply for one of those. But she'd have to agree to help the prosecution in going after her traffickers, and down here that's like asking somebody to testify against Al Capone. The cartels and the traffickers are no different than the mafiosos in the US. If you're a threat, they'll kill you." David paused. "Besides, even if she did all that and got the humanitarian visa, it still wouldn't help with her F-1 application."

****

After what seemed like a lifetime, 'Mr. David' as Max called him walked to the door and invited Luisa back inside the conference room.

"Take a seat."

The teenager did as she was told, choosing to sit next to the blonde woman with the kind eyes.

The man Luisa was once afraid of, but who she now viewed as a saint, turned in his chair to face his young charge.

"I'll be honest with you," Max said. "You've been through enough in your life that you deserve to have people tell you the truth without any sugarcoating."

Luisa nodded her head. "Okay. What's wrong?"

A small smile flashed across Max's face and he glanced over at David Hargrove. "See – I told you she's smart." He paused. "There's a problem with your paperwork, Luisa. The other ladies in the group are from Mexico, so we can prove their identities with Mexican birth records."

"Which means we can get them new passports," Shannon added.

"Okay . . ." Luisa replied. *What does that have to do with me?*

"You're not Mexican," Max said, answering her unspoken question. "You're Honduran, in Mexico illegally, and we can't find any record of your birth or identity in the Honduran files that we have access to."

"But . . . I am Luisa Dominguez. I'm fifteen years old. My birthday is July 23, 1997."

Max nodded. "I know, honey. But so far that isn't enough. In order to get a passport, we have to do more than know who you are. We have to be able to prove who you are."

"Without a valid passport, Luisa, I can't issue you a visa," David explained. "And without a visa, you can't go live at the Jacobbsen's ranch."

Tears flooded into the teenager's eyes and streamed down her cheeks. "I . . . I . . . I can't . . . I can't go b-back there."

Max jumped out of his chair and rounded the conference table to kneel down in front of Luisa, wrapping his skinny arms around her in a bear hug.

"Shhh, shhh. Don't cry. No te llores. You don't have to go back. Don't worry."

"B-but you j-just s-said –"

"We'll figure out the paperwork," Max promised. "That's David's job. No te preocupes. Don't worry. And in the meantime, if you need to, you can stay a little bit longer with Mr. and Mrs. Barrón."

Luisa's tears turned to sniffles and she raised her head to look at the three Americans in front of her. "You promise? I don't have to go back?"

Max wrapped his arms around her again and kissed the top of her head, how Luisa always imagined a dad would have done. "I promise. You never have to go back."

FIFTY-ONE

After Max and Luisa left the Consulate, David returned to his office and picked up the phone. Punching numbers with his index finger, he put the receiver to his ear and listened as the line rang.

"Bueno, Francisco Rodriguez."

"Francisco," David said with a smile, "so glad I caught you. It's David Hargrove up in Guadalajara."

"Oh, hey, David, how are you?" the man answered in heavily-accented English. Although he was also an American citizen, Francisco grew up in Honduras with his mother's family.

"I'm doing well, man, I'm doing well. Thanks. Listen," David said, not wanting to waste any time, "I have a favor to ask."

"Okay, sure. What is it?"

David sighed. "Well, I'm working on an F-1 visa for a girl here in Mexico, but she's from Honduras. She doesn't have any papers."

On the other end of the line, the embassy worker in Tegucigalpa laughed. "Good luck with that."

"I know, I know. That's what I thought at first. But this girl has been to Hell and back – she was a sex slave for the last two years. Now she's got an offer for a free ride at a school in the US. I really want to make this happen for her."

The line went silent. After a few seconds, Franscisco asked: "Do you have anything to go on? Name? Parents? Last known address?"

"I've got fingerprints, a name – although probably not her full name, and a hometown."

The other man sighed. "The fingerprints might help. Send me everything you have and I'll see what I can do. No promises, though."

****

Francisco Rodriguez was right . . . having the young woman's fingerprints did help. Combined with her name, birthday, and place of birth, it was enough to convince the National Persons Registry to issue a new identification card.

186

"If only that was enough," the Embassy worker grumbled as he rode the elevator down out of his office building. He was headed to Luisa Dominguez's hometown, a tiny village deep in the jungles of the nation's southwest mountains. *'Good luck finding it on a map'*, Francisco thought, repeating the words that his grandmother told him over the phone. No one in the Embassy knew where to find the town of Tepeu, named after the Mayan sky god, but he knew his grandmother would. The elderly woman was an encyclopedia of Honduran names, dates, and locations. *'Travel parish to parish. The priests will know how to find each other. They can direct you. It could take several days to get there, my boy. Especially if the rains have washed out the mountain roads.'* Rodriguez sighed. *Several days in the mountains. Fabulous. This girl better be worth it.*

Getting in his government-issued white sedan, Francisco drove west-northwest away from the capital city of Tegucigalpa toward the district of La Paz. It was there, on the northern end, in the general direction of San Pedro Sula, where he was supposed to encounter Luisa's village.

Fourteen hours and one very uncomfortable night sleeping in his car later, Francisco Rodriguez, agent of the United States government, arrived in Tepeu. Population: seventy-nine.

Walking up to the first person he saw, Francisco said: "Excuse me, can you tell me where to find the priest?"

"¿El padre? Él no está. Regresará la semana que viene."

Rodriguez's jaw dropped open and his shoulders slumped. "He's not getting back until next week?"

"Sí, la semana que viene."

Francisco sighed and looked up at the sky, rubbing his hands through his hair. "Okay, thank you."

"Who are you looking for?" a voice called out.

Turning to the side, he saw a young boy leaning against a concrete building.

"The priest," Francisco replied. "Father Daniel Lecca. The old man says he won't be back until next week."

The little boy laughed. "Don't listen to him. He doesn't like strangers. Come on," he added, waving over his shoulder. "Father Daniel lives over here."

A grateful Rodriguez followed his guide over mud-packed ground, through a series of bushes and vines, and past more snakes and spiders than the city-dweller cared to acknowledge.

"Ahí," the boy said, pointing toward a one-story concrete structure with a large cross carved into the wooden door.

Francisco nodded his head. "Gracias." Walking up to the parish hall, he knocked twice and hoped that the boy – rather than the old man – had been telling the truth.

A few seconds later, the wooden door creaked and swung open. A man no older than Francisco himself stood in the entryway. Black shoes, black pants, and a black short-sleeved shirt gave every indication that this was the person he drove from Tegucigalpa to meet. *All that's missing is the white collar.*

"Father Daniel?"

"Yes?"

Francisco breathed a sigh of relief. "I'm here to talk to you about a former parishioner of yours. Luisa Dominguez."

****

Five days later, David Hargrove knocked on the front door of the Barrón's home. He didn't normally visit the residences of visa applicants, but this was no normal application. He wanted to deliver the news in person.

Señora Barrón let him inside.

"You owe me HUGE, Max," David said as he walked into the living room. "Not that you didn't owe me before," he continued, "but you owe me HUGE now."

"What are you talking about?"

"This," the consular official said, then dropped a manila envelope on the coffee table between him and Max. "Papers for the Honduran girl."

Max's eyes lit up and he grabbed the envelope off of the table. "You got papers for Luisa?!"

The Hondureña, who had been listening to the conversation from the upstairs balcony, ran down the stairs and threw her arms around David's neck. "Thank you thank you thank you thank you! I get to go to the United States?!"

Hargrove peeled himself free from Luisa's grasp and stepped away from her. He was never one for letting strangers touch him, and even after four years of working with Max he still hadn't gotten used to all of the displays of affection from the grateful young women.

"Yes, you get to go."

Unaware of David's aversion to hugs, Luisa wrapped her arms around him again. "Thank you thank you thank you!"

Seeing the look of panic on the other man's face, Max smiled and got up from the couch to rescue him.

"See, Hargrove, I don't owe you anything. This isn't payment enough for you? That happiness? That joy?"

David eyed Luisa warily and sighed, putting his hands up in front of his body as a defense. "Keep her from hugging me again, and we'll call it even."

Max's blue eyes sparkled as he laughed. "Deal. Here, take a seat. Luisa, you sit on this other couch with me. I want Mr. David to tell us how he worked his magic." Max winked at the teenager and smiled, and again she couldn't help thinking how much she wished she had a dad like him when she was growing up.

"It wasn't easy," the State Department official began, leaning back against the couch and crossing one ankle over his knee. "At the end of Luisa's interview, Shannon scanned her fingerprints. Standard procedure for the visa application. But I called a buddy of mine at the Embassy in Tegucigalpa, he pulled a few favors, and we got the National Persons Registry to create a new identity card based on the fingerprints."

"That's all you would need, right?" asked Max.

"No," David replied, shaking his head. "In order to get a new passport issued, you need to either turn your old passport back in or have your original birth certificate and one other official Honduran document with your name and picture on it. Not to mention that a minor seeking a passport has to have both parents present or written permission from both of them."

"So . . ."

"So," David continued, "after we got the ID card, based on what Luisa told me about her hometown and her great-grandparents, my friend went to her old church parish. The priest there had a baptism record for a Luisa Emilia Dominguez de Losa, born July 23, 1997, and baptized three weeks later by Father Ignacio Quinones. With the identification card and the baptism record, my friend at the Embassy convinced them to issue Miss Dominguez a new passport."

Luisa gasped. "I remember Father Ignacio. He was always so nice to me. He and my great-grandfather went to school together when they were kids or something like that."

Max, a devoutly religious man, smiled. "Amazing. A baptism is a sign of rebirth in Christ – the start of a new life. Your infant baptism, Luisa, is allowing for your new life in America."

"What about my mom's approval?" the teenager asked.

David sighed and his voice turned somber. "I'm sorry, but records show that your mom died last year."

"How?"

"Drug overdose, it seems."

The young woman snorted and rolled her eyes. "Figures."

"With the mother dead and no known father," David explained, "we were able to get that requirement waived."

"So I'm in?" Luisa asked, turning to face Max. "I can go?"

Her new guardian smiled. "It looks that way, yep."

"Yes!" Luisa yelled, throwing her arms around Max's neck. "Thank you thank you thank you thank you!" she said, transferring her show of gratitude to a new recipient.

The young woman then leaned back, sat up straight, and placed her hands in her lap. "I swear, I'll be the best student you've ever had at your school. I'll follow all of the rules and I'll study hard and I'll always be nice to everybody. You'll never regret having me there. Se juro. I swear."

Max laughed and placed his hand on Luisa's shoulder. "I believe you. Why don't you go tell the rest of the group the good news?"

After Luisa bounded out of the room like a five year old on Christmas morning, Max turned to his fellow American and nodded his head. "Great work, David. Really – great, great work. And you're right . . . I do owe you one."

190

FIFTY-TWO

A week later, with passports, visas, and new wardrobes in tow, Luisa and her six classmates said goodbye to Mr. and Mrs. Barrón and climbed into yet another van.

I like this van, though, Luisa thought with a smile as she wedged herself between Sofia and Lola. *This one is taking us to the airport!*

Seven teenage girls and two adult males boarded a 757 at Guadalajara International Airport, joining one hundred other passengers who were bound for the United States. Their trip would be a long one, and Max warned the group to prepare for an exhausting day.

All of the warnings in the world, though, couldn't have contained Luisa's excitement. Never in her life did she ever dream that she would fly in an airplane. Or move to the United States. *Or, for a while there, live a life free from prostitution.*

After a first leg of three and a half hours, the Wilberforce Academy traveling party arrived in Atlanta, Georgia. Before boarding their next flight to San Antonio, the group had to pass through Customs and Immigration.

It's the same as the booths at the Guatemala-Mexico border, Luisa thought as she looked over at the row of cubicles manned by United States Customs officials. It gave the teenager some comfort to have a small sense of familiarity at a time when everything else in her life was changing.

Lots of different lanes. Separate lines for US citizens and non-citizens. Luisa continued to rattle off the similarities in her mind. *Wait your turn, step up to the booth. Present your identification and documents.* Luisa wasn't worried there. Señor Max and Señor David created folders for each girl, complete with all of the necessary information. *Answer the questions they ask. Thank goodness they speak Spanish.* Panic flashed across Luisa's face. *They speak Spanish, right?*

"Señor Max – they'll speak Spanish, right?"

Her guardian smiled and nodded. "Yes, they will."

Luisa let out a deep breath. *Phew. Okay. Answer the questions, look into the camera for a picture – no smiling allowed. Then I get my documents back, walk through the back door of the booth, and just like that . . . I'll be in the United States!*

"Next!"

Luisa smiled. *My turn!*

After exiting the booth, Luisa walked over to rejoin Señor Max and some other students while they waited for the rest of the group to pass through Customs inspection. The young women smiled and giggled and hugged each other in excitement. They had made it to the Promised Land.

Luisa looked around the pristine white-washed airport with amazement. In many ways it was similar to the one in Guadalajara, but on a bigger, nicer scale. Restaurants everywhere. Shops everywhere. Signs in English that Luisa couldn't read and, surprisingly, signs in Spanish too. Announcements over a loudspeaker also came in two languages – another surprise and another element of comfort in a foreign land.

"Ready?" Max asked when their group was complete again. "We don't have all that long to wait before our next flight leaves, so if we want to get something to eat we should get a move on."

Luisa nodded her head in agreement and followed Max and Jesús away from the Customs counters and into the massive Hartsfield-Jackson Atlanta International Airport.

"Stay close, ladies," Jesús said over his shoulder. "This is the busiest airport in the world . . . we don't want anybody getting lost."

Luisa took a step closer so that she was rubbing shoulders with Lola. All of the travelers were wearing specially-designed red 'Wilberforce Academy' golf shirts, in part to continue the group bonding that Max stressed but also to make it easier for the two men to keep track of everyone.

Luisa glanced around at her new classmates, smiling and laughing with each other, and a wave of sadness passed over her. It was crazy, she knew, to be sad at such an amazing moment in her life. *But I can't help it*, the young woman thought. *I can't help but think of everyone who isn't here with me. Abuela. Josefina. Bianca – although maybe she and Felipe made it.* A part of Luisa even wished that her mom was there to see it. Her, Luisa Dominguez, a Hondureña and former sex slave, in the United States legally and on her way to a private boarding school. With a chance to go to college. *What I wouldn't give to see Mami's face when she learned how far*

I've come. How much I've survived. No thanks to her. Luisa shook her head. *No, no thanks to her. All thanks to God and his angel, Señor Max.*

"Okay ladies," the angel said, breaking into Luisa's thoughts. "This is our gate. C-17. Now, there are seven of you so I'm going to take half at a time to use the bathroom and grab some food. The others will stay here with Jesús. Sound good?"

Luisa smiled. She appreciated how Max always asked the girls if they liked his plans. She knew he probably wouldn't change them even if she said no, but she still liked the fact that he asked. For the first time since her abuela died, Luisa felt as if her opinion mattered to someone. "Yes sir," she answered. "That sounds good to me."

****

Another two and half hours on a plane and three hours in a car brought Luisa to her ultimate destination: Resurrection Ranch. Nestled between the two tiny towns of Sonora and El Dorado, Max and Esmerelda Jacobbsen's West Texas retreat was the exact definition of 'the middle of nowhere'. And they liked it that way.

All seven of the ranch's new residents fell asleep on the ride from San Antonio, and it was dark when Señor Max drove through the gates, over the cattle guard, and onto his property. There would be a celebration the next day to welcome the girls: an 'Independence Day' party complete with food, decorations, and music. But, for now, they would rest.

Walking into a two-story building that served as the students' dormitory, Luisa found her name on a festive sign covering one of the doors. Every new resident was given a roommate, with one group of three in a corner room on the end. Roommates were assigned both to save space and to help lower the amount of time that the ladies were left alone at night.

The only sore spot of the entire day for Luisa was when she saw Sofia's name next to hers on her door. *There are worse things in life*, she thought before stepping inside. *Especially because this room is light years different than the one I had in Monterrey!*

The beige carpet was plush and soft, the walls were painted in a pale pink, and two twin beds sat opposite each other. Navy blue comforters with matching sheets and pillows covered the mattresses. They each also had a desk, a chair, and a flat, rectangular item that Luisa would soon learn was a laptop computer.

Luisa knew she would sleep peacefully through the night for the first time since she left Honduras over two years earlier. Actually, since she left her abuela's house a year before that. There would be no loud city noises, no gunshots, no yelling, and no strange sounds coming from other rooms. Only peace, quiet, and crickets. The young woman smiled and shook her head in disbelief. *I don't know what I ever did to deserve this, but thank you, God. I'm the luckiest girl in the world.*

Luisa climbed into bed, closed her eyes, and drifted off to sleep. The smile never left her face.

FIFTY-THREE

The next morning, a wet, sticky piece of sandpaper scraped across Luisa's face and woke her up. Her mouth and eyes squeezed shut in an instinctive reaction, and she tried to roll away from her attacker. But that only resulted in the same sandpaper sliding over her jaw, cheek, and ear.

"Ahhhh!" Luisa screamed, sitting up so fast in her bed that she fell off the side onto the floor.

"Oww . . . shit that hurt."

Tears welled in Luisa's eyes and she grabbed her elbow with her free hand to try to ease the throbbing pain in her arm.

Sofia, Luisa's roommate, hopped out of bed and squatted next to her on the floor, examining Luisa's arm. Several of the other dorm residents appeared at the doorway, all with expressions of concern on their faces.

"What is it?"

"What happened?"

"Are you okay?"

"Oh my gosh – a dog!"

Lola's comment caused Luisa to open her eyes and look toward the center of the room. Standing beside her bed, wagging its tail and smiling at her with bright amber eyes, was the owner of the wet, sticky sandpaper. *Otherwise known as a tongue*, Luisa thought. *Ugh. I hate dogs.* Scrambling back onto her bed, she scooted as far away from the animal as she could and tucked her knees to her chest for protection.

Lola shared no such fear of dogs. She pushed past the other girls in the doorway and plopped onto the floor. Luisa's four-legged intruder needed no further invitation, climbed into his new friend's lap, and commenced licking all over her face.

"Lola, stop," Luisa called out. "That's gross. It might bite you. It could have diseases or something."

Her housemate laughed and pushed the dog far enough away to be able to answer without catching a mouth full of slobber. "Don't be silly. He's so sweet!"

"Gus! Here you are. I've been looking all over for you."

Señor Max stood in the doorway of the bedroom and smiled. "Good morning, ladies. Sorry about the intrusion. Gus here obviously wanted to welcome y'all to the ranch. C'mon boy," Max added and slapped his hand twice on the side of his leg. "Let's go. You can see them all later."

The big brown ball of fur climbed out of Lola's lap and trotted out of the room, wagging his tail the whole time.

"Breakfast is in thirty minutes," said Max. He then turned and left, leaving everyone alone in Luisa's room.

****

Later that morning, on her first full day at Resurrection Ranch, Luisa decided to explore her new home. Upon arrival the night before, she and the other students were given a welcome packet that had a letter from the Jacobbsens, a schedule of 'orientation events' (*whatever those are*, Luisa thought), and a map of the 1,000 acre ranch.

Taking the map out of the folder, Luisa waved goodbye to her roommate and set off to see the sights. Growing up in the mountainous jungles of Honduras had turned Luisa into an adventurous outdoorswoman, but the last three years had been a series of stifling confinements – first in the one-room apartment in San Pedro Sula, then in cars and trucks and trains, and, of course, the 'Happy House' in Monterrey. Luisa loved the idea of spending the next several years in such a large, open space.

The first stop on her self-guided tour was the same as her starting point: the student dormitory. It was two stories tall with twenty rooms on each floor and four communal bathrooms, one on either end of every hall. The younger girls were on the first floor and paired with a roommate. Luisa didn't know it, but those were strategic decisions made by the ranch's head counselor, Señora Jacobbsen. The first floor meant that jumping from the window would be futile, and roommates meant less time that the girls would be alone – both efforts to reduce the risk of suicide. Guilt, despair, hopelessness, and worthlessness were all triggers, and they were all felt by the students at Wilberforce Academy.

Leaving the dormitory, Luisa crossed over a small grassy area called 'the quad' and arrived at the center of campus activity: the Gomez building. Named after Señora Jacobbsen's family, the Gomez building housed classrooms, faculty and staff offices, the cafeteria, and a small gymnasium. It was where Luisa would eat, learn, and play. Gomez was also where she would have daily therapy sessions and twice-weekly group counseling. Similar to the other structures surrounding the quad, the one Luisa was standing in front of was built in the Spanish colonial style – complete with thick stucco walls, a red tile roof, and lots of open air courtyards and walkways.

A bronze plaque on one of the walls near the entrance to the building caught Luisa's eye. Walking closer, she saw that there was the outline of what looked like a man's face, with a name, dates, and some words in English that she couldn't read.

William Wilberforce
1759-1833
Politician, Philanthropist, Abolitionist

"You may choose to look away but you can never say again that you did not know."

"Hmm," Luisa said and shrugged her shoulders. "Maybe that's one of Señor Max's relatives."

Continuing her campus tour, Luisa walked past a small chapel, the Jacobbsen's one-story, three-bedroom house, and a series of small cabins for the workers who chose to live on the ranch. Crossing a bridge that spanned a dried-up creek, Luisa saw a small pond with a dock, several storage sheds, and – in the distance – the building she had been looking for: the barn. Despite her fear of dogs, Luisa loved horses. Several farmers in her rural village kept horses to pull plows and wagons, and more than once the little Dominguez girl was found in a neighbor's barn, curled up in a stall next to the big animals.

The irony of her living situation in Monterrey, in a converted barn, was beyond the young woman's understanding.

After walking through the eight-stall building and petting all of the horses she saw, Luisa went back outside into the bright Texas sunshine. Several horses were roaming in a field behind the barn, and Luisa couldn't resist running over to the paddock fence and climbing up to lean on the top rail.

"Hola bonitos," she called out with a smile. "Bonitos bonitos caballos."

"They are pretty, aren't they?" a male voice said, and Luisa turned around to see Señor Max walking toward her.

The teenager nodded. "So pretty."

Luisa and Max stood in silence for a few minutes before the ranch owner asked: "how would you like to work with the horses while you're here?"

"Work with them?"

"Sure," Max said, nodding his head. "Every student is assigned a different chore, and I can put you down as working in the barn if you want. Not every young lady wants to spend her time mucking out stalls or standing around smelly horses, so if you do then the job is yours."

"Oh my gosh, yes. I would love to!"

"Good." Max paused. "I actually came out here looking for you. I wanted to apologize for my dog busting in on you this morning. He thinks every room belongs to him."

"It's okay," Luisa replied. "I'm afraid of dogs, but I'm afraid of a lot of things."

Max nodded his head. "Most people are afraid of a lot of things, if they're honest. But I'll make sure Gus stays away from your room until you're ready for him to come back. How does that sound?"

"Good."

"Good." Max paused, unsure if he would be overstepping with his next question. Luisa was still new, but he wanted to ask anyway. "If you don't mind telling me," he began, "why are you afraid of dogs?"

Luisa cut her eyes sideways, opened her mouth to respond, and then stopped. She sighed and looked back out at the horses in the paddock in front of her.

"You don't have to answer if you don't want to."

"No, no, it's okay," Luisa said with a sigh. "There were some stray dogs roaming around in my village when I was a kid," she began, "but I never had a dog as like a pet or anything." A small laugh escaped her lips. "And we definitely didn't have any pets with my mom in San Pedro Sula."

The smile left Luisa's face and the sparkle faded from her eyes.

"Señor had dogs. Guard dogs. One of them bit me once. I'm not sure why." Luisa climbed down from the paddock fence, crossed her arms over her chest, and walked back toward the barn. Max had to jog to catch up.

"After I escaped and was brought back," Luisa continued, talking to herself as much as the man walking beside her, "Señor threw me in a storage closet in the back of the house. He stationed one of his German Shepherds outside. If I got anywhere near the exit, the dog would start barking and growling and slamming his paws into the door so hard that I thought it would bust open. No bathroom breaks; no food; no water. Just me on the concrete floor in the far corner of the closet. For three days."

"What happened after three days?" Max asked.

They had reached the barn by that point, and Luisa sat down on a bale of hay by the entrance. "Emilio drove me to Mexico City. Back to El Agente's warehouse. He was driving and I was in the trunk. For ten hours."

Max joined Luisa on the bale of hay and patted her hand with his. "No more dogs until you're ready. I promise. Now what do you say we go see what's cooking for lunch, huh?"

Luisa nodded. "Yeah, lunch sounds great."

FIFTY-FOUR

The first day of summer classes dawned bright and beautiful, with the West Texas sun streaming through spotted clouds to send rays of warmth and hope down upon the students of Wilberforce Academy.

Luisa had an extra spring in her step as she joined her fellow schoolmates on the short walk from their dormitory to the classroom building. The teacher at her village school in Honduras moved away when Luisa was nine, and they hadn't been able to find a replacement. Luisa's mom had no interest in her daughters' education, so this was her first day of school in six years. The young woman smiled. *I can't wait*, she thought.

Before actual classes began, all thirty-five students at piled into the cafeteria/auditorium for a welcome speech by the school's headmaster: Max Jacobbsen.

"It's the same speech every year," Luisa overheard one girl saying. "You'd think he could come up with something different to say. Or at least only make the new students sit through it."

"Oh it's not so bad," the person walking next to her replied. "Better listening to him than doing schoolwork."

Luisa made sure to sit on the other side of the room from the two older students. She was determined to have a good day and didn't want them to spoil her mood.

After all of the young ladies were seated, Señor Max climbed up the stairs onto a small podium at one end of the lunchroom.

"Good morning!" he said in a booming voice.

When no one responded, Max repeated himself: "good morning!"

"Good morning," the students replied in unison.

"Welcome to Wilberforce Academy, ladies!"

Looking out at the small audience in front of him, Max smiled. He always referred to the students as ladies, not girls. It was subtle, perhaps imperceptible to some, but he wanted to emphasize that they had value and worth. That they were important.

"Today is the first day of a new school year and I'm so excited to have all of you here. The rest of the teachers and staff are as well.

This past week has been very busy, I know, especially for the new arrivals who are still trying to get settled into life here at the ranch. But now the semester begins and I hope you ladies will love learning as much I did when I was a student."

Eyes in the audience avoided looking his way and the girls shifted back and forth in their seats. School had never been a fun activity for them.

"Before you head off to your classrooms," Max continued, "I want to tell y'all a little story about how the school got its name. Have any of our new residents ever heard of a man named William Wilberforce? There's a plaque with his name and image on the wall by the front door."

Silence filled the small auditorium.

"It's okay, most people don't know who he is. I know the older students do, since they hear me give this same speech every year." Max smiled. "William Wilberforce lived a long, long time ago in England. Does everybody know where England is?"

The older students raised their hands and nodded their heads while the new girls sat motionless.

"Well, England is a country on the other side of the ocean. And back when Mr. Wilberforce was alive, people on one side of that ocean would kidnap other people, turn them into slaves, and ship them back around the world to be sold. Does that sound kind of familiar?"

With eyes downcast, the students nodded their heads in the affirmative.

"I thought it might," the headmaster replied, a sadness filling his voice. "The only difference was that, back then, selling people that way was legal. There were big open-air markets and advertisements in newspapers. The government in England knew about all of it and said it was okay. But William Wilberforce believed that it wasn't okay to sell people and ship them around like cattle, so he decided to try to stop it."

"He didn't do a good job then," Sofia called out, and several of her classmates murmured their agreement.

"Well, I can see why you would think that," Max replied. "But actually he did. It took a long time, almost thirty years, but he finally got the government in England to make the slave trade illegal. He's

201

one of the heroes of the abolitionist movement . . . the effort to end slavery."

Max saw the looks of disbelief in the teenagers' eyes. Slavery might be illegal, but to them it was still very real.

"Now, I know there's a lot of work to do before we end slavery once and for all. And I'm not saying I'm the same as William Wilberforce. Not even close. All I'm saying is that, even with all of the evil in the world, there are still good people. And that one person can make a difference. Never forget that, ladies. One person can change the world."

After Max's speech ended, the girls left the cafeteria and separated into their classrooms. Unlike prior semesters, which followed a 'one-room schoolhouse' approach, there were now two different groups of students at the Academy. One was an advanced class with girls who had either been at the ranch longer or spent more time in school before they left home, and one was a beginner class for students who had farther to go in their studies.

Luisa was placed in the beginner group along with her roommate Sofia, chatterbox Lola, and all but one of the other girls from her entering class.

The young Hondureña enjoyed the headmaster's speech, and her excitement for the day hadn't dampened. She believed in the message that the Jacobbsens gave her. *This is my chance to start over*, Luisa thought as she settled into her new desk in her new classroom. *This is my chance at a new life.*

****

A few minutes later, a short, thin young woman who looked to be about ten years older than Luisa walked into the classroom and stood at the front.

"Okay, class, can I have your attention please? Thank you," she said. "I'm very excited to welcome all of you to your first day here at Wilberforce Academy. I'll be your teacher this year. We're all going to learn a lot and have fun in the process!"

Maureen Ramirez looked out at her fresh crop of students with a smile that they didn't return. All the teacher saw was uncertainty and fear.

202

"Well, before we start on our lessons for today, I want us all to get to know each other. I'll go first."

Speaking in Spanish, the blonde-haired, blue-eyed instructor continued: "my name is Maestra Ramirez." Maureen knew that titles were important in Mexico, and that the girls would call her 'Teacher Ramirez' instead of 'Miss Ramirez'. The same went for architects, lawyers, and any other profession that could be given a title. "My grandparents were from Cuba," she said, "so that explains the Ramirez. I'm twenty-five . . . not too much older than all of you. I actually grew up down the street from the Jacobbsens in Palo Alto, California. I kept in touch with them after they moved to Dallas and then here, and when they found out that I was a high school teacher, they offered me a job at their school. This is my first year here, so I'm new like you."

Maureen smiled, the kind of smile empowered by education, optimism, and youth.

"Now," the teacher continued, still smiling, "I want to go around the room and hear a little bit about each of you. Please tell me your name, age, hometown, and how old you were when you left school." Ms. Ramirez looked over at a tall brunette in the back corner. "Let's start with you, please."

"Me?" the girl asked. "Umm, okay, my name is Raquel. What else do you want to know?"

"Your age, your hometown, and how old you were when you left school."

"Okay. Umm, well, I'm sixteen. I'm from Mexico City. And I was thirteen when I left school."

"Good," the teacher replied. "Next. Right in front of Raquel. Yes, you."

"My name is Katia," the chipper young woman replied. "I'm also sixteen. I'm from Chihuahua. And I was fourteen when I left school."

"Okay. Next."

The students proceeded around the classroom listing off the requested information.

"Lola. Fifteen. Torreón. Fourteen."

"Sofia. Sixteen. Tepexpan. Twelve."

"Blanca. Seventeen. Iguala. Fourteen."

The last one to go was Luisa Dominguez.

"My name is Luisa," the young girl said. "I'm fifteen. I'm not from Mexico, actually. I'm from San Pedro Sula . . . it's in Honduras. And I was nine when I left school."

Several people in the room gasped.

The teacher had done her homework, had known going in that the students would likely be many, many years behind in their schooling. High school still wasn't mandatory in Mexico in 2011, and Maureen knew the statistics associated with that. Sixty-four percent of adults in the country without a high school degree. The Mexican government spending one-tenth as much per student as the US. Children leaving school early to work because their families needed the money.

But nine years old? Teacher Ramirez hadn't expected that.

Maureen took a deep breath, smiled, and tried to keep sadness from arriving in her eyes. *The last thing these girls want or need is my pity.*

"Nine years old," Ms. Ramirez nodded, marking down the number in her notebook beside Luisa's name. "That would put you in third grade. Okay." The teacher smiled again, something which was quickly becoming her default facial expression. Smiles could mask all kinds of emotions. "I liked third grade. It was one of my favorites."

Anger, shame, and embarrassment began to disappear from Luisa's face and her lips curved up into an almost-grin. Her teacher breathed a sigh of relief. *Good. I can't have her giving up on herself before we even get started.*

FIFTY-FIVE

Starting on the second day of school, classes at Wilberforce Academy commenced every morning at nine-thirty. Luisa's day, however, began earlier than that. She took an immediate liking to the horses on the ranch, so one of her assigned chores was to feed them every morning. And horses, the teenager soon learned, were early risers.

After spending time with her fuzzy, four-legged friends (and saying hello to the stable cat, Macy), Luisa would return to her dorm room, shower, change clothes, and grab a bite to eat before dashing off to her eight-thirty therapy session. Since she was already awake with the horses, Luisa volunteered for the before-school time slot with Dr. Jacobbsen.

Esmerelda Gomez-Jacobbsen was nice, smart, and beautiful. Luisa was starstruck the first time she saw her, and ever since that day the Hondureña had loved spending time with Señor Max's wife. The fact that the fifty-six year old woman was her psychologist didn't bother her at all. In fact, it made Luisa like her more.

Daily therapy was the norm on the ranch, and it was required for all first-year residents. Depending on a girl's progress, her sessions could be reduced over time, but the first full year included individual counseling five days a week and group meetings every Wednesday and Saturday.

One Friday morning, Luisa settled into a large, overstuffed chair in Dr. Jacobbsen's office and pulled her feet under her body to sit cross-legged.

Her therapist looked up from the notepad she had been writing in. Luisa always sat cross-legged during their sessions, and it made Esmerelda smile. *Despite everything she's gone through*, she thought, *Luisa still has some of that little girl innocence about her.*

"So," the Stanford-trained psychologist began, "how was yesterday?" Esmerelda started most of her meetings by asking about the current day, but since she met with Luisa in the morning that had to be adjusted.

"Yesterday was good," the teenager replied, picking out a piece of her long, black hair and twisting it between her fingers. It was a

205

nervous habit that Dr. Jacobbsen made note of during their first session.

"School is hard," Luisa continued. "I can read okay because my abuela taught us how to read the Bible. But I don't know any of the stuff that the other girls know. They stayed in school for so much longer than I did."

"That's alright," Esmerelda replied, brushing her own black hair away from her eyes. "I heard from your teacher that you're a very fast learner and are catching up quickly."

Luisa pursed her lips together and sighed. "Doesn't feel like it."

"Keep at it. You'll get there. How is everything else going? Have you been sleeping okay?"

The young woman shrugged her shoulders. "I guess. Sometimes. No, not really." Luisa's answer became more and more honest with each attempt.

"Did you have a nightmare again last night?" Trouble sleeping was common amongst the ranch residents, and Dr. Jacobbsen and the other therapists tried their best to treat the underlying cause of the insomnia. They recommended chemical sleep aids as an option of last resort.

Luisa nodded in response to the question. "Same one. I close my eyes at night and all I see is them. Clients. Guards. Snarling faces and glaring eyes. Weapons being swung at my head. Hands reaching out to strangle my neck." Luisa blinked back tears. "I'm afraid to sleep, Doctora. Every time I close my eyes, I'm taken back to Mexico. There are flashes of it playing constantly in my head – the room, the men, the pain. No matter how much my mind tells me I'm in a different place, no matter how much I know I'm safe, my body says something different. It has a memory all its own. It's still not over. I'm still there . . . it's like there's a broken record stuck repeating every night and every client." Luisa sighed. "I know I'm safe here, but I'm still so afraid that they'll show up one day and take me back."

"That's not going to happen, sweetheart. Not as long as you're here. Keep telling yourself that. You're safe here."

The teenager and the therapist continued talking for the rest of the session, covering topics that still barely skimmed the surface of the fire blazing beneath. Esmerelda knew she couldn't push too hard – couldn't force the young woman to talk before she was ready.

From reading Luisa's file, she knew the Hondureña was sold into slavery by her mother. That betrayal, as well as Luisa's missing sister, held the key to unlocking and releasing the pain that Luisa was holding inside of her. *Getting there is going to take a while, though*, Dr. Jacobbsen thought. *It always does.*

****

Later that night, after dinner, evening chores, and lights out in the dormitory, Max and Esmerelda sat together on the couch in their living room. The Jacobbsen's house was separate from the students' living quarters but not far away in case they were needed. As headmaster and primary counselor, the couple was always on call.

"What is it?" Max asked when his wife sighed for the fourth time in ten minutes.

"I keep thinking about something one of the girls told me during therapy today."

Max wanted to ask which one, but he didn't. Doctor-patient confidentiality extended everywhere, even to him.

"Anything I can do to help?"

"Maybe. Well, yeah actually," Esmerelda said, sitting up straight and turning to face her husband. "Right now all of the staff can wear pretty much whatever they want to . . . they don't have uniforms."

"True."

"Can we change that? Can we make all of the workers wear like red golf shirts or something?"

Max wrinkled his forehead and thought for a second, then shrugged his shoulders. "I don't see why not."

Esmerelda's brown eyes sparkled with gratitude at her husband's agreement to her proposal.

"But what's the reasoning behind it?" asked Max.

"I think it will help the ladies feel safer. I mean, they know about our rules for visitors – how people have to be met at the front gate and accompanied at all times, but I think it would help if they were able to tell right away, from a distance, if somebody wasn't supposed to be on the ranch. Imagine what would go through your mind," Esmerelda continued. "You've lived through unspeakable horror, and every day you worry that those people will hunt you down and find you. You're walking to class one morning and Jesús or another worker has his back turned to you so you can't see his face. From behind, with his height and build and complexion, he looks like your old pimp. Imagine the terror that would flood your body."

Max put his arm around his wife's shoulders and pulled her closer to him. "I get it. You're right. I don't know why we didn't do it sooner. We can order the shirts tomorrow."

FIFTY-SIX

With employee uniforms ordered and set to be delivered in a week, Esmerelda was in a great mood the next day as she crossed the center of the campus quad to go to Saturday's group counseling session. Six girls and a psychologist were in each meeting, and group therapy was a chance for the girls to express their feelings in a safe space while surrounded by people who could understand what they had been through. It was also a time when Esmerelda and her staff tried to teach the teenagers about healthy relationships and boundaries. Making them more self-aware and increasing their logical reasoning skills was a huge step in the recovery process.

Group sessions were almost always open format, with the young ladies encouraged to talk about whatever came to mind. The first person to speak that day was Laura, a pretty brunette who had been under the control of her boyfriend in Mexico City before being sold to The Broker.

"One of my earliest memories is of my dad telling me that he was glad I was born a girl. So that, if he ever needed to, he could rent me out to men." Laura paused. "I was still too young to understand why anyone would want to rent me. Now I know."

Esmerelda nodded her head and remained sitting in silence. Her job in these group sessions was more to observe than to counsel – to let the girls comfort each other as fellow survivors. It was a struggle for her, though, to not become just as jaded as the teenagers who arrived at her ranch twice a year. Hours upon hours of therapy sessions had exposed her to levels of trauma and abuse that were hardly fathomable. Women kept in cages. Teenage girls given commands like dogs and beaten if they didn't comply. Abused by fathers, brothers, uncles. Sold by mothers. Laura's comment was the latest in a long line of terrible tales. *In most places in the world, fathers want sons*, Esmerelda thought to herself. *China has an outrageous gender imbalance because of the preference for male heirs. But Laura's family wanted a girl . . . because they knew they could be her pimp.*

Statements like that struck hard at Señora Jacobbsen's faith in humanity. She was trained to deal with trauma, but a person – victim or therapist – could only see so much of it before it began to eat away at their soul.

The one that haunted her the most, that still kept her awake at night, was the brunette named Isabella who was part of the first group Max rescued from The Broker. Isabella was seventeen when she arrived at Resurrection Ranch.

"How long did you spend in the life?" Esmerelda had asked the young woman on her first day.

Isabella didn't reply. Her head was up and her eyes were facing the therapist, but there was no life in them. Brown pools of despair stared empty back at Dr. Jacobbsen.

"You were in Acapulco, right?" she asked, trying to start a conversation with her new client.

The teenager continued to sit silently in her chair. By that point, Esmerelda was used to the nervous habits of trauma victims: jittery arms and legs, eyes darting back and forth, picking at finger nails or the edges of their clothing.

But with Isabella there was nothing.

Hands resting in her lap, shoulders slumped, head tilted slightly to the right, and a face as blank and emotionless as her eyes. The only way that Dr. Jacobbsen knew the girl was still alive was when she blinked.

It was like that every time the therapist and teenager met. Six weeks of silence. Isabella didn't speak in class, either, and the rest of the girls said she never uttered a word in the dorm.

"I'm worried about her," Esmerelda had told her husband numerous times. "All of the girls are in pain; all of them are traumatized. But I can talk to them. I can reach them. Wherever she is . . . I can't get there."

"She'll come around," Max had replied. "Give her time." From his purchase report and the little information he gleaned during her visa application interview, Max knew that Isabella spent six years in one of the most notorious brothels in Acapulco. Dozens, sometimes hundreds of clients a day. "It takes time to recover from what she's been through."

Dr. Jacobbsen had sighed and leaned her head on Max's shoulder. "But what if she never does?"

The next morning, Isabella didn't show up for school. A sick feeling gathered in Esmerelda's gut as she bounded up the stairs of the dormitory and sprinted down the hall to the young woman's room.

The door was locked.

"Isabella!" she said, pounding on the door. "Open up! It's Dr. Jacobbsen. Open the door, sweetie."

Seconds later, Max arrived with the master key.

When they entered the bedroom, the first thing the couple saw was two bare feet dangling in the air – her body suspended by a belt tied to the clothes rack in the closet.

It was after Isabella's suicide that new rules were put in place on Resurrection Ranch. First-year students were given roommates . . . *if there was another girl in the room that night,* Esmerelda often thought, *she might not have been able to kill herself.* All first years were also moved to the bottom floor of the building in an attempt to prevent any head-first dives out of second-floor windows. Clothes racks were replaced by shelves. Belts were no longer permitted as part of the wardrobe.

That was also when Esmerelda's husband, Max, had insisted on hiring two additional psychologists to help lighten the load. She was grateful for the help, but the trauma specialist was still troubled. *Not as troubled as these poor girls, though*, she thought, giving her head a quick shake to bring herself back to the present.

On the other side of the circle, a seventeen year old named Blanca began to speak.

"My family doesn't know about this," she said. "About what I've become. I left home when I was fourteen to get a job at a factory. I was supposed to send money back to my parents and younger brothers and sisters. I guess they think I forgot about them since I don't send money anymore." Blanca used her hand to wipe tears off her cheeks. "Maybe they think I'm dead. That would be better than them thinking I abandoned them." She paused. "Yeah, I hope they think I'm dead."

Sofia nodded her head in agreement. "I can't imagine if my family knew what has become of me. I'm so glad they're so far away. I left home because I thought they were mean and overprotective. I wanted my own space and my own life." She snorted. "Boy was I ever wrong."

Dr. Jacobbsen noticed that one of her favorite students, Luisa, kept shrinking lower and lower in her chair as everyone else took turns talking about their loving, caring families and how their relatives would hate to hear about their work as prostitutes.

"What about you, Luisa?" asked Lola, the chatterbox of the group. "Do you think your family knows?"

Luisa kept her eyes glued to the floor and nodded her head up and down.

"They do know?"

Luisa let out a deep breath and lifted her head up to look at her classmates. The tears that had pooled in her eyes poured out over her cheeks.

"My mom knows. She's the one who sold us."

A few of the girls gasped in shock, and the members of the group looked back and forth at each other, uncertain how to respond.

Finally, Lola leaned forward in her chair. "Us?" she asked.

"My sister and me," Luisa explained. "I was thirteen; Josefina was twelve. She got bought by somebody else at The Broker's house in Mexico City."

"Your *mom* sold you?" Sofia asked.

"For how much?" Lola questioned.

"Por Dios," said Blanca. "It doesn't matter how much."

Luisa shrugged her shoulders and looked back down at the floor. "I don't remember how much. She wanted to get rid of us and figured she'd try to make some money in the process." Luisa paused. "It doesn't matter anyway. Señor Max said that she's dead now." Luisa dug her sandal-clad toe into the tile floor in front of her. "Like I said, it doesn't matter."

The therapist felt compelled to jump in. "It does matter, Luisa. All of you matter. All of your stories matter. You don't have to talk about it right now if you don't want to, but it does matter. It is important. *You* are important."

Luisa nodded her head and swallowed back more tears. "I know," she whispered.

A bell rang in the classroom and interrupted the conversation. It was noon – lunch time.

"Okay ladies," said Dr. Jacobbsen. "That's all for today. Remember: if any of you want to talk about anything, you can always come see me."

FIFTY-SEVEN

Resurrection Ranch placed a very high emphasis on the recovery and restoration of the girls' mental health, which meant that therapists working at the ranch outnumbered the teachers 2:1. Not all of the mental health professionals lived on campus . . . some of them commuted in from the tiny neighboring towns of Sonora and El Dorado. All were sworn to secrecy by employment contracts and patient privacy laws, and all held sessions throughout the day with the girls. On this particular day of the week, Wednesday, the students participated in group therapy for an hour in place of their usual physical education class.

Walking back into the academic classroom after therapy ended, Luisa sighed and plopped down at her desk with a thud. The only remaining subject for the day also happened to be her least favorite. Her nemesis. The bane of her grade point average.

English, she thought with disdain.

"Okay ladies," her teacher said with a smile, clapping her hands together to get their attention. "Let's all return to our seats. We also want to welcome Señora de la Paz," Maureen added, gesturing toward her supervisor sitting in the back of the room. "The advanced level class is taking a test right now and Max and Esmerelda's son, Brandon, is being the proctor, so the señora was kind enough to offer to sit in and help us with our English lesson."

Groans and sighs filled the room. Luisa wasn't alone in her dislike of the foreign language.

"I know, I know," replied Maestra Ramirez. A few short weeks into the semester, she was already well aware of the girls' feelings on the subject. "The sooner we start the sooner we can finish."

Desks creaked and chairs scraped across the floor as the students settled in for their remaining hour of instruction.

Forty-five minutes later, with school almost over for the day, Maureen Ramirez turned around from the whiteboard to face her class.

"Alright," the young teacher said, "the last thing we'll do today is review what we've learned so far of the English alphabet. Would anyone like to volunteer?"

Silence settled over the room.

"If no one volunteers then I'm going to pick someone."

All of the girls kept their hands lowered and their eyes averted.

Ms. Ramirez sighed. "Okay. Let's see . . . Luisa. We'll start with you."

Luisa's head shot up and her eyes grew wide.

"Me?"

"Yes ma'am. Come on up here to the front."

Luisa rose from her desk and walked up to her teacher, dragging her feet the whole way.

"Good. Now, repeat after me, okay? A – apple."

"Eh – ahpole," said Luisa.

"No, no, be a little more nasal with it. Aaaaaple."

"Ahhhhpole."

Maureen sighed. "Close enough. B – baseball."

"B – beísbol."

"Wow, good."

Señora de la Paz cleared her throat in the back of the room. "Ask her how she would spell baseball."

The younger teacher, standing in front of the class, nodded her head. She was, after all, still at the ranch on a trial basis. The señora said she wanted to observe the students' progress today, but Maureen suspected that she was the one who was truly being observed – and graded.

"How do you spell baseball?" Señorita Ramirez asked in English.

Luisa squinted her eyes and tried to translate what sounded like a question. "Beísbol."

"No, how do you spell –"

"¿Cómo se escribe baseball?" asked the older woman in the back.

"Oh, oh, okay. B-e-í-s-b-o-l," Luisa answered with a smile, proud of herself for remembering how to say each letter in English.

"Not quite," replied her teacher. She stepped over to the dry-erase board on the classroom's front wall and wrote 'baseball' in big block letters. "See? B-a-s-e-b-a-l-l."

"Bahseeball," Luisa said, sounding out the word how she had been taught to.

"Baseball. The 'e' is silent."

214

Luisa was confused. *Silent letters? Why have them if they don't make a sound?*

Seconds later, the bell rang and signaled the end of the school day. *Oh thank God*, Luisa thought, never happier to be finished with class for the rest of the afternoon.

"Ugh," she complained to Sofia as they walked back to their dorm. "I'll never be able to learn English. It makes no sense."

"No kidding," her roommate agreed. "A silent letter? Why have a letter in the word if you're not going to make that sound?"

"That's exactly what I thought!" Luisa shook her head. "I don't get it."

FIFTY-EIGHT

Three months later, on an autumn Friday afternoon, Luisa was in her dorm room finishing her homework. Unlike many high school students, weekend homework at Wilberforce Academy wasn't postponed until Sunday evening. Sundays were for church and for rest, so weekend homework was done on Friday night or Saturday. Tonight's topic was biology – a subject that was giving Luisa fits.

Cooler temperatures had finally begun to arrive on the West Texas ranch, and Luisa opened her window to let in the cool breeze. She could hear Gus playing and barking in the quad, a sometimes welcome distraction from the textbooks in front of her. Despite their inauspicious beginning and Luisa's lingering fear of most dogs, Max was correct in predicting that the big chocolate lab would win her over. *I love that dog*, she thought with a smile.

A soft knock on Luisa's door startled her. She had been so focused on her homework and Gus that the rest of the world slipped away.

A second knock came.

"Who is it?" she asked.

"Brandon," answered a male voice, and Luisa recognized it as belonging to Max and Esmerelda's son. She closed her textbook, using a pencil to mark her page, and got up from her desk to answer the door. Luisa couldn't quite believe that this was her home now. A room with a window, a desk, a computer (!), a bed she didn't have to share, and a door she didn't have to open unless she wanted to.

I'm the luckiest girl in the world, Luisa thought as she twisted the knob and opened her door.

Still uneasy around most men, forever expecting the worst, Luisa only opened the door enough to be able to see her visitor's face.

"Umm, hi," she said, not sure why the younger Mr. Jacobbsen – Joven Jacobbsen as the girls called him – would be at her room.

"Hi," he replied with a smile. If he were back in college, Brandon would've asked if he could come in or made some kind of wisecrack about Luisa not opening the door all the way. But this wasn't college, and he knew better than to say or do anything to make any of the girls feel uncomfortable.

"I'm sorry to bother you like this, but your teacher asked me to talk to you."

"¿La maestra?"

Brandon nodded. "Your teacher, yeah. Look, maybe we could go over to the mess hall and grab something to drink? That's probably a better place to talk, no?"

A few minutes later, Luisa found herself seated on a wooden bench at a long, indoor picnic table. On the other side of the table was Brandon Jacobbsen, the ranch owners' son and resident heartthrob. She fiddled with the glass of water in front of her, avoiding eye contact out of fear that she was somehow in trouble with her teacher. *If la maestra sent Brandon to deal with me, then that means Max and Esmerelda know too and I'm in big trouble. But I haven't done anything wrong . . . have I?*

"Look, sir, I don't know what I did but I'm really sorry and I promise I'll never, ever do it again."

Laughter filled the empty dining room as Luisa's tablemate reacted to her outburst. "First of all," he replied, "don't call me 'sir'. That's my dad. I'm Brandon, okay?"

Luisa nodded. "Okay."

"Secondly," he added with a grin, "if you don't know what you did, how can you promise that you'll never do it again?"

The color drained from Luisa's face and she looked back down at her water glass. "I . . . I . . ."

Male laughter once again filled the room, but this time it had a softer, gentler tone.

"I'm messing with you. Don't worry," Brandon said, "you haven't done anything wrong. In fact, you've done something right."

Luisa's gaze peeled up from her glass to look across the table through thick black eyelashes.

"Something right?"

Brandon nodded. "Yep. Señorita Ramirez said that you're one of the smartest girls in class, even though you started off way behind, and that she wanted me to talk to you about what it's like when you apply for and go to college here in the US."

Luisa was glad she wasn't taking a sip of water when the younger Mr. Jacobbsen finished his sentence, because she knew she would've choked on the drink.

"C-college?"

"Yeah, college."

The teenager shook her head. "I'm not smart enough for college. And even if I was, I mean even if I *were*, I definitely don't have any money to pay for it."

"That's what scholarships are for. Trust me: if Maureen says you're smart enough and Señora de la Paz agrees with her, then you're smart enough."

Luisa stared at the young man sitting across from her. He was eight years older, but light years younger as well. He knew who his father was. Had a relationship with him. His mother loved, supported, and cared for him. He'd never lived a day on the streets; never watched a man die; never had anything precious stolen from him. He was charmed.

Yes, Brandon Jacobbsen had everything that Luisa ever wanted. And now he was sitting with her at a mess hall table telling her that she could one day have a similar life.

College, she thought in disbelief. Only eight percent of people in her native Honduras attended a university, and even fewer graduated. The idea that she, Luisa Dominguez, the daughter of a prostitute and a former prostitute herself, could not only attend college but attend college in the United States? It was too good to be true. *It has to be*, she thought. *He's pranking me.*

Much like his dad, Brandon Jacobbsen had the ability to read people's emotions and sometimes, it seemed, their minds.

"I'm completely serious," he said in response to Luisa's disbelief. "It will take a lot of work. You were even farther behind than most of the people are when they arrive here. But you've also improved at a much faster rate. It won't be easy," Brandon added, "but if you're willing to go for it then we'll help you every step of the way."

"That's another reason why your teachers asked me to talk to you, actually. To see if you'd be willing to do extra tutoring sessions with me. They have their hands full with the rest of the students, but I've got time for some one-on-one work. What do you say?"

Luisa couldn't quite believe that Joven Jacobbsen was telling her the truth, but she didn't want to give him the chance to take back the offer either.

"Yes," she said. "I'll do it. I want to go to college."

Brandon smiled. "Great. Why don't we get started tomorrow afternoon? If memory serves me correctly, Mom is taking some of y'all into El Dorado tonight to see a movie. Aren't you leaving soon?"

"Oh! I almost forgot about that!" Luisa climbed up off of the wooden bench and smiled down at her new tutor. "Thank you so much for helping me. You won't regret it. I promise!"

FIFTY-NINE

Luisa's life at Resurrection Ranch continued on in that manner for the next several years. Her weekdays were full of classes, chores, tutoring, and therapy. Saturdays brought homework, extra tutoring, and a group counseling session, while Sundays were reserved for church and rest. There were the occasional trips into nearby El Dorado for a movie or shopping using money earned from doing chores, and once per semester each class of girls got to travel to either Austin or San Antonio for a weekend field trip. They stayed in posh hotels, ate at fancy restaurants, visited symphonies and art galleries, and gained exposure to a culture that many of them had thought only existed in the movies.

The end of each semester brought with it a certain sadness when the older girls graduated and moved away. Most of them returned home to Mexico, some to jobs and some to universities. A few lucky Wilberforce Academy graduates got to stay in the United States to attend college there. But, regardless of destination, they all had to leave the ranch to make room for the next semester's new arrivals.

Sofia, Class of 2015, graduated six months before Luisa was scheduled to. They day she packed her bags to leave for the University of Guadalajara was one of the saddest moments that Luisa experienced while at the ranch. Despite their rough beginning, the two girls had grown very close and stayed roommates up until the last semester. After three and a half years, Sofia was as close a friend to Luisa as Bianca had been. Almost a sister to her like Josefina. Almost.

"Call and email me every day. And we're going to have Skype dates all the time," Luisa said, wrapping her arms around her friend and squeezing her tight.

"All the time," Sofia repeated. She reached up to wipe tears off of her cheeks. "After you graduate, you're going to come visit me in Guadalajara."

"I'll visit so much that you'll get tired of seeing me," Luisa said with a smile. She also had tears in her eyes.

"Okay ladies," Max said, interrupting their goodbye. "Time for us to leave. We don't want Sofia to miss her flight."

The two teenagers embraced again, then Sofia tore herself away from her best friend and stepped up into the passenger seat of Max's SUV.

"Bye," she said, waving and smiling despite her tears. "I'll miss you!"

"Bye!" replied Luisa with her own wave and smile.

The SUV then rolled away from the student residence and down the dusty West Texas driveway.

An arm wrapped itself around Luisa's shoulders, and the young woman recognized it as belonging to Señora Esmerelda, Max's wife. "She's going to do great," the psychologist said, "and so will you."

Luisa nodded her head and sniffed back the remainder of her tears.

"What do you say we go get some ice cream?" Esmerelda asked.

"That sounds perfect."

With her arm around her patient's shoulders, the two women walked side-by-side toward the community kitchen.

"How are your college applications coming along?" Señora Jacobbsen asked.

"They're all finished except for one."

"When is it due?"

Luisa groaned. "Tonight."

****

Luisa pulled her long black hair into a ponytail and scooted her chair closer to her desk. Taking a deep breath, she placed her fingers on the keyboard.

All of her other college applications were submitted weeks ago, but Luisa wanted this one to be perfect and was down to the wire. It was due by midnight.

Luisa sighed and leaned back in her chair, then looked up at the ceiling of her dorm room. She and Sofía spent countless hours painting it midnight blue and painstakingly adding little bright stars everywhere. The girls even traced the constellations onto the ceiling, including Luisa's favorite: Leo. It was her Zodiac sign, with her July 23rd birthday, but Luisa would have loved Leo even if it wasn't her sign. Lions were fierce. Strong. Kings and queens of the jungle. All of the things she wanted to be.

"What else would you like us to know as we consider your candidacy?" Luisa repeated the troublesome question staring at her from her computer screen.

If it were any other school, any of the other ten she was applying to, Luisa would've said something different. Something about how she loved to ride horses and worked part-time in the on-campus stable, or how every Sunday she made a traditional Honduran dinner for the other girls in her dorm. Or maybe how she wanted to be an international human rights lawyer one day and had a poster of the abolitionist William Wilberforce hanging in her bedroom.

If it were any other school, those essays would have been good enough. But this wasn't any other application. This was Harvard. Something more would be required.

Luisa re-read what she had written so far. Pages detailing what she experienced in Monterrey. Paragraphs bringing to light her former world of darkness. Sentences struggling to describe in words the horror and despair she felt in her soul.

"Luisa – dinner!"

The voice calling out up the stairs broke into the young woman's thoughts as she worked to finish her essay.

"Be down soon!" she replied, then narrowed her eyes and returned her focus to the computer screen in front of her. *Time for the grand finale*, she thought.

With her fingers flying over the keyboard, Luisa concluded her essay.

When people think about the prettiest places in the United States, they often mention Yosemite National Park, the snow-capped Rocky Mountains, the Grand Canyon, or the wild and wonderful Pacific Northwest. I have learned in school that those places are gorgeous examples of America's natural beauty. I hope to visit them all one day. But, for me, they aren't the prettiest place in the United States. That honor belongs to . . . West Texas. I know, I know, but hear me out. The flat, barren, more-cows-than-people former oil mecca shows the United States' true beauty to me. Because the true beauty of America isn't her mountains, or lakes, or Great Plains. It's her people. Her people and the spirit of unbridled passion and possibility that they carry with them everywhere they go.

When I was little, los Estados Unidos was nothing more than a dream. A fantasy-land far, far away. And when I arrived in this country three years ago, my own passion and sense of possibility were broken. Stripped bare and absent after years of believing I was unworthy of any kind of life beyond the slavery in which I found myself. But now, with the help of doctors, teachers, therapists, friends, and my ranch family, I am ready to bring my own American spirit to the campus of your university. Ready to learn, explore, and one day return to my native Honduras – carrying with me an education and a determination to make sure no other little girl ever has to learn the price of her life.

Want to give the author your feedback on the story? Write a review at Amazon.com!

ABOUT THE AUTHOR

Danielle knew she was born to be a writer at age four when she entertained an entire emergency room with the – false – story of how she was adopted. *Price of Life* is Danielle's fifth novel. She is a graduate of Georgetown University (Go Hoyas!) and Harvard Law School. Danielle lives in Georgia with her chocolate lab, Gus.

Find out more about Danielle and her books on her website: www.daniellesingleton.com.

Follow Danielle on Twitter: @auntdanwrites

Like Danielle's Facebook page: www.facebook.com/singletondanielle

Read Danielle's blog: www.daniellesingleton.wordpress.com

CPSIA information can be obtained
at www.ICGtesting.com
Printed in the USA
LVHW080401201218
601182LV00020B/1515/P